TANGLED ROOTS

A Mystery

G. G. VANDAGRIFF

DESERET
BOOK

SALT LAKE CITY, UTAH

Visit us at DeseretBook.com

Library of Congress Cataloging-in-Publication Data

Vandagriff, G. G.
 Tangled roots / G. G. Vandagriff.
  p. cm.
 ISBN-13: 978-1-59038-745-0 (pbk.)
 1. Women genealogists—Fiction. I. Title.
 PS3572.A427T36 2007
 813'.54—dc22   2007002448

Printed in the United States of America
Malloy Lithographing Incorporated, Ann Arbor, MI

10 9 8 7 6 5 4 3 2 1

TO

MY MOTHER-IN-LAW

Marguerite Vandagriff

MYSTERY FAN AND FAITHFUL INSPIRATION

Acknowledgments

To Sandra Whitaker for her unflagging support as a dear friend and reader of many revisions of this manuscript.

To Suzanne Brady for her superior editing skills, enduring friendship, and encouragement to go ahead with this project.

To Jana Erickson for her professionalism and dedication to producing a polished book.

To Earlene Fowler for her mighty example of beautiful and inspiring writing.

And to my husband, David, for his never ending patience, love, and commitment to me.

A Word about Timing

The two previous books in this series took place in the 1990s. This one occurs during the winter after *Of Deadly Descent* concludes. Because the era is pre-Internet to a large extent, genealogical research is done the hard way.

Prologue
1936

The single shot sounded a dull thud. Somehow silencers made the whole act of murder a bit anticlimactic.

He looked at what he had done. His victim sat slumped at his precise walnut desk in his Old World library as though he were some sort of an English gentleman granting an interview. Well. No longer. He wouldn't tyrannize anyone anymore.

The murderer laughed as a whimsical idea occurred to him. He would put the gent to bed. There was no one around but the tyrant's daughter, who was fast asleep in another wing of this hideous pile of a house.

Letting himself out of the mansion half an hour later, he laughed again. His burst of sound turned into an icy cloud in the freezing air. He was well satisfied. He'd gain his end by other means. No one even knew of his existence, let alone his relationship to the dead man. That was the pure, elegant beauty of it. He would contrive.

Chapter One
1994

Alex Campbell tried to concentrate on her new case as she drove the final leg from Kansas City to Chicago. But the closer she got to her destination, the more the past intruded. Of course, it was winter now, and a quilt of white shrouded the vast lawns in front of the North Shore mansions. Behind them, Lake Michigan foamed like a sullen witch's brew, dark pewter with roiling white caps. Last August, when everything was green and the lake sparkling, she had been on this same road, bent on confronting her parents after eighteen years. It had been a disastrous event, culminating in a murder.

Her life had changed beyond all recognition in the intervening months. It seemed futile to tell herself she was a new person now, facing new challenges. These surroundings triggered an automatic response not only to the horrors of last summer but to adolescent dramas played out long ago.

The self-assured, thirty-six-year-old widow of a world-renowned photographer wilted away, leaving an insecure, frightened teenager uncertain about what awaited her in that daunting neo-Georgian mansion in Winnetka, Illinois, she had once called home. Would it ever be any different? Her father was dead. She had forgiven her mother and moved on. Hadn't she?

Her growing anxiety dismayed her. Wasn't forgiveness enough? She hadn't expected these childish fears.

What would Dr. Goodwin say? She wouldn't ask her. Today's interview at the North Side Treatment Center was not about her problems. It was about Holly Weston, a sixteen-year-old drug addict. She would focus on the job, not the past. This was the first time she had used her genealogical skills for the psychiatric hospital, except when she had done a genogram of her own family while her mother was recovering there. She knew firsthand how valuable these psychological family trees could be. Dr. Goodwin was convinced that there was something amiss in young Holly Weston's family. A secret.

Though they made her uneasy, massively dysfunctional families also fascinated Alex. She felt compelled to heal them in order to make the world safe. Her friend Daniel should understand that.

As she drove up Sheridan Road, the twisting street with its elite dwellings continued to elicit unwanted memories. Was Holly's life as empty as her own had been with an alcoholic mother and a workaholic father? Were her problems with drugs a cry for help? Or was her acting out due to some other factor that Alex might uncover in the genogram she was about to begin? Ancestors could be a blessing or a curse or sometimes both. The sins of the fathers echoed in unpredictable ways. That's what genograms helped determine. What was Holly's sense of reality? Did it bear any relation to the actual facts? Or was her whole world some sort of cover-up, as Alex's had been?

She kept coming back to herself. Maybe Daniel had been right, and this *was* going to be painful. In the winter light, the undulations of Sheridan Road were full of shadows, particularly as she drove down into the heavily wooded hollow south of Highland Park. The thick stand of bare black-brown trees gave her the sense of a lifeless prison overhung by circling carrion birds. She shivered. *I'm not a child anymore. I'm a grown-up. I pay taxes.*

She didn't want to think of the conversation with Daniel last night after the opera. But now every word and nuance replayed itself in her mind.

* * *

"Alex, I'm sorry, but I have to tell you, I really don't like the sound of this new job of yours," Daniel said.

They had come back to her crazy, half run-down apartment building in the artistic community of Westport, Missouri. Necessity had compelled them to use the fire escape, as the elevator of the Baltimore was permanently out of order. The mellow strains of a cello sounded through the wall she shared with her Hispanic neighbor.

"Why not?" Alex demanded, feeling her hackles rise. "It's a great opportunity to be near my mother."

"Why do you want to work at a psych hospital of all places?" he inquired, his Kelly green eyes probing hers.

"You work at a psych hospital," she countered.

"I'm a psychologist. You're a genealogist. And the way you run your business, that seems to be extremely hazardous to your health. If you go, you should at least take Briggie."

Restraining more violent gestures, Alex pushed herself away from her cherry parson's table and stood up. "I knew *Madame Butterfly* was a mistake," she said. "Don't be so melodramatic. There aren't likely to be any murders in this case. And my mental health is just fine, Dr. Grinnell."

He took a deep breath of resignation and ran his fingers through his ginger-colored hair. "I hear myself and know I'm blowing it, but when I see these red flags, they're like triggers . . ."

He stood up, too, and began pacing her small living room with its white Bauhaus couches facing one another. The silver-gray walls were hung with chrome-framed posters—photographs of Florence, Venice, Rome, and Genoa. Stewart's last commission.

Stopping at the square glass coffee table, Daniel picked up her husband's book, which invariably exercised some kind of magnetism over him. Paging through the photo essay on Scotland, he looked as though he were seeking something definite that continued to elude him.

His preoccupation with Stewart calmed her. Here was a substantive barrier she could hide behind while the intimacy of the opera cooled. Daniel was always trying to find a way to relate to her loss.

Over the last year, the pain of Stewart's sudden death had at last started to numb. He would always be a presence in her life, but that presence was starting to be accompanied by a gentle nostalgia punctuated like lightning with times of searing horror, anger, and despair. Being a psychologist, Daniel knew that.

As she sat down on the couch, she observed, "Therapists think they are the modern equivalent of the knight errant."

"Come on, Alex," he said, sitting down beside her. His look was entreating. "You don't have to be a psychologist to see that you've had more than your share of shocks in the past six years."

"Look. I'm dealing with it, okay?" Why did she have to feel so powerfully connected to this solid man with the wrestler's frame who had seen her through the worst period of her life? "You don't really know me. You always see me as a victim. I'm stronger than you think."

He took her hands and, looking down at them, smoothed them

with his thumbs. Smiling reluctantly, he said, "I know you're strong. Dang good at karate, too. For a yellow belt."

Unfortunately, he had a very nice smile. "I haven't had time for lessons lately," she said, pulling her hands away. "I've been out of town."

"Yes. I noticed. And now you're going out of town again."

"It shouldn't take long. And I'm really looking forward to helping these people. You can understand that, can't you?"

Looking at her steadily, he said, "I know I'm an idiot sometimes. Don't shut me out, Alex."

He had been so endlessly patient with her uncertainties. Reaching out, she stroked the hair back from his forehead and said with a grin, "You haven't ambushed me lately. I'm ready. I got one of those super soaker squirt guns."

"I actually thought the opera was more fitting in this weather," he said, returning her grin. "I assaulted you with Puccini."

"You have the most peculiar ideas of courtship, Daniel Grinnell. Hari kari? I like squirt guns better."

*   *   *

The memory of the last exchange made her smile. She would go to the treatment center and begin her job. She was a professional, after all. Half owner of RootSearch, Inc. It was a crazy business, maybe, but it, combined with the nurturing of her colleague, Brighamina Poulson, and the gospel of Jesus Christ, had succeeded in rescuing her. She was no longer dangling all alone in the universe by a single, frayed thread of will.

As Alex pulled into the parking lot of the red brick, black shuttered hospital, she thought how ordinary and reassuring it looked from the outside. Kind of like a bank. No one would ever guess that terrible battles were fought within its walls.

Pulling down her visor mirror, Alex quickly finger-combed her shoulder-length black ringlets and applied a little lip gloss to her full mouth. Her eyes, looking tired again, had purplish smudges beneath them, a common condition due to her Celtic pallor. In Scotland, where she and Stewart had lived, they had accused her of having Irish blood, with blue eyes "put in by a smutty finger."

Dr. Goodwin was expecting her. The swan-necked Audrey Hepburn look-alike, dressed in a yellow woolen suit with large black buttons, welcomed her warmly. They had fought wars together.

"It's good to see you again, Alex. I'm glad you decided to take this case. How is your mother?"

"Doing well. She's using a walker because of her MS. But I don't think she's relapsed."

"Good. If she can keep away from liquor while she's facing multiple sclerosis and living alone, she's an incredible woman."

"I took this case mainly to be near her. I don't like her living alone, either. But she won't leave that house and come to Kansas City with me. And that's where my business is." She squared her shoulders, feeling anything but professional in her jeans and black turtleneck. Perhaps she should have worn her suit, but she had opted for comfort while traveling. "Tell me about this case."

The doctor settled behind her desk and toyed with a pencil, bouncing it by its eraser. The room was meant to be soothing with its rose-colored walls and prints of begonias. "I'm not really sure what we're looking at here. Holly seems to be in a deep state of denial. I can't get her mother to open up to me at all, so I don't know anything about the family system. That's crucial in dealing with a sixteen-year-old."

Dr. Goodwin stuck the pencil incongruously behind her ear. She was about Alex's own age and tended to shed her professionalism the longer they were together. "Whenever I try talking about the family, Mrs. Weston goes all pruney. I thought we might have more luck if you spoke with Holly's grandmother, Mrs. Harrison, who lives in Lake Forest. I just found out about her because Holly likes her dog." She sighed deeply. "That's about all I've been able to get out of her. She's extremely hostile."

Alex's heart quailed, so she sat straighter. She didn't like being around angry people, but she would deal with it. "I'd like to visit with Holly first, I think."

"Yes. That would probably be a good idea. There's something going on in that family. I can sense it. I think Holly may be out of the loop."

"That sounds familiar. You think the answer lies in this genogram?"

"Psychological family trees are absolutely vital in a case like this. As you know from your own experience, the facts can be a big surprise. The construction that families choose to put on those facts is what tells us what we really need to work on."

Oh, yes. Alex had had experience. An uneasy feeling told her that that experience just might prove more of a trial than a help.

Chapter Two

Before visiting Holly, Alex went to the cafeteria for a salad. She had missed lunch and was feeling a little light-headed. The cafeteria looked more like a restaurant with faux marble-topped tables, pastel upholstered dining chairs, and subdued lighting. In spite of its denizens, sitting one to a table, Alex felt a tremendous emptiness here. She shivered again as she had in the dark hollow on Sheridan Road.

It had been about six months since she'd brought her mother here to dry out. Alex didn't know Amelia Borden as anything but an enraged alcoholic.

In addition to the recent onset of multiple sclerosis, she was still undergoing the painful rehabilitation of an addict, which Alex had come to realize is never really over. There were so many lost years to make up for. Twenty to be precise. And her mother now wanted very much to know the woman Alex had become. Alex had been out of touch with her parents at the time of her marriage to Stewart, so her mother had never seen the tall man with the black beard and piercing black eyes who had died such a fiery death in the terrorist crash of Pan Am Flight 103, over Lockerbie, Scotland, in December 1988.

Amelia had never visited the little white cottage with the black door at the edge of Scotland's Loch Fyne. She had never known the great clan of Campbells—Alex's family for ten years. She hadn't seen the mists on the heather or the frightening majesty of the great gorges. All Amelia Borden would ever know of Stewart were his photographs. To Alex, this loss could never be replaced for either one of them. And as she watched her mother struggle with the disease that was debilitating her body, she had come to realize that Amelia viewed her current suffering as a judgment.

Looking around her at the bland décor meant to foster calming thoughts, Alex thought of the battle her mother was fighting. Seeing her determination to win back her life had made it easier to forgive her for the years of barrenness and fear she had experienced as an adolescent, but some days, like today, the images, though unbidden, persisted.

Alex recalled the terrible, empty feeling of walking into the mansion in Winnetka every day after school. She could hear the sound of her own footsteps on the parquet floor. It would have been different if the house had been truly empty. But she had known it wasn't. Her mother was upstairs, insensible, stretched across her bed, fully clothed. Not only was there was no one to buffer Alex from the world but the horror of that world had all too often been concentrated in her own home. Her mother's terrible rages had appeared from nowhere, which made them all the more frightening. Alex had felt she must never put a foot wrong, never trust in a seeming moment of tranquillity, for it might only be the lull before the storm. Even eighteen years after leaving home, her clearest memory of her mother's face was as a rigid, screaming mask with flaring white nostrils.

Despite the fact that she now knew the reason for her mother's behavior, she couldn't remake her adolescence. The pain and isolation and, most of all, the unwillingness to trust anyone but herself was too deeply ingrained in her emotional makeup. Especially since Stewart's death, she had felt impelled to maintain absolute control of her world. Otherwise, otherwise . . . she couldn't even contemplate the horror of revisiting that suffering, reentering that crazy universe where pain touched every molecule of her existence.

She had known during her marriage that there were walls inside her. She remembered a particular day when she and Stewart had been hiking through a narrow, open gorge that descended forever below them, the wind whipping angrily around their faces. She had held her husband's hand, and he had led her across the trail to the other side and then enfolded her in his arms. But she had resisted feeling safe, just as she resisted feeling safe in their little white cottage. And Stewart *had* left her. It hadn't been his fault, of course, but she hadn't trusted that he would be there always, and it turned out she had been right not to.

Pushing her half-eaten salad away, Alex stood up. She now had no desire whatever to visit Holly. Why was Daniel always right?

* * *

The girl was sitting on her bed, bunched up against the wall. Her short magenta hair was ragged, and she wore razor-slashed jeans. A gold ring pierced her nose. Alex knew instantly that she should never have ventured into this interview while feeling so vulnerable. There was too much anger in this room.

"Hello, Holly." She greeted her with a smile. "I'm Alex. Dr. Goodwin is my doctor, too."

"Who are *you?*" the girl challenged.

12

Deciding not to sit down, Alex viewed the patient's room for some kind of clue to the personality beneath the suspicion. Although Holly's temporary domicile was painted psych-hospital rose, she had hung it with neon posters of rock stars. The only other possession of hers in view was a Susan Conant dog-lover's mystery on the bedside table. She was a surprisingly neat child. Alex remembered her own immaculate room. It had been her way of exerting control over her surroundings.

"I'm just a family historian. I see you like Susan Conant. Do you have a dog?"

The girl looked at the book and then back at Alex, her eyes uncomfortably shrewd. "Of course not."

Remembering the comment Dr. Goodwin had made about her grandmother's dog, she asked, "I understand your grandmother has a dog that you like."

Holly shrugged and began to pick at a black-painted toenail, keeping her eyes away from Alex's. "Lord Peter's all right," she said grudgingly. "I haven't seen him lately. Mother thinks Granny's crazy."

"What do you think?"

"Who cares?" She looked away again, but not before Alex could see the tears forming in her eyes.

"Maybe I do," Alex said softly.

"I'm not sick, so you can quit all that stuff," Holly said bitterly.

"I never said you were."

"You think I'm a druggie." The tears clotted her heavily mascaraed lashes, but her eyes were now narrow with accusation.

Alex was still standing. She didn't know what to say.

"That's what they told you, isn't it?" Holly demanded.

Wetting her lips, Alex nodded. Dr. Goodwin had said Holly was in denial. It seems she was right. The anger made sense. But the tears?

She decided to risk it. "I went through some pretty awful times

13

when I was your age. I wish I'd had someone to help me through them."

Holly didn't answer. The mascara was running down her face.

"Let me explain something to you that might help you understand why I'm here," Alex said, guessing that Holly might like to be treated as an adult. "We live in family systems that include a collection of beliefs. Whether you like it or not, your family system is your reality. From the time you were born, everything you saw and did was filtered through that reality." She took a step further into the room. Feeling as though she were taming a wild animal, she continued, "But sometimes that view of the world is skewed. What we're trying to do here at the Center is to determine what the truth is in your family system."

"I'm *not* a druggie!" Holly suddenly burst out, careless of Alex's explanation. She rubbed her eyes defiantly with the back of her wrist. "I'm not like the other creeps here!"

The girl was scrunched up in a smaller ball now, as though getting ready to strike. Honed by years of living with incalculable rages, Alex's sensitive antennae picked up the signals. Holly was now seeing her as part of the system that had turned against her. She trusted no one. Her fury was palpable.

Suddenly Alex sensed that Holly was going yell at her. She held her breath.

"You don't believe me, do you?" The girl's face was contorted, her eyes hard and accusing. "No one ever believes me! I'm just a prisoner in this crazy hospital!"

Alex bit her lip. This wasn't her mother screaming at her, she told herself. This really didn't have anything to do with her. "Holly, I'm just trying to figure everything out . . ."

The girl continued shouting. "Everyone just wants me to be a nice little druggie, with ordinary little druggie problems. Well, I'm not a druggie! Do you hear me? I'm not a druggie! It's my family that's got the problems, not me!"

She paused and stood, her small body trembling with fury, her hands clenched at her sides. Alex felt as though her insides were being heaved up by a steam shovel. Holly's wretchedness was eerily familiar. The powerlessness. The conviction that everyone else was seeing the wrong picture. The certainty that you were the only sane person in a world gone mad.

"You're just part of the whole setup." Holly's voice was breaking into sobs. "I won't put up with those doctors prying into my life, and I won't put up with you. This is *my* room! Get out of here and don't come back!"

Alex was trembling. She backed slowly out of the room, murmuring, "I'm sorry, Holly. I promise . . . I only want to help you."

But she wasn't in any position to help Holly. She was eighteen years old again, banished to Paris for a reason she couldn't understand. Her parents didn't want her. They lived in a world that was hedged up against her. They were a united front, and she was only one. Alone.

She stumbled blindly through the halls to the door that locked Holly away from everyone who should love her. Alex thought she could almost hear the eerie hoot of a river barge echoing from the River Seine.

Briggie. I need Briggie.

Finding her way out of the hospital, Alex got into her car and fumbled in her purse for her cell phone. Why was this terror and helplessness resurfacing? She wasn't eighteen! And the family situation was long since past. Years and years past.

Alex's panic started to ease with this mental assertion. But she was very disappointed in herself. *I'm not getting it somehow. If I were truly forgiving, I would be past all this. If my faith were stronger . . . if I were a better person . . . if I really believed what I say I believe . . .*

Her friend and business partner would put her back on course. Briggie probably came the closest to being someone Alex completely trusted. This Mormon grandmother had rescued her after Stewart died, taking her from Scotland back to the States to live with her in Independence, Missouri, introducing Alex to the gospel, and teaching her her trade. Together they formed RootSearch, Inc., based in Briggie's big white-framed house. Alex had been baptized just over a year ago.

"Hello?"

"Briggie, this is Alex. What are you up to?"

"Watching Oprah. She has Harrison Ford on today. Don't you think he should have won an Oscar by now?"

Alex grinned and felt the last vestiges of her panic fade. "He was nominated for one. I don't think he cares about Oscars, though."

"He just says that. I can tell it hurts. I hate it when he's in R-rated movies, because then I have to wait to see them on TV. How's Chicago?"

"A little more difficult than I thought it would be. Not genealogically, but emotionally."

"So. Dr. Daniel wasn't so far wrong?".

Alex paused, momentarily wishing she hadn't given up swearing. "No. I hate it that he's always right. It's not fun to be seen through like that."

"How's your mother?"

"I haven't seen her yet. I'm not looking forward to it."

"You sound really woebegone, Alex. What's the matter?"

"I miss you," Alex admitted. In her heart, she could see her dear friend, stalwart and unflinching in her Royals sweatshirt, her white hair standing on end as it usually did when she was immersed in a genealogical puzzle.

"Do you need me?"

Alex tried to put her need into words. "I need someone who will remind me of who I am *now*. I'm getting this all mixed up with past stuff. There's a lot of rage here." She hesitated. "Briggie, I need someone here who loves me."

"Your mother loves you, child."

"But I can't *feel* it! I know I *should*. But the past keeps getting in the way. Maybe I'm just not a very forgiving person."

"You're trying to do this all by yourself, aren't you?"

"What do you mean?"

Briggie sighed audibly.

"Scripture study and prayer don't solve everything," Alex said defensively.

"Neither do therapists and psychiatrists. We've all got to have a little help. Now, I'm not the only one who loves you. God loves you, Alex."

It was Alex's turn to sigh. "I know that in my head, Briggie. But I can't feel it. It's the trust thing again."

"But you trust me?"

"You know I do."

"Well . . . I guess that's something, anyway. I can be there tomorrow. All I've got on the schedule is knitting."

"Knitting? What in the world are you knitting?"

"A Royals afghan for Richard."

Richard was Daniel's father—a dyed-in-the-wool St. Louis Cardinals fan who detested the Kansas City Royals as an upstart expansion franchise. Alex laughed again. Richard would probably turn purple.

"I hate winter," Briggie said fretfully. "No baseball, no fishing, hunting . . . nothing."

"You can stay at the house with Mother and me. I have a feeling this case is going to be difficult. No one's talking."

"Well, I'm always ready for a challenge. I'll take Maxie over to Daniel's and drive up tomorrow morning."

Alex hesitated. "I suppose you have to leave the cat over there?"

"Marigny is the only one who can do anything with him. You know how spoiled he is. He's never gotten over all the kids leaving." Marigny was Daniel's daughter.

"Well, could you avoid discussing my emotional state with Daniel?"

"You're afraid he might be on the next plane?"

"No. I just don't want him to know he was right."

Chapter Three

Well, she couldn't put it off any longer. After all, this was what she had come to Chicago for, wasn't it? Alex turned into the driveway of her old home. The brick and mortar of the house her grandfather had built stood solid in its garden of snow. This time it was going to be different, she reminded herself. Her mother was not going to be drunk or hostile. She was truly looking forward to Alex's visit. She had called her mother on her cell phone twenty minutes ago to let her know she was on the way.

Amelia Borden greeted her at the door. "Honey! It's so good to see you! But you look so tired. Did you have a terrible drive?"

Awkwardly hugging her mother, the walker between them, Alex said, "I broke it into two days. I've just come from the treatment center."

A brief look of vulnerability flashed in Amelia's eyes, but she banished it swiftly. She was a smaller, shrunken version of the woman Alex had left eighteen years ago. Her hair was still a careful strawberry blonde, her deep blue eyes now free of their alcoholic haze, but she had the ravaged look of a woman much older than her fifty-six years. Had she been as worried about this visit as Alex had been?

Hoisting her luggage, Alex asked, "Is it okay if I have Daddy's room? The guest room has always reminded me of the Brontë sisters."

"But I've redone it," her mother exclaimed. "Just for you! Come see."

"But can you go upstairs?" Alex indicated her walker.

"I've had an elevator installed," she said with some smugness. "I've been busy."

"I guess you have." So far, so good. As during her visits to the hospital, Alex felt as though she were conversing with a woman who was not her mother but a polite stranger.

They walked through the black and white marble entry with its pampas grass and Picasso into the hall. There, the large coat closet had been converted into an adequate elevator that carried them slowly to the second floor. Following her mother awkwardly along the sage green carpeted hallway, they came to what had once been a drab and dark bedroom. Amelia flicked on the overhead light. "Ta da!"

The room was now painted a pale yellow, trimmed in white. It was fragrant with her mother's special brand of rose potpourri, which sat in an open glass bowl on top of a white chest of drawers. There was a white canopy bed suited for a young girl, adorned by a navy and yellow hand-tied quilt.

"Oh my gosh, Mother! Did you make that quilt yourself?"

Looking pleased with herself, Amelia said, "Well, it's only tied. My bridge group helped me. I wanted it to be special."

Alex was disheartened that she couldn't feel the pleasure her mother obviously intended. Instead, she felt guilty and subtly manipulated. Her mother had gone to all this trouble to make up for the past, and she couldn't feel gratitude. What was wrong with her?

"It's beautiful," she said, putting down her suitcase. "So cheerful." Then, turning to her mother, she added, "I hope you don't mind, but Briggie's coming tomorrow evening."

"Briggie's coming?" Dismay flattened Amelia Borden's once sharp voice.

Of course her mother would rather die than admit it, but she was jealous of Alex's friend. "I'm having trouble with this case, and Briggie taught me everything I know," Alex told her.

Her mother bowed her head. Okay. Wrong thing to say. Alex added, "Besides, she loves to come to Winnetka and see you. She's all alone in that big house."

Amelia began to weep. In the past, tears had been one of her weapons. Alex stiffened.

But her mother just sniffed and blew her nose into a tissue. "Do you think she'll bring her deer rifle this time?"

Relieved, Alex forced a chuckle. "You never know with Briggie. I think she just had it bore-sighted, if you know what that means."

* * *

The following morning Alex drove up the shore to Lake Forest. The evening with her mother had gone well after the initial awkwardness. Though she hated to cook, Amelia had gone to the trouble of making a tuna casserole. They had watched *Charade* afterwards, with Amelia providing popcorn and hot chocolate. Alex had gone to bed and lain awake wondering at how strange it felt to be in her childhood home. Was it really home?

The Harrison residence proved to be a long way from the road on the lake side, almost hidden behind high, thick hedges. As Alex rolled to a stop, she had a fleeting thought that it resembled Thornfield in *Jane Eyre*. Surely, the place couldn't be as spooky as it looked. The windows were small-paned and few in number. The stone house had numerous chimneys and towers with leafless ivy creeping up its facade like some deadly fungus. Behind it, the lake was a dull gray mass, threatening to swallow the whole picture. *Made-to-order Gothic,* she thought.

Mrs. Harrison answered the door promptly to the sound of furious barking. "Good afternoon. You must be Mrs. Campbell." Looking down at the small black dachshund that was guarding her with stalwart vigilance, she said, "It's perfectly all right, Lord Peter. This is a friend."

Tall and plump, she didn't look the typical grandmother, nor did she seem to go with the grotesque house. Her hair was white and arranged in a North Shore bouffant, her dark brown eyes keen and clear. Dressed in tweeds and pearls, she gave an Old World impression. Alex felt as though she were back in Scotland.

"Good morning. Yes, I'm Alex Campbell. From the North Side Treatment Center."

"Dr. Goodwin called. I've been expecting you." The brown eyes brightened. "Come in."

Preceding them down the hall, the sleek little dog was now wagging his tail. The interior of the house was a surprise, gaily painted in hues of yellow and pale pumpkin. Alex inquired, "Do you live here all alone?"

"Oh yes. Except for my menagerie. I've quite a collection of pets. It worries my son-in-law. He and my daughter inherit. Pet stains on the Aubusson, you know. But I'm very careful."

Alex sniffed, detecting only a faint odor of dog. A large orange cat appeared and began rubbing against her black slacks.

"Here, Tuppence." Mrs. Harrison scooped up the inquisitive feline and led Alex to a spacious terra-cotta red living room with white moldings and cornices. A bright crystal chandelier shed its beneficent light on the walls and all the carefully polished antique furniture. In the corner stood a cage containing a brilliant macaw that greeted her, "Right. And Bob's your uncle."

"Mrs. Campbell, this is Professor Moriarty, but I generally just call him the Professor." Turning to the parrot, she said, "Isn't it nice to have a guest?"

Obviously, Gladys Harrison was a reader of British detective fiction. This endeared her to Alex immediately. "Did you know before this morning that Holly is in the Center?" she asked as she and Mrs. Harrison seated themselves on a coral and cream Regency-striped couch.

"Yes, dear." Holly's grandmother didn't seem overly troubled. "She'll get over her problems in time. She's got to discover her backbone, that's all." She ran her fingers lovingly through her cat's coat. Lord Peter settled himself resignedly at her feet, laying his small muzzle on her heavy brogues. "I have great faith in Holly. She's a lot like me, you see. I noticed it when she was tiny. She never wanted to take the same road as other people, which has always caused a bit of an uproar. My daughter is very traditional."

Alex hid a smile. Was there more to Mrs. Harrison than tweeds and pearls? Her surroundings certainly belied her stated dislike of tradition. Alex got out her pencil and paper. "I'm a professional genealogist and have been hired by the center to do a genogram of your family. It's a little like a family tree, but it records psychological and medical information, too. Is this all right with you?"

"Whatever will help Holly," Mrs. Harrison assented. She continued to stroke Tuppence.

Alex took a deep breath. Had she at last found someone who was willing to talk? "This *will* help her, I think. A lot of times our problems come from our family systems—the way we were taught to view reality. You say Holly's like you?"

"Oh yes. Though it's probably—what do you call it? A genetic throwback. I mean she wasn't raised the least like me. Her mother took her to the zoo and had her portrait made regularly and was a room mother and all that. Grace always tried her best."

"What do you think went wrong?"

"Went down like jackstraw," the Professor commented.

"I firmly believe we bring our characters with us," Gladys said with a gentle smile. "Holly wasn't cut out for Grace's idea of childhood. I wasn't either. My granddaughter's always been a little bit of an adventuress, as we used to say."

"So you were an adventuress?" Alex was hardly able to credit it, looking at the serene woman in front of her.

"Oh, goodness, yes. I didn't have what you'd call a peaceful childhood. My father was murdered, you see. Right here in this house." Mrs. Harrison's voice was almost complacent.

Alex stared. The family secret. Dr. Goodwin was right. But the woman said it with such apparent calm that she had difficulty believing her words. Could Alex talk about her own father's murder so dispassionately? To a stranger? Never. She still had trouble discussing it with her friends. *Daniel was going to flip. Was there some dark cloud that followed her around?* Taking a deep breath, she sat taller.

"I'm so sorry, Mrs. Harrison."

"Oh, call me Gladys. And that was all a very long time ago."

"Okay." She hesitated, feeling unable to treat the matter as cavalierly as her hostess was doing. But she was here to do a job. "So, for the purposes of the genogram," she went on, trying to match Mrs. Harrison's calm, "how old were you when this happened?"

"Sixteen. It was in 1936. It was quite shocking in a little town like Lake Forest. He was rich. It was in all the papers. I found him. Nightmares. For years." For the first time she seemed a little agitated.

Alex waited. The woman twisted the old-fashioned diamond

rings on her fingers. As though sensing her distress, Lord Peter gave a whine and nuzzled her ankles.

"He was shot in his bed," she said, reaching down to stroke the dachshund's ears. "I don't use that room."

It was hard to believe this was the defining experience of this woman's life. But it had to be. How could you be untouched by your father's murder? Alex couldn't begin to count all the ways her own experience had changed her life. Distrust. Regret. Horror. The list went on and on. But there was a certain rote quality about Gladys Harrison's recitation, as though it weren't quite real to her anymore.

Alex couldn't refrain from asking, "Did they ever find out who did it?"

Looking unseeingly at her macaw grooming himself under one wing, Mrs. Harrison said, "No. It was never solved. I became very wild, I'm afraid." Defiance marked her voice. Clearly, whatever she felt, it wasn't grief. To her cat's evident displeasure, she continued to stroke her dog. Tuppence leapt from her lap and stalked away. "You see, Daddy was very repressive, and I decided that now that he was gone, I was going to be an actress. I bleached my hair platinum blonde and went to Hollywood."

There was no doubt that this seemingly staid North Shore matron meant to shock her. Could she really be telling the truth? Alex assessed her surroundings, hopeful of finding a clue. Nothing. Except for the slightly eccentric macaw, the house was vintage North Shore respectability. Assuming a bland expression, Alex continued her sketch. "You must have had some interesting times there."

"I had some bit parts, nothing big. But I met all the stars—Jean Harlow, Claudette Colbert, Clark Gable, Greer Garson, Humphrey Bogart. Mother refused to send me an allowance, so I worked in Beverly Hills as a maid." She smiled sweetly. "I ran off with an actor once. We took a boat to Cuba. Danced the tango."

Alex was reluctant to think her kindly hostess bonkers. Perhaps, in her solitude, she lived on a diet of old movies on cable TV. And Golden Age detective stories, obviously.

Clearly lost in her story, Gladys Harrison tilted her head to one side as though listening. Then she sobered. "But those sorts of things never really work out, of course. Not like the movies. It was a dreadful mistake, and I lived to regret it. I was such a thoughtless child, wasn't I, Lord Peter?" She addressed her dog, looking lovingly into his adoring eyes.

"And then I met Mr. Harrison. He 'rescued me' from my life of dissipation. I was about nineteen then. It was very good of him to overlook my failings. He was twenty-nine and idealistic, you see. He said he was representing Clark Gable in a lawsuit when he met me coming off the set. I had been filling in as an extra in a ballroom scene." She smiled broadly now and looked directly at Alex. "I could hardly believe it, but he told me later that he took one look at me and knew he was meant to marry me."

Alex didn't know how to respond. Surely this was nothing more than an old woman's fantasy. For crying out loud, if it were really true, would she tell a stranger all these things? And how exactly should she depict the story on the genogram? Then her unruly imagination broke free and ran away with her. Darned if she couldn't see the tall, willowy blonde (as she must have been then) with a touch of languid glamour dancing the tango with a Rudolph Valentino look-alike and attracting the very correct young lawyer in the white starched shirt.

"He asked me out for coffee," Mrs. Harrison continued. "I was in a mess. My actor friend had just left me, and I was feeling low. Mr. Harrison—Robert—was very kind. I guess he could see I really wasn't meant for Hollywood. I mean it was clear I couldn't go on starving as a maid between ballroom scenes for the rest of my life."

Alex cleared her throat. "I can see that," she said. At this point the woman stood and went over to an antique oak sideboard covered with pictures. She handed one to Alex. It was framed in bird's-eye walnut and had the smooth, finished look of a studio portrait from the thirties.

"This is my Robert. He's pretty good looking, don't you think?"

Alex nodded obediently. "He could have been an actor himself. He reminds me of Leslie Howard."

"You know, that's just what I've always thought. Anyway, we married and eventually moved back here, where he went to work in the family steel business. It was so strange. My mother acted as though I'd never left. I dyed my hair back to plain brown, of course."

End of adventure. Well, this was exactly the sort of thing she had come for. True or false, it was all part of the family's reality. Drawing a circle for Mrs. Harrison's mother, she asked, "It sounds as though she was what we call in denial. What was her maiden name?"

"Norman. Sarah Norman."

"I probably should explain that on genealogical charts women are known by their maiden names. And your father's full name, please?"

"Lloyd Williams. A good Welsh name, he always said. He was the son of our family legend. A coal miner who came from Wales to Pittsburgh and later made a fortune in steel. My grandfather was the one who built the house: William Williams."

More storybook drama. It had needed only this. A rags-to-riches tale. Oh well. It was easily checked. One thing about the North Shore. Everyone knew how everyone else made his money.

She worked steadily on her genogram. Messy, messy, messy. If Gladys Harrison were telling the truth, there appeared to be almost too many potential sources of dysfunction—excessive wealth, murder, self-deception, denial, acting out.

"Did you have any brothers and sisters?"

"Just one brother. He passed on some time ago. His name was Lloyd Jr. Wife died before he did." Taking a sulking Tuppence onto her lap again, Gladys Harrison narrowed her eyes, seeming to concentrate. "They had a daughter, but she was killed in a hit-and-run accident down in Texas. Austin, I think it was. So that's the end of that line. It's sad."

Alex hastily sketched in these new family members. Could Mrs. Harrison relate any tale without some kind of dramatic twist? But she was mainly interested in the primary line of descent to begin with. She could get the other details later.

"Dr. Goodwin told me that Holly's mother was your only child."

"Yes. It's odd that we all have such small families. Even Grandfather, the steel millionaire, you know, had only one sister. My Aunt Bronwyn. They immigrated together. The Welsh usually have such big families."

At this point, Alex could only be glad that the family was small. She already felt like the victim of an avalanche. Most of the time, her genealogical researches were painfully slow. She wasn't used to getting so much so fast. Of course, every detail would have to be verified. How far back did she really need to go? Just on the off chance, she would go back as far as she could. Who knew at this point what would help Holly?

Lord Peter sniffing at her toes, Alex extended the pedigree of Gladys Williams Harrison back to her grandfather, William Williams, and gave him a father and a sister.

"Holly's mother's name is Grace?" Alex read out the address she had in Wilmette.

"Yes," Mrs. Harrison confirmed.

"And her husband is George Weston?"

"Yes. Insinuating sort of man. I've never understood what made Grace marry him, if you want the truth." Alex did want the truth, of course. Or Gladys Harrison's version of the truth, anyway. She added

Grace and George to the growing picture. Lord Peter sighed and lay on the Aubusson, his head on his paws.

"May I see it?" asked Holly's grandmother.

"Of course," Alex said. "It probably looks like a jumbled mess to you, but hopefully something here will help Holly."

The former "adventuress" looked over the genogram, benignly accepting its assessment of herself and her relations. "Yes, you've got it all down. What will you do now?"

"Talk to Holly's parents, probably. Thank you so much for giving me such good information. You were more than helpful."

"Well, Grace isn't going to like it, I can tell you. Whatever you do, don't show her that. She likes to keep the family history tightly under wraps."

Alex looked up from her drawing. "Does she?"

"She lives in a fantasy world, I'm afraid. I guess you'd call it denial." Mrs. Harrison shook her head sadly.

The macaw added his two cents' worth: "Queer as Dick's hatband."

Beaming at her clever bird, Mrs. Harrison said to Alex, "Do try to get Holly to come and visit me when she can. I'd like to get to know her better, poor child."

"I don't have much say in things like that," Alex said cautiously. "The North Side Treatment Center is a lockdown facility, you know. She can't come and go as she pleases."

At length, she left Mrs. Harrison alone with her menagerie.

*　　*　　*

"Alex?"

She had vaguely expected Daniel, but it was Charles, her recently discovered third cousin calling her on her cell phone. Her pulse raced

Gladys Harrison's Genogram

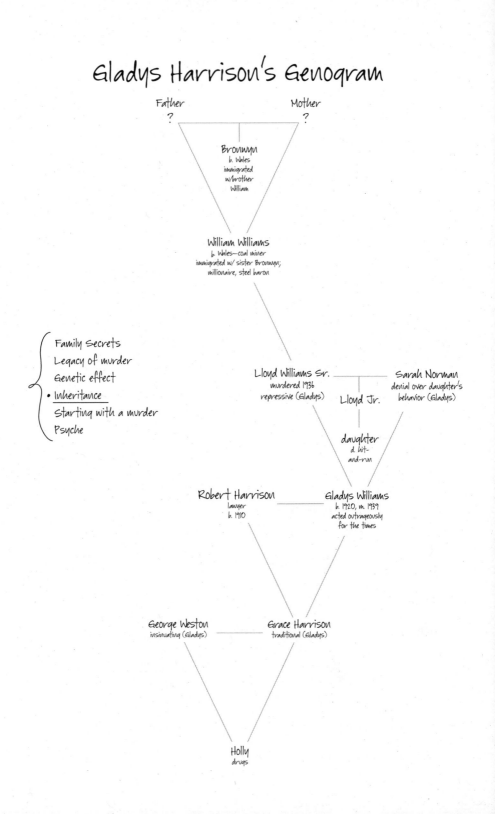

Father
?

Mother
?

Bronwyn
b. Wales
immigrated
w/brother
William

William Williams
b. Wales—coal miner
immigrated w/ sister Bronwyn;
millionaire, steel baron

Family Secrets
Legacy of murder
Genetic effect
• Inheritance
Starting with a murder
Psyche

Lloyd Williams Sr.
murdered 1936
repressive (Gladys)

Lloyd Jr.

Sarah Norman
denial over daughter's
behavior (Gladys)

daughter
d. hit-
and-run

Robert Harrison
lawyer
b. 1910

Gladys Williams
b. 1920, m. 1939
acted outrageously
for the times

George Weston
insinuating (Gladys)

Grace Harrison
traditional (Gladys)

Holly
drugs

at the sound of his British public school accent. The glamorous Charles had that effect on women, she chided herself.

"Hello."

"Are you in Chicago yet?"

"I arrived yesterday. How are you?"

"Doing well, thanks. How's the job going?"

She had to tell someone. "You won't believe it, but the woman I just interviewed claims her father was murdered. I have some reservations, but still . . ."

There was a pause on the other end of the line. "Is this one likely to get you run down in a dark alley?"

"If it happened at all, it was in 1936."

"You don't have your bodyguard," he said, referring to Briggie. "Need me to fill in?"

"You and Briggie weren't much help in Oxford, if you remember." She recalled the previous summer after her father's death, when she had gone to England to find his cousins and heirs. It was then she had met Charles. Unfortunately, lust for the fortune had led to another murder, that of their cousin Philippa. The murderer had taken Alex completely by surprise. She had very nearly been killed herself. "My karate wasn't much help, either. But since I don't really believe in ghosts, I think I'm going to be okay this time."

"I'm glad to hear it. But it sounds like a potentially ghastly setup."

She laughed. "There was a murderer in your family, remember."

"Well, that just proves the point. However, the burning question is, will you have dinner with me tomorrow night?"

She sensed the familiar offhand quality in his question. There was much unresolved tension in Charles. For good reason, he was as wary of a new relationship as she was. It was a relief to know that he would keep his distance as a matter of course.

"I'd like that."

Chapter Four

"It never happened," Grace Harrison Weston told Alex firmly. "My mother never went to Hollywood. It's just a story she's made up."

Alex couldn't say she was surprised, though she had certainly taken to Gladys Harrison more readily than she was taking to her daughter, Holly's mother. Grace was a tiny, sharp woman with restless hands and none of her mother's graciousness. Her face was taut across the cheekbones and eyes. Alex guessed at recent plastic surgery. Tinted blonde, her hair was drawn back in a hammered silver clip.

Wetting her lips, Alex took a deep breath. She was obviously going to have at least two versions of the same genogram. But that was probably par for the course in this kind of thing.

They were sitting in a living room starkly different from Mrs. Harrison's. The furniture was angularly modern black leather and chrome. Abstract art (originals, or at least lithographs, from what Alex could tell) hung on the walls, and a black marble floor was warmed by only a few rugs of Native American design.

"And the murder of her father?"

"Well, he died in bed. He certainly wasn't shot. The doctor wouldn't sign the death certificate." Holly's mother's almost black eyes were hard and bright. "In the end, the coroner thought it must have been some form of barbiturate mixed with alcohol."

"So it could have been a suicide?" Surely Mrs. Weston must know Alex could look up death certificates. Was she likely to fabricate?

"Possibly. What does all of this have to do with Holly? We're talking about her great-grandfather!"

Alex wished she were better prepared for this task. For the psychological aspects, she could only rely on what she had learned in therapy herself. She could see that tact was called for in this case. Unfortunately, she wasn't particularly tactful. "We need to know more about Holly's family so we can tell more about her perception of reality—what's true and what's false."

"I'm not sure I like this," Grace said flatly. "Holly is only sixteen. I don't want to overwhelm her with all the problems on her family tree."

"Holly is already overwhelmed, Mrs. Weston." Dr. Goodwin had filled her in on Holly's state of mind. "In acute denial, with signs of paranoia," she had told Alex.

"Are you a psychologist?" the woman before her demanded suddenly.

"No. I'm a genealogist."

Grace Weston stood up. "It's clear that you're not qualified to deal with her. She's a very sensitive girl who needs psychological help, not ancient family fables. If they insist on this approach at the North Side Treatment Center, I'm afraid we'll have to move her. Holly doesn't need all this mumbo-jumbo."

Alex set her jaw and wrote by Mrs. Weston's circle: *Flat denial of her mother's story. Fear of what may be uncovered?* She rose to go.

At that moment a short man with a graying goatee walked into the room, hands in the pockets of his expensive charcoal woolen slacks. His head was tilted to one side, and he looked at her like an inquisitive, heavily feathered owl. His eyebrows almost obscured his little black eyes.

"Who is this?" he asked.

Grace Weston replied, her voice heavy with scorn, "A genealogist. The North Side Treatment Center sent her. She's supposed to ferret out all the family secrets. But I'm not having any of it. Holly will have to be moved."

Alex stiffened as Mr. Weston's interested eyes assessed her. He *was* insinuating. In this, she agreed with Gladys Harrison.

"Now, dear, anyone would suppose we had something to hide. Don't you think it would be better to have Holly stay where she is? The security is so good."

His wife sniffed, just like the women in British novels.

"I'm not trying to make trouble, Mrs. Weston," Alex said. "I just want to help Holly."

"Does this woman have a name, dear?" George Weston asked. "You haven't introduced us."

Alex stepped forward and offered her hand, determined not to be intimidated. "Alex Campbell. I assume you're Holly's father?"

Very white teeth gleamed above the black and gray goatee. "Yes. George Weston. What's that you have there?"

Instinctively, she held her work to her chest. "It's just Holly's genealogy on her mother's side. I got it from Mrs. Harrison."

"Ah. Gladys. Our *raconteur*. I suppose she claimed her father was murdered?"

"Well, yes. But your wife was telling me it didn't really happen."

"Let's just say that Gladys has a rich fantasy life. You saw her parrot?" The smile again.

Alex decided she could find out the facts easily enough and that it might be politic to appear to swallow the Westons' version of things. She returned Mr. Weston's smile and hoped she looked ingenuous. "Actually, I was hoping to make an appointment with you. I would like to find out about your side of the family tree."

He laughed. "Oh, my family is very boring. No romantic old mansions, family scandals, or Cinderella Welsh coal miners. We were very *Leave It to Beaver*. My mother was June Cleaver to her marrow. That's why Grace married me, you know. After being raised by a drama queen, she wanted a bit of predictability in her life."

If she let them think she agreed with them, perhaps they wouldn't move Holly and she'd really be able to help her. "Well, sometimes older people like to embroider a little," she confessed. "I've learned to take what they say with a grain of salt."

Grace Weston smiled graciously, abandoning her frigid manner. "Yes, Mrs. Campbell. I think that would be best."

The couple walked her to the door. Alex couldn't shake the feeling that she was being let out of a fortress or maybe a meat locker. There were three locks on the door.

*   *   *

Alex called Dr. Goodwin on her way home, relating the facts of her two conversations. "At a guess, I'd say Mrs. Weston is probably right and Mrs. Harrison is indulging in fantasies."

"There's where the genealogist part comes in," the doctor said. "You ought to be able to get the facts. There's some reason behind the fabrication, whoever's doing it, and frankly, I wouldn't put it beyond Mrs. Weston to try to hush things up. That's why I called you in. I sense she's under a terrible strain of some kind."

Pondering her words, Alex nodded. "Yes. I got that impression, too. But Mr. Weston seems to be normal, just taking his mother-in-law in stride." She pondered her facts. "I should be able to get something on the marriage. Where it took place, anyway. Lloyd Williams's death certificate will tell how he died. And, of course, there are the newspapers. He was a prominent man. Somewhere there will be an account of the murder or suicide or whatever it was."

"Yes. Let me know what you find out."

*   *   *

It seemed, outwardly at least, that Amelia was resigned to Briggie's visit. She and Alex were having herb tea in her sitting room, which was furnished with rose-covered furniture, an antique walnut desk, and bookshelves containing all the latest best-sellers.

"It will be good to see Briggie again," Amelia said. "I have a feeling that things are never dull when she's around. Do you think maybe I could help with the case?"

"Do you really want to?"

"Actually, I do. I think it would be good for me to apply my mind to something constructive."

Did she really want her mother involved in this part of her life— the part she and Briggie had built together? To say no would certainly wound her. "It's bound to be a wild ride. It always is, with Briggie around."

"I don't mind. If you don't think a cripple will slow you down." Amelia may not scream anymore, but she was not above being manipulative.

"I'm sure we could use the help," Alex said finally. They would find something safe and simple for her to do. Phone calls or something.

Arriving at about five o'clock, Briggie was her brisk, sure self, dressed in royal blue sweats, her weather-beaten face creased in a happy smile.

"Amelia! Alex! I drove as fast as I could. Kept the smokies at bay with my CB."

"I'm going to help with the case," Amelia said proudly.

Briggie flashed a look at Alex and then gave Amelia a hug. "Good. It sounds like we can use all the help we can get. Now, are you going to fill me in?"

"First things first," Amelia said, briskly taking control of the situation. "I thought we'd go to Hackney's for dinner. My treat."

"That sounds great!" Briggie had an enthusiastic appetite. "I've only had a hot fudge sundae somewhere around noon."

"Then the sooner we get you settled, the sooner we can eat," Amelia said.

The time-honored steak house of the North Shore was busy, even at 5:30 in the afternoon. An American's fantasy of a Scottish hunter's pub with dark green and tartan plaids, Hackney's smelled of hamburgers and onion rings. Alex's mother made her way awkwardly through the crowd with her walker and when they were seated ordered very little—a half sandwich and a salad. Briggie ordered onion rings and a Hackneyburger. Alex compromised with a plain burger. The decor always made her feel festive, though real Scottish eating establishments looked nothing like Hackney's and wouldn't know how to fix a hamburger if the country's independence relied upon it. All around them, middle-aged and elderly denizens of the North Shore dressed in Polo shirts and madras celebrated the meal with apparent conviviality. They always appeared to have come straight from the golf course, even in winter.

"So. What is it that's giving you problems?" Briggie asked.

Alex enumerated the points one by one on her fingers. "Holly, our client in the treatment center, claims she's not on drugs but that her family is the one with the problems. The grandmother claims her father, wealthy steel baron, was shot in bed and that she ran away to

Hollywood where she had an affair with an actor, eventually married a lawyer, and moved back here. Her daughter denies all of this, saying it's pure fiction. Except the part about her grandfather. There was something fishy about his death, but according to her, he wasn't shot but rather died of some kind of overdose. Holly is just extremely angry."

Amelia gave a little shiver. Briggie considered her and then patted her arm. "It sounds like what Daniel would call 'a bit dysfunctional.' Take deep breaths."

Alex watched her mother. "It is, actually. This is bound to call up ghosts, Mother. Are you sure you want to hear more?"

"Certainly, I do. Here." Abandoning her dinner, Amelia rummaged in her black leather Coach bag and pulled out a stenographer's pad. "Just let me take notes."

Surprised at her mother's efficiency, Alex said, "It seems to me that the first thing we have to do is find out who's telling the truth. I thought we'd start with what Gladys Harrison calls the 'murder.' We ought to be able to get a death certificate and an obituary."

"Then we can move on to the questionable Hollywood marriage to Robert Harrison. Do you know what year it was supposed to have been?" Briggie asked, her keen little brown eyes narrowing as though she were seeing back through the years.

"Let's see." Alex pulled out her genogram sketch and laid it on the table where both other women could see it. "She says she ran off at sixteen. That was in 1936. She married when she was nineteen, making it 1939."

"Shouldn't be a problem then," Briggie said. "What county are we working in?"

"The marriage would have been in L. A. County, I imagine. The Harrison house is in Lake County. I looked in my *Handybook,* and they have death records back to 1877. The county seat is Waukegan, which is almost to Wisconsin. It'll be a drive."

"We'll start with the death records tomorrow." Briggie polished off her onion rings. "As soon as we have a death date, we can go to downtown Chicago to the Newberry Library and see if they can find us an obit in the *Tribune.* If he was that rich and there was any sort of scandal, it'll be there."

"Maybe we can work with California by fax."

"They're kind of touchy about their records there. Want to know why you want them. My daughter can help us."

Amelia, eating in silence, followed this conversation with her head as though it were a tennis match. "These poor people," she said finally. "They won't have a shred of privacy left."

Her mother had a lifelong aversion to any kind of scandal. That fact had led to most of Alex's problems. Her voice sharp, she said, "Maybe you don't want to be involved in this after all, Mother."

She watched as Amelia put down her fork and composed her face. "I don't suppose this information will go beyond Dr. Goodwin at the treatment center, will it?"

"It depends on what we find," Briggie told her. "If there was a murder and we uncover fresh evidence, of course the police will have to have it."

Alex's mother crumbled a piece of sourdough bread between her fingers. "Those poor people," she repeated.

"What if someone *was* murdered, Mother? If he was, it was never solved, you know," Alex said perversely. She didn't believe there really was a murder, but a part of her wanted to scare her mother off. How much reality could she take now that she wasn't numbed by alcohol? "Who can tell what kind of havoc that has caused in this family?"

"You're thinking of our family, aren't you, Alex?" Amelia asked, heaving an enormous sigh. "Secrets."

"Yes. It should be obvious from our experience that those kind of secrets aren't healthy for a family."

Briggie studied the genogram, and Amelia scrutinized her table knife, testing its edge with her thumb. "Dr. Goodwin agrees with you," she said finally.

"Do you really want to be part of this, Amelia?" Briggie asked. "We go for the jugular."

Alex's mother straightened her spine and, putting down the knife, looked Briggie in the eye. "Yes. Yes, of course I do." Then she sagged, bringing both hands to her temples. "It's just that sometimes I think no one has a *normal* life. I want everything to be simple, like it used to be when Alex was little. Before . . ."

"Everyone's got problems, Mother," Alex said briskly. "As Briggie puts it, 'Welcome to mortality.' "

"God's in control, Amelia," Briggie assured her. "Remember your Twelve Steps. We're in his hands. We'll sort this out with his help."

"I think probably Briggie is the most normal person I know. She should have been your mother, not me." Amelia's voice was mournful.

We've been heading this way since yesterday, Alex reflected ruefully.

Briggie intervened. "Honey, there's no way of knowing what I would be like if I'd had to walk in your shoes. I think you're a very strong lady." Putting her plump hand on Amelia's wasted arm, she gave it a gentle squeeze. "Look at the way you're fighting this MS. You've stayed sober through it, even when Alex and I were in England. My life has been a walk in the park compared to yours."

Amelia dropped the subject, allowing herself to be calmed, but Alex could tell that her feelings hadn't changed. Unfortunately, it happened to be true that Briggie *had* been more of a mother to Alex than her own mother had.

Chapter Five

"Daniel sends his love," Briggie reported the next morning as the two of them drove up the North Shore towards Waukegan. With Briggie in the car, there were no ghosts in the dark hollows. Amelia, tired from the outing the day before, had been convinced to stay on the couch. Alex hoped this meant she was having second thoughts about helping them. "He really meant it, bless his heart," her friend continued.

Alex shook her head. "I know. He's kind of like my Greek chorus, wailing and wringing his hands in the background. I wish he could learn to cheer me on instead."

"How is this case bringing up the past? The facts are very different."

"Oh, I wouldn't say that. Maybe it's just that I sympathize with Holly's situation, but I really don't think she's on drugs. I think her parents have stuck her in that hospital for some other reason. Like when I was sent to Paris." She tightened her hands on the wheel. "I really thought I had dealt with all the stuff with my parents, Briggs.

41

I mean, you *know* I've forgiven my mother. I understand why she did what she did, and I love her and want to be with her. But it's hard. Why am I still hanging onto all that emotional garbage I went through as a kid? Isn't forgiveness enough? Isn't knowing the truth enough?"

"What's happening, Alex? Why don't you think you've gotten over it?"

"When Holly started screaming at me, at first it was like I was a child again, trapped with this crazy person. Mother. Then, in some way, I was Holly, too. It was very confusing. I ran away."

Briggie was quiet. "I don't know, honey. I honestly don't know. I've never had to go through what you've gone through. You're willing to forgive. That's the main thing." Opening her carryall, she began rummaging through it as though looking for an answer. "I think maybe you need some deeper kind of healing for all the stuff that's programmed into your nervous system. It's something you and the Lord are going to have to work out." She took out a stick of gum and, unwrapping it thoughtfully, stuck it in her mouth.

Alex bit her lip. So Briggie didn't have an easy answer. It had been childish of Alex to suppose she would. God was there for a reason, and Briggie had never claimed to replace Him. Where did that leave her? With prayer, probably. She shook her head. She had a real problem with humility. It came from all those years of living with Stewart. Mr. "I-did-it-my-way." No, it was too easy to blame Stewart. It was just that it was so hard to surrender that tight little knot of pain inside of her. She didn't want to undo it. She was scared she might lose control. Of her pain. Of her anger.

But she believed in God. He had carried her, rescued her from a senseless universe. Briggie might have been His instrument, but she never would have prevailed if Alex hadn't come to share her beliefs. Somehow, she needed to let go and really trust the Lord or she knew she would never be a really whole, functional person again. She wouldn't be able to truly love.

Traveling in silence for a while, Alex gradually became aware that the car behind them had been tailgating for some time. The road was narrow here, and there was no place to pull over. She checked her rearview mirror.

A string of cars was following them up the winding two-lane road. "Those cars are following kind of close," she said uneasily. "I wish they'd back off."

"Any chance someone's a little too interested in what we're doing?" Briggie asked.

"Don't be dramatic, Briggs. This isn't one of those kind of cases."

"There was that murder."

Alex sighed and looked in her rearview mirror again, taking note. "I can see you're determined to believe Gladys. I should have expected it. Okay. A black car. I don't know what kind, but I'd recognize it again. Then there's a metallic blue van, a red sports car, and another black car—a smaller one."

"Honey, it's obvious you didn't have any brothers." Briggie craned her neck and looked out the back window of Alex's Honda CRX. "The first black car is a Ford Taurus, the van is a Toyota, the red sports car is a Toyota MR2, and the smaller black car is a Honda Civic. This is a kind of Honda Civic, too, for Pete's sake."

"Well, that must be a newer model. I didn't recognize it."

None of the cars parked anywhere close when they stopped at the Lake County Courthouse.

*   *   *

The death certificate, to Alex's surprise, bore out Grandmother Harrison's claim. Her father *had* died of a gunshot wound. The

43

coroner's verdict, a copy of which they also obtained, determined "murder by person or persons unknown."

So Gladys Harrison *had* been telling the truth, and for some reason, Grace Weston hadn't wanted Alex to know it. Did her own husband even know the truth? She doubted it.

Alex held back a groan. She knew Briggie and murder investigations. Her friend was like a bull terrier. And what was Daniel going to say? She'd promised him no murders this time.

Having the documents certified took some time, so Alex and Briggie adjourned down the street to a shabby-looking grill called Ernie's. It smelled strongly of coffee grounds and bacon, the booths were orange plastic, and the tables were chipped walnut formica. Waukegan was definitely not a North Shore kind of town.

"Hang on to your hat," Briggie said after they had both ordered hot chocolate. "Here we go again."

"What would Grace Weston hope to gain by lying? These certificates are in the public domain."

"Well, I've never met her, but maybe she's one of those people who proclaim things and think everyone will believe her just because she's who she is."

"Dangerous. Poor Holly. How many ways has her world been distorted? No wonder she's paranoid." Alex looked out the window at the winter street. Dried leaves the size of her hand were blowing down the sidewalk. Skeletal trees and power lines stretched against the sullen winter sky. "This is like déjà vu, Briggs. I'm glad Mother stayed behind."

Briggie pondered. "I wonder what Holly's mother will do when she's confronted with the truth?"

"Throw us out, I expect. Try to get Holly's hospital changed. Maybe we'd better keep it to ourselves for the time being."

Her colleague nodded as the waitress brought their hot chocolate.

She was an attractive woman of indeterminate age in a western-style brown shirt, bolo tie, and Wrangler jeans, wearing a hair net over her blonde hair. Her name tag said she was Earlene.

"While we're here, we ought to see if there's a copy of the will on file. Now that we know we're dealing with a murder," Briggie said.

Earlene looked startled. "Excuse me, but are you detectives or something?"

Alex smiled. Briggie said, "Sort of. We're professional genealogists."

"Oh." Looking at them uncertainly, her pencil tucked behind her ear, she moved away.

Sipping her chocolate cautiously, Alex found it was surprisingly good. Not instant. "Does it follow that we *have* to solve this? I mean, the police were unsuccessful. What makes you think we should or even could solve it after all this time?"

Briggie stirred her chocolate with a spoon. "We've got a seriously messed-up family here, Alex. Isn't this what doing genograms is all about? Finding out the truth?"

"I suppose you're right." Gazing outside, she realized she really didn't want to leave this booth and go back out into the cold wind.

"We've got to give it a try. If it's something related to the genogram, we'll find it. If not, then it will remain just another unsolved mystery."

"Mother isn't going to like this at all."

"That's her problem, then, Alex. She doesn't have to be involved if she doesn't want to."

"She's jealous of you. She wants to be in this part of my life."

Briggie smiled and patted Alex's arm across the table. "I'd gathered as much."

Leaving Ernie's, they made their way back through the cold to the overheated courthouse, this time visiting the dimly lit, ancient probate court. As Briggie filled out the request, Alex sat on a scarred wooden bench and tried to order her thoughts.

She eventually noticed a man sitting at the end of the bench. He was reading a paper, so she couldn't see his face, but she automatically remarked him as odd, for he was wearing Nikes with a pair of expensive khakis. Daniel would never be guilty of such a breach of taste. Especially in this part of the world. Penny loafers or something yuppie-like were meant to go with khakis.

The will was short, obviously a carbon copy, and typed on a very old machine that had made it fuzzy and hard to read. Accompanying it was a trust, handwritten in the custom of many years before. The lighting in the courthouse was poor.

Briggie consulted her watch. "Almost lunchtime. Let's go back to that little grill. It's my kind of place."

Alex agreed. "I can't read anything in this light."

Earlene was still on duty. Briggie ordered a Reuben sandwich with fries. Alex decided that Ernie was probably unacquainted with fresh vegetables in the wintertime, so she passed on the club salad and ordered chicken noodle soup.

Her colleague spread the documents out on the table. "Let's see. This handwritten document is the original trust of a William Williams leaving his fortune to the oldest son and 'his children in perpetuity.' If the oldest son's line dies out, the money is to revert to his other children and their heirs, with the exception of his daughter Gwenyth."

"What's wrong with Gwenyth?" Alex asked.

"I don't have any idea. The shorter typewritten document is Lloyd Williams Sr.'s actual will. It is dated 1930 and leaves the residual fortune made by him to his children equally in trust and continues the terms of the trust of his father. It looks like he decided to interpret his father's trust literally. Even though Gladys was a girl, he left her half."

Briggie put the will aside when her lunch was served.

"Homemade noodles," Earlene commented. "Sauerkraut on the Reuben is homemade, too. Our cook's a Kraut, himself." She smiled, revealing beautiful teeth. "That fellow over there—friend of yours?"

Alex raised her eyebrows, looking in the direction of their waitress's cocked head. The Nike Man sat studying the menu one booth away from them.

"He asked to be seated near you," Earlene explained. "I thought he might be some kind of kook, you being involved in a murder an' all. Told him that table hadn't been cleaned yet." Indicating the booth next to them, her hazel eyes were wide with curiosity. She probably thought she'd walked into a case straight out of the *X-Files*.

"Thanks," Alex said. "I have no idea who he is."

Digging into her greasy Reuben with relish, Briggie had a one-track mind. "I think we ought to visit Gladys. I'd like to meet her. And she's likely to be the best authority on her brother. Do you suppose he murdered his father?"

Earlene stayed where she was, her red lips parted slightly.

"I think we should keep our voices down," Alex answered in a low monotone. "That man behind you was at the courthouse. Do you think it is possible we're being followed?"

The waitress whispered, "D'you want me to call the police?"

Startled, Briggie looked up from her sandwich. "This isn't anything we can't handle," she assured the woman.

Earlene moved away with obvious reluctance, glancing at Nike Man as she passed his table.

Briggie lowered her tone to match Alex's. "You know I don't like to take chances. Would anyone know what you're working on?"

"Grace Weston tried to stop me. But why would she have me followed? She couldn't have killed her grandfather. He died before she was born."

Considering this, Briggie took another bite of her Reuben. "Doesn't make sense." She shrugged. "But where there's murder, I don't rule anything out. You saw him at the courthouse? What's he look like?"

"Middle-aged. Nondescript. If he hadn't been wearing Nikes with his khakis, I wouldn't have noticed him."

"Honey, I wear Nikes with my skirts."

Alex smiled. "I guess that really doesn't qualify him as a full-fledged kook, then. Maybe he's just lonely or something."

Chapter Six

On the way to the Williams mansion, Briggie checked the cars behind them. "None of the same cars are behind us, but then, if he was listening, he'd know we were going to Gladys's place, so he wouldn't have to follow so close."

"I expect he was just an ordinary guy. Earlene 'got the wind up,' as they say in your favorite detective stories."

They had called Gladys Harrison from Waukegan, and she was expecting them at 2:30. When they arrived, she greeted Briggie with the same warmth she had shown Alex. Lord Peter scooted around their feet, barking excitedly.

"Hello. You're from the treatment center, too?"

"This is my business partner, Brighamina Poulson."

"Great to meet you, Mrs. Harrison. Thanks for letting us come."

Dressed in yet another set of tweeds, pearls, and brogues, Gladys led them once again into the terra-cotta room. Professor Moriarty warned, "Doing it a bit too brown," and fluffed his plumage. It occurred to Alex that the parrot had been educated by someone intimately familiar with Georgette Heyer's Regency romances.

Tuppence recognized Briggie immediately as a cat person and threaded herself lovingly through her ankles. Briggie stopped to admire the animal.

"Beautiful coat," she remarked. "Marmalade."

"Thank you," Gladys Harrison said. "I'm afraid I spoil Tuppence. She eats a lot of albacore. This is dear Lord Peter."

The little dog ran around in circles, apparently delighted at the company. Alex and Briggie seated themselves on the Regency-striped couch.

"Tuppence?" Briggie said. "As in Tommy and Tuppence? Agatha Christie?"

Gladys smiled sunnily. "So few people understand the allusion."

"And Lord Peter is Lord Peter Wimsey, of course," Briggie went on.

"Not quite up to snuff," Moriarty pronounced.

"And this is Holmes's nemesis," Gladys said fondly, speaking of her parrot.

"Professor Moriarty?" Briggie had a twinkle in her little brown eyes.

"Right." Even though she had to be in her seventies, the woman gave them a naughty look as she sat in a needlepoint chair. "I understand you put a bee in my daughter's bonnet." She laughed. "She doesn't like me talking about the past. Me, I think it needs airing. Grace has spent her whole life trying to keep a lid on things. I wouldn't be surprised if that control is what Holly's trying to escape. She's got my grandfather's fire, that girl. She's Welsh to the bone."

"Your grandfather?" Briggie asked. "The one who made the fortune?"

"Yes. William Williams. He didn't die until I was about ten, so I remember him a little. He was very fierce with great white eyebrows.

50

You know, the kind with long hairs like wires that twist all around? He was real small. My grandmother, who was much younger, was taller than he was. I guess he didn't get enough to eat as a youngster. Did I tell you his father was a coal miner and that he started life the same way?"

Alex nodded vaguely, studying the genogram in her hands. Was everything Mrs. Harrison told them true? She now supposed that it might be.

Briggie asked, "What was your grandmother's name?" Tuppence had unceremoniously leapt into her lap. Briggie petted her absently.

"Angela. She was a Duncan. My mother drilled it into me from the time I was tiny that I was a Duncan of the Lake Forest Duncans. They were not only rich but had moved here from the East and were considered 'old money.'" She swept the room with her arms. "She decorated and furnished this house. It was her pride and joy. She was a patron of the arts and that sort of thing. But Grandmother Williams never had much time for me or any of my grandfather's Welsh relations. I liked them, of course."

"What about your father's brothers and sisters? We didn't talk about that last time," Alex said as she fleshed out her chart with new facts.

"Devil of a fellow," the Professor informed them.

"I had an Uncle William, my father's older brother, but he died just before Grandfather. They didn't ever talk about it. I suspect it may have been suicide."

Alex raised her eyebrows at Briggie.

"Being closemouthed seems to run in your family," Briggie remarked, apparently accepting Gladys's pronouncement. "But maybe it was just too painful to talk about it. That wouldn't be strange. Someone might have been to blame or thought they were to blame."

Gladys Harrison smiled her serene smile as though she liked

nothing better than stirring things up. Lord Peter had settled in his favorite position, his head on her brogues. Alex still found it difficult to take everything she said at face value.

"Any other siblings?" Briggie asked.

Gladys replied. "My Aunt Gwenyth. She married a Dr. Gustav Gunther. My grandfather never liked him because he was first-generation German. She was virtually disowned. I don't think she inherited under Grandfather's will."

The woman paused and reached down to stroke Lord Peter's ears. Then she went on, her voice definite. "In fact, I know she didn't. It wasn't an ordinary will but a trust fund set up for my father. Grandmother reconciled with Aunt Gwyneth after Grandfather died, and I think she left her all of her Duncan money." Smiling wistfully, she added, "I got to know Aunt Gwenyth quite well eventually. My father was fond of her, and she often came over to the house. She had a German shepherd, of course."

"Whew!" said Briggie. "I really appreciate your helping us like this. It sounds like your grandfather was a strong personality. If Holly takes after him, I can see where she might have a few blowups with her mother."

"Poor Grace. Don't judge her too harshly. I am fond of her, you know."

"What it boils down to, then, is that all the Williams money went to your father?" Alex persisted.

"That's right. Under the trust."

Looking at her colleague, she plunged on, "I believe you told me you had a brother who died."

"Yes. Lloyd Jr. I'm afraid he was a big disappointment to my father. He was only twenty when Father died, but already he'd been in trouble. Rich-kid syndrome, I guess you'd call it today."

"Anything that could have any bearing on Holly's problems?"

Briggie asked, adding, "We appreciate your frankness with us, Mrs. Harrison."

"All rolled up," squawked the macaw.

Gladys sighed, for the first time looking bothered. "Well, I suppose it wouldn't be difficult for you to find out that Lloyd was the number one suspect when Father was killed. Even though it was never proven, it gave our family the sort of notoriety that is never really lived down on the North Shore." There was sadness in her eyes now. "When Lloyd married, they moved away. Even though it was half his under the trust, he never lived in this house after his marriage. When Mother died, he turned his half of it over to Robert and me. So Grace grew up under a cloud." She got up and went over to stroke her parrot. Perhaps she felt her daughter's defection far more than she let on. "It would have helped if they had just proven it one way or another. I think she's suffered more from it than Lloyd did. Underneath that armor of hers, she's actually pretty sensitive. Or anyway, she used to be."

Seeing her hostess's sudden melancholy, Alex wondered how much of the woman's serenity was assumed. As she worked to fill in the remaining places on the genogram, she once again felt overwhelmed by all the information. It was very poignant that in spite of all these relations, the woman before her lived alone in the family home. That enforced separateness might account for her volubility. She was probably starved for company and wanted to entertain them.

Alex handed the genogram to Briggie for her approval. From this perspective, it looked as though the murder *was* central to Grace's problems and therefore Holly's. Would solving the murder heal this family or wrench it further apart? With so much money involved, it could easily be a genealogical matter. The problem was, except for Lloyd Jr. and Gladys herself, there seemed to be a dearth of suspects.

Their hostess insisted that they stay for tea. When asked if she

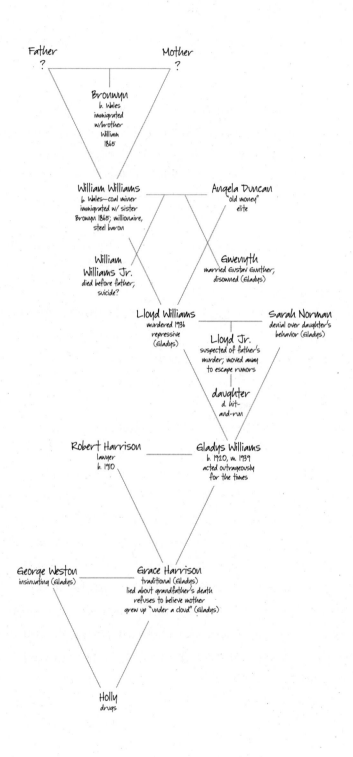

Father
?

Mother
?

Bronwyn
b. Wales
immigrated
w/brother
William
1865

William Williams
b. Wales—coal miner
immigrated w/ sister
Bronwyn 1865; millionaire,
steel baron

Angela Duncan
"old money"
elite

William
Williams Jr.
died before father;
suicide?

Gwenyth
married Gustav Gunther;
disowned (Gladys)

Lloyd Williams
murdered 1936
repressive
(Gladys)

Sarah Norman
denial over daughter's
behavior (Gladys)

Lloyd Jr.
suspected of father's
murder; moved away
to escape rumors

daughter
d. hit-
and-run

Robert Harrison
lawyer
b. 1910

Gladys Williams
b. 1920, m. 1939
acted outrageously
for the times

George Weston
insinuating (Gladys)

Grace Harrison
traditional (Gladys)
lied about grandfather's death
refuses to believe mother
grew up "under a cloud" (Gladys)

Holly
drugs

perhaps had any herbal tea, Gladys replied that yes, she had some chamomile for when she needed to relax. Both Briggie and Alex requested it.

Gladys prepared tea in the customary British manner Alex had become used to in Scotland. Her china was Royal Doulton, blue-and-white flowered.

"My grandfather always insisted on tea in the afternoons. We lived with him and my grandmother, you know. All of us together in this great big house."

Whatever she thought of her father, it seemed clear that she had tender memories of her grandparents.

"How many years has it been since your husband died?" Alex asked gently.

The woman looked at her with her slow, serene smile. "Oh, my Robert's been gone since 1980. Now tell me about *your* families."

Alex left this to Briggie, who was enjoying a gingersnap. With her nine children scattered to the four winds, she always had plenty of stories to tell.

"My youngest is living in Brazil of all places," she told Gladys. "He went there on a mission for our church, and when he came home he never could settle down. Couldn't even pray unless it was in Portuguese. Missed the food and the people."

"What on earth does he do in Brazil?"

"Teaches entrepreneurship at a university in São Paulo. He made a little money on a high tech start-up," Briggie said offhandedly. Warren was actually a multimillionaire who was volunteering his expertise, trying to lift the curse of poverty from his beloved Brazilians. Briggie supported him in his efforts but missed him and his children terribly.

"Well, I call that wonderful," said Gladys. "You must have raised that boy right." She sighed. "I'm afraid I didn't do too well by my

Grace. All she seems to care about is appearances. What about you, Mrs. Campbell?"

"Please call me Alex. I'm a widow, too, although I don't have any children." She took a sip of her chamomile tea and forced herself to be more forthcoming than she usually was. "Right now I'm staying with my mother in Winnetka. I actually grew up on the North Shore, like you. But our business is based in Kansas City."

At this point, Briggie began regaling Gladys with humorous anecdotes of their adventures. Her tea finished, she had taken Tuppence on to her lap again.

"You'd be amazed at the places we've found the clue that filled in the blanks on a pedigree. I always was a fan of Agatha Christie, but as they say, truth is stranger than fiction. One time the evidence was in the sleeve of a sleazy video!"

Gladys's laugh trilled out. "Oh, you two must have so much fun." There was a wistfulness on her face that tore at Alex's heart.

Briggie put her arm around Alex's shoulders as they walked to the car. "I'm sure glad I have you, kiddo."

"Likewise. What a waste. All that zest for life, and she's just shut up in that old house."

"I think I'm going to encourage her to write her life's story," Briggie said. "Holly should have it."

"She'll have to smuggle it to her. And I doubt if Holly would ever believe it. She's been too brainwashed."

* * *

Daniel called late that afternoon before her date with Charles. Seeing his name on caller ID, she answered with mixed emotions. "Hello?"

"Alex?"

"Hi, Daniel. Is Maxie running up your draperies yet?"

"Marigny's got her in the gym downstairs. She's going to keep him there this time. How are things?"

She wondered how much she could tell him without alerting his protective radar. "Progressing," she said finally. "We've got an interesting case. Everyone has a different version of reality."

"How's the patient? Holly, I think you said?"

"She's in pretty sad shape, I'm afraid. We've got some serious work to do. It's turning out that the genogram is really going to be valuable in this case."

"Then I'm really glad you're doing it. I actually called to apologize."

Alex laughed a little ruefully. "I was telling Briggie you're my Greek chorus, standing in the background wringing your hands."

"I'm giving up hand-wringing."

She was agreeably surprised. "Are you sure?"

"I've resolved to. I've taken up weight lifting again as a cure."

"Daniel, you really don't need to worry about me, you know. I'm having a great time with this. I just had to ask Briggie to come up because it's really complicated, but we're going to 'get to the bottom of it,' as she always says."

He was silent for a moment, and she was conscious that perhaps she had explained a little too much. She decided a little discreet confiding would lend the picture more verisimilitude. She was alone in her bedroom, getting ready to go out.

"Mother is having some problems with Briggie being here. I expected it. She's decided she wants to help us on the case."

"And how do you feel about that?"

"Mixed. I'm glad she's showing an interest in real life, though."

"Yeah. But it makes it kind of hard to stand back and let her heal when she's zeroing in on your territory." As usual, Daniel had put his finger on the problem.

"She's pretty handicapped with the MS. Maybe we can put her to work on the telephone or something," Alex replied.

There was a short silence, unusual in a conversation between them.

"Look," Daniel said finally. "Maybe you're right about the knight thing. Maybe I'm a carryover from the Middle Ages. I'd like better than anything to rush off to some kind of joust with your handkerchief tied to my lance."

Alex laughed at the image.

"What I'm trying to tell you is that the *very last* thing I want is to be fatherly or brotherly or anything like that."

Grinning, she said, "Thank goodness."

"Well, if you were here, I'd give you a convincing demonstration, whether you liked it or not."

The words were said so masterfully that she was glad she wasn't there. She wondered if she would be proof against Daniel in a masterful mood. He might just flatten her fences. He was already too close.

"I've been thinking that maybe I analyze things too much," he went on. "I've always known I couldn't push you. I've tried to stand back and let you come to me on your terms, Alex."

"But you don't," she burst out. "You can't seem to help acting like a therapist. It's an uninvited intimacy."

There was silence. "Are you telling me there's no hope?"

Was she? "I just wish you didn't see me the way you do," she said. "It's not your fault."

"What do you mean?"

"You know all my weaknesses."

"And you know mine," he responded unexpectedly. "I have a father who drives me crazy and treats me like I'm still a kid, a daughter who's trying to be a femme fatale at the age of fourteen, an ex-wife who ran off with her golf instructor and left me with this huge chip on my shoulder . . ."

"But, Daniel," she interrupted, genuinely startled. "I never think of you that way. Is that really how you feel?"

"Of course it is. You're not the only one with issues, for crying out loud. And besides all that, I'm only five foot ten."

Unable to help a laugh, she said, "My gosh. You make me feel like such a self-centered diva. I'm sorry. It honestly never occurred to me that you had any insecurities."

"Oh, for Pete's sake. Do I seem like a mental health poster child or something?"

"Yes," she said. "Sort of a short version of Superman."

"How sickening. No wonder you've kept your distance."

"A woman likes to feel that she has something to work with," she told him lightly. "Now that I know about your inferiority complex, I feel more like I'm needed. You're so self-sufficient, Dr. Grinnell."

He sighed audibly. "I'm only a man, Alex. And believe me, the last thing I see you as is a client. When can I come visit you?"

She was instantly back in the treatment center hearing Holly scream. *I've got to get a handle on myself first.* Then another idea intruded upon her anxiety. It was an unwelcome stranger. Even though he had done so in a comic vein, Daniel had just bared his soul. He had been attempting to level the playing field. Did she want to play by these new rules?

"I'm not really sure, Daniel. Briggie and I are pretty busy."

"Well, let me know if there are any murderers to chase down," he said, switching to a breezy tone. "I wouldn't want to miss the fun again."

Was he omniscient? She was assailed by memories of Daniel's assistance in the case of her father's murder last year. Together they had hung on as if they were riding double on a bucking bronco. In some ways it had been horrible, but the heat of their ordeal had forged a bond between them she couldn't shrug off. It was the genesis of her present dilemma. Her voice soft, she said, "If I need a karate black belt, I'll be sure to let you know."

When they hung up, she felt she had barely escaped with her defenses intact.

Chapter Seven

The restaurant was as elegant as she had known it would be—a tiny bistro off Michigan Avenue renowned for its wine and vegetarian menu. There were high ceilings, linen tablecloths in pale pink, red roses on every table, and a maître d' in evening dress.

But at first Alex registered none of these details. Charles was awaiting her in the foyer. He was the kind of man who always caught the gaze of every woman in the room. This time was no exception. Carrying himself with complete assurance, he could be His Royal Highness himself. This, together with his Greek god features and fair hair, gave him extraordinary presence. He wore a navy dinner jacket. She was glad she had decided on her turquoise sheath with her mother's pearls. This was about as dressy as she ever got.

She hadn't seen Charles since the day they had said farewell at Heathrow, and here in Chicago he seemed larger than life. After the conversation with Daniel, she was feeling slightly vulnerable. But she and Charles were on different terms. She doubted he would make any emotional demands.

But he *was* intimidating. Lifting her chin, she told herself she had rubbed shoulders with the greatest photographers in the world and solved two murders. She wouldn't let herself be intimidated.

He was standing by the maître d's stand, gazing into the dining room.

"Hello, Charles."

"Alex. At last." Moving forward, he placed a peck on her cheek. Charles always kissed the women in his life.

They followed the maître d' to a prominent table. *He must realize what snob value Charles has,* she thought.

Unfortunately, it was very noisy. A man with a beaked nose and a fringe of silver hair in surprisingly casual clothes was soon seated alone next to them, and Alex suspected he had nothing better to do than listen to their conversation. This made her acutely reticent.

"How's the legal tangle coming?" she asked, trying to be heard above the din. Charles was in the United States to sort out the complicated mess of Borden Meats. Though she had always thought her father was the sole owner of the company, her researches had unveiled a whole other branch of the family in England. It now appeared that they were all joint heirs of the Borden meatpacking fortune.

"We may have a buyer for the business." Alex detected a spark of triumph in Charles's eyes. This was his first venture into entrepreneurship. At Oxford he had been a theater critic and a tutor at Christ Church College.

Through all three courses, they talked only about the complex estate they had inherited from their shared great-great-grandfather. The grilled Portobello mushrooms on saffron rice, meatless lasagna, and creamy tiramisu were excellent, but Alex felt more and more as though she were discussing business with a very well-mannered stranger. It wasn't until after the dessert that she gave him her colleague's message. "Briggie asked to be remembered to you."

He grinned his first true grin. "The redoubtable chaperone has come to watch over her *jeune fille*, then?"

"I'm not a *jeune fille*, and Briggie is certainly not a chaperone," she said with feigned heat. "Besides, I'm living with my mother, in case you had any designs on my virtue. Briggie's come to help me with my work. It's turning out to be pretty complicated."

"Let's get out of here," he said suddenly, stacking currency on top of the bill. The ice was finally broken. He was the old, impatient Charles.

She gave a little smile, a short, genuine laugh, and then relaxed. It was far too cold to walk down Michigan Avenue, so Alex suggested taking a cab to the Drake. They could sit in the lobby and he could have coffee or whatever he liked and she could have a cup of herb tea.

There, in the cozy surroundings that reminded Alex so vividly of England, they sat side by side on a blue velvet loveseat. At least they were rid of the bald man. Charles put his arm across the back of the seat, the tips of his fingers barely touching the silk of her dress.

"How did you leave everyone in England?" she asked, resuming the tenor of their previous conversation.

"Hang my relatives. How are you really doing, Alex? You seem a bit out of sorts."

"What do you mean?"

"Well, for one thing, during dinner you kept pulling at the neck of your dress. And you can't seem to keep still. It's not me, is it? I mean, I'm just Charles."

"No," she said carefully. "It's not you. It's a combination of things."

"Anything you want to talk about?"

There was nothing she wanted less. Charles didn't know of her personal struggles, and she wanted to keep it that way. It was bad enough to have one man in your life who thought you were a basket case. In England, Charles had known a strong, self-possessed Alex who had saved his life.

Just then, she spotted their silver-haired friend from the restaurant behind a potted palm. He was close enough to hear their conversation, although he appeared to be reading the evening paper. This made her more determined than ever to keep her own counsel. Sitting up straighter, she said flatly, "No. It's just a difficult case. Briggie and I will deal with it."

He put the hand that had been so near directly on her shoulder and peered into her face with concern. For a moment, his cool blue eyes remained fully on hers, but when he saw her deliberate calm, he adopted a similar attitude. They talked airily of his mother and cousins until Charles had finished his coffee.

"This has been great," she said, looking up with determined good humor. "You've got to come to dinner on Sunday to see Briggie and meet my mother."

He smoothed her cheek with a finger. "That would be lovely. Shall I see you to the train?"

Alex nodded, and they rose to hail a cab. At the station, Charles left her with another chaste peck on the cheek. Though the evening had been far from comfortable, in Charles's presence she had felt once again like the competent woman he had known at Oxford.

*   *   *

"I can't help thinking how much Gladys would enjoy this expedition to the Newberry," Briggie exclaimed the next day. "I hate to think of her sitting in that house all alone."

"Maybe we can take her downtown one day," Alex suggested. "I wonder how long it's been since she's shopped on Michigan Avenue."

They were almost at the library now, that most distinguished of genealogical institutions. Its Italian Renaissance-arched façade always made her blood run quicker. There was nothing like being "on the chase." Fortunately, they had brought their credentials proving them to be serious genealogists.

The lady at the information desk was small and desiccated, with ancient spectacles that looked pre–World War II. Her dyed black hair was permed into a fuzzy cloud, and she wore a magenta knit suit of very good quality. With such a jumble of contradictory indicators, Alex hadn't a clue to her real personality or how she would greet them. The Newberry was famous for its Tartars.

This lady proved to be one of them. She looked askance at their casual attire. Briggie was wearing her white polyester slacks and blue Royals sweatshirt, and Alex, her jeans and black turtleneck. When they gave her their business card, she examined it minutely. Alex then handed over the contract between herself and the treatment center that requested her to do the genograms.

The magenta lady was, at length, satisfied. She directed them to the newspaper index for the *Tribune.*

Looking up the name of Lloyd Williams provided them with a long list of dates and issues, but Briggie noted down only those that occurred after the death date in January 1936. After they had requested these issues on microfilm, Alex and Briggie sat down in two leather wing-backed chairs to wait.

"So we're to see Charles on Sunday?"

"That's the plan."

"Who's going to cook?" Briggie wanted to know.

Alex hadn't considered this. All of them hated to cook. Stewart had been the chef in their family, Briggie had burned out cooking for eleven every night, and Amelia appeared almost helpless in the kitchen. While they were debating this issue, they were paged to retrieve the microfilms they had asked for.

First, they read the obituary, which gave a sanitized version of the death, listing the birth and death dates of Lloyd Williams, which Alex added to her chart. Born July 25, 1895. Died January 12, 1936. Obviously, the source of the obit had been a socially conscious wife, for much was said about Lloyd's father, the great steel magnate, and his mother, the celebrated Angela Duncan.

Moving on from there, they got to the real news. It had made the front page. "STEEL MAGNATE'S HEIR FOUND SHOT IN BED."

Following this were sparse details doled out by the local police: no weapon was found on the scene, all the doors to the house were locked when the shooting had been discovered, the caliber of the bullet had not yet been determined.

Later versions of the story zoomed in on the family, quickly establishing Lloyd Jr. as the prime suspect. He had no alibi. He was at odds with his father over problems with money and women. He, of course, would not have been deterred by locked doors. And he stood to profit.

The newspapers did not entirely rule out Gladys, however. The odd arrangements of the will were revealed, along with rumors of strained family relationships. The possible suicide of Lloyd's brother, William, was even resurrected.

No weapon was ever found. There was no trace of a weapon connected with the Williams family. All the evidence against the family was circumstantial. The tenor of the articles suggested the Williams's wealth and position precluded a trial that might misfire badly. So in the end, the coroner ruled the death, "murder by person or persons unknown."

But the newspapers hadn't let it rest. They had continued to follow Lloyd Jr. through every step of his life as the "son of the murdered Lloyd Williams Sr." This was even mentioned in a small article inserted at the time of his marriage. No wonder the poor man had left the area.

Gladys's departure was also mentioned, but as she had been discreet, no one knew where she had gone, and follow-up was impossible. Briggie pointed out that speculation might have led to a libel action. None was made. As with Lloyd Jr., the facts were simply reported.

"Well," Briggie said, "I really don't see that this gives us a whole lot more information."

"Except the locked doors and the lack of a murder weapon," Alex told her. "We didn't know about that before."

"That seems to point to someone in the family, but would anyone be that stupid?"

"I imagine the police wondered the same thing."

"Well, what next?"

"Let's make copies of these, and then I suppose we need to verify that Gladys went to Hollywood."

*   *   *

Among Briggie's many children was a daughter who lived in Riverside, California. While this was certainly not many miles from Los Angeles as the crow flies, it was actually a nightmarish journey over gridlocked freeways and never-ending suburbs. However, Lorna Jean promised faithfully that, as requested, she would get a babysitter for her six children and drive into Los Angeles on Monday to the county recorder to see if she could find a record of a marriage between Gladys Williams and Robert Harrison some time in 1939. In return, Alex promised her that RootSearch, Inc., would reimburse her for gas, baby-sitter, and time. She determined to send her a gift basket of Crabtree & Evelyn bath products as well. From her experience of L.A. as portrayed on television, Alex felt as though she were sending Briggie's daughter on a dangerous mission.

After making the call that evening, she and Briggie held a council of war at the dining room table. They had dined on a green salad and spaghetti sauce mixed with canned clams over linguini noodles. Alex considered it one of her better efforts.

"I wonder about that daughter of Lloyd Jr.'s who died last year," Briggie remarked. "You just have a circle here. No name. She would have come into her father's money when he died. Hit-and-run, huh? I wonder who came in for her money."

"I forgot about her," Alex said. "I don't even have a name. I remember feeling completely overwhelmed by everything Gladys was giving me at the time, but I don't know how it could be important. She was born after the murder."

"Get your mind off the murder for just a minute. This could be suspicious all by itself. We need to find out if she had any heirs. I think it's important. This family is screwy."

Amelia entered the room at this point, a brilliant smile on her face. She stood a little taller and only touched her walker with the tips of her fingers. "Guess what. My legs. I just stood up, and suddenly they seemed to have gotten a little stronger."

"That's wonderful!" Alex rose and embraced her mother in genuine pleasure. "Can it really be a remission? Do such things happen?"

"Oh, yes," said Briggie. "That's one of the good things about MS. It can go into remission for a long time."

"Now I can help you on the case!" Amelia crowed, looking at the chart on the table. "What have you found out?"

"Holly's grandmother's story is true," Briggie told her. "Her father was murdered." She showed her a copy of the article from the *Tribune.*

"Oh, dear," said Amelia. "Does the poor girl know?"

"No," Alex said. "Fortunately, that's not our business. We just have to give the facts to Dr. Goodwin, and then she will decide what to do with them."

Her mother exchanged a glance with her. "I wish Dr. Goodwin had been in my life twenty years ago," she said.

Alex bit her lip. How different would their lives have been if her mother had decided to face the crisis in her life head-on instead of escaping into an alcoholic neverland? She would never know. As Briggie said, you acted the script you were given. It wasn't any good dwelling on might-have-beens.

That night Alex determined it was time to take her friend's advice, and she went straight to the Lord. Kneeling by her bed in serious prayer, she pleaded, "I'm not very good at this, Heavenly Father. Please help me heal these old wounds. Please help me to go forward with my life, not backwards. Please help me to feel real forgiveness and love." But she held her hurts tightly to her, binding her aching chest with her arms. How could she ever let go? The idea of being "as a little child" was terrifying.

Chapter Eight

The next day being Saturday, Alex slept late and woke up to the gray winter morning with a feeling of malaise. Lying under the quilt her mother had made, she gave herself a pep talk. Mother was better. That was a cause for rejoicing. Briggie was here, and they were making progress on the case.

She went over the facts in her mind. They wouldn't hear from Lorna Jean until Monday. But she felt increasingly sure that Gladys's Hollywood adventure was true. So where did they go from here? The murder. The family. Lloyd Jr., Gladys, and Sarah Norman Williams, the wife of the murdered Lloyd Williams Sr. What did they know about her? Nothing. But something prodded her brain. For some reason the later newspapers hadn't focused on her as a suspect. What was it?

Drawing on her navy blue terry cloth robe, she padded downstairs to her mother's sitting room where they had left the copies of the newspaper articles they had found yesterday. Reading through them again, she came upon the sentence, "Mrs. Williams, visiting her

70

sister in Canada, was notified of the death of her husband by telephone."

Well. That disposed of Gladys's mother satisfactorily. But it left only Gladys and her brother. She would stake Stewart's diamond, her most valuable possession, upon Gladys's innocence. Lloyd Jr. Had he really murdered his father? How would they ever find out?

Briggie walked in. "Alex, what's the name of that great pancake place? I think we should take your mother out this morning to celebrate her remission."

"Walker's Original Pancake House," Alex said instantly. "Oh, Briggie, that's a great idea."

After a sumptuous brunch, at which Alex consumed an entire sizzling, fat apple pancake, she, Briggie, and her mother took a drive up the Shore. The early gray overcast skies had succumbed to a strong wind off Lake Michigan, and now the sky was cloudless with crystal sunlight casting long shadows on the trees, so that they drove in and out of the light as though they were traveling through tunnels.

"It's been a long time since I've done this," Amelia said. "Your father and I used to take you on Sunday drives when you were little. Do you remember, Alex?"

"Yes," she lied. In fact, everything earlier than age sixteen was blocked in Alex's mind. There were pictures in the attic that proved she had had a happy childhood, but she could remember very little of it. She knew that she needed to be willing to go there. To succumb to the hurt. To be willing to feel it and look past it.

Wrenching her mind from this path, she found herself thinking of Holly. What were Holly's memories of early childhood? She was much closer to them than Alex was. Maybe she could remember something that would help. But Holly mistrusted her, to put it mildly. How could she ever force her way into that room again? Shouldn't she respect Holly's boundaries?

Now she was sounding like a therapist. Distancing herself. She wrinkled her nose. *Face it.* What she was really afraid of was that the girl would start screaming again, making her relive her own ordeal. But she had a job to do.

She tried to think of what was *really* best for Holly in the long run. Her mother had lied to her all her life. Possibly her mother had stuck her in the treatment center for reasons only known to the elder Westons. She had denied her the company of a nurturing grand-mother. Didn't Alex owe it to Holly to find out the truth? She was the adult. Holly was the child. She was helpless to get herself out of that prison. Alex hadn't been able to help herself when she was a child, but she could help Holly.

Drawing a deep breath, she asked, "Do you mind if we go by the treatment center on our way back? I just want to visit Holly for a couple of minutes."

Her friend, who was driving, looked at her quickly. "Are you sure?"

"I've just thought of something I want to ask her. Besides, what else is there to do?"

Saturdays were generally long days for the patients at the treat-ment center. With no planned activities, those without passes to the outside world could only watch television, videos, or stare at the four walls. Holly was doing the latter.

"It's you," she challenged when Alex entered. "I thought I told you to stay out."

Looking squarely at Gladys's scrappy granddaughter, Alex tried to detect what was beneath her hostile exterior. Under their heavy black makeup, her eyes were both wary and desperate. She was like a cor-nered animal. Alex's mind flew back to the methods Briggie had used to coax her out of her own corner.

Leaving Holly plenty of space, Alex remained standing in the doorway. "Holly, you feel like everyone's ganged up against you, don't you?"

The girl looked down at her black toenails. "How would *you* feel if you were sixteen years old and you were forced to go to prison for something you never did?"

"When I was eighteen, my parents sent me away. I never knew why. I wasn't allowed to come home again."

"Why would they do that?"

"It turns out that it was for my own safety. But I didn't know that until last year. Even though I understand now, it still hurts."

Holly turned sullen. "It's not like that with me."

"What do you mean?"

"Why do you care?"

"Maybe because I know just a little bit of what you're going through. I believe you, Holly. I don't think you've been taking drugs."

"Are you serious? All the doctors think I'm a druggie." Her eyes were narrowed in suspicion.

"I'm coming at this from a different place than the doctors are. I recognize how you feel." She moved further into the room. "Like I told you, I've been there, Holly. You feel like you're the only one who knows the truth, don't you?"

The girl nodded, looking down.

"Why don't you share it with me? Why did your parents put you in here if it wasn't because of drugs?"

She looked up at Alex, her brown eyes regarding her skeptically. "You won't believe me."

"Try me. I won't tell anyone if you don't want me to."

"It wouldn't do any good. Everyone believes my parents."

Alex hesitated and then decided to go with her instincts. "Holly, I've already proven that your parents are lying about something. A great big thing. It wouldn't surprise me at all to hear that they are lying about you."

The girl's eyes widened. "No kidding?"

"No kidding. So what's the real story?" Alex came all the way into the room and sat down.

"I think they must have, like, spent my inheritance or something," the girl said in a small, hesitant voice. "I already get a big allowance from Granny, but, like, I get my trust money when I turn eighteen. Anyway, I'm supposed to."

Alex raised her eyebrows in question.

"I've got friends," she asserted stubbornly. "They think, like, if my parents can prove I'm a druggie then, like, I won't get control of my money."

"You think they're trying to prove you're mentally incompetent?"

"Yeah. I told you you wouldn't believe me."

Alex said thoughtfully, "I suppose that could be the reason. It makes sense." Was Holly right? If so, why had Mr. Weston insisted on keeping her at North Side because of the security? "Holly, did your parents seem scared of anything?"

"Yeah. At least my mom is. She's, like, totally paranoid. She wouldn't let me go anywhere by myself. Like, she even drove me to school and back."

"That's weird," Alex acknowledged. "I wonder why. When did this start? Has she always been that way?"

Holly considered. "No. Not really. My mom's never been cool, but my dad is. He hasn't really changed. But suddenly, like, Mom's gotta have me under her thumb. It's been that way since," she looked at the ceiling, calculating, "since I broke up with Peter."

"And that was . . . ?"

"Last April."

Alex tried to put the pieces together. Was it possible that Holly's treatment had nothing to do with the genogram? Why had she assumed it had? "Did Peter threaten you or anything?"

"No way. He's cool. He taught me to ski last winter. We had a blast."

Alex didn't feel comfortable asking her why they broke up. "Did anything else happen around that time?"

Holly shrugged. "I don't, like, hang out with my parents much. I keep to my space."

Standing, Alex said, "Well, I don't know what's going on, but I promise you I'm going to try to find out."

"Mom won't like that," Holly informed her.

"I know. But your grandmother will."

"Granny?"

"She says you remind her of her grandfather."

"The steel dude?" Holly let out a childish peal of laughter. "That's too much. Mom goes, 'Your grandmother lives in a dream world. Don't ever take her seriously.' She, like, hardly lets me talk to Granny. How could she know what I'm like?"

Alex wondered. Had the older woman merely projected her own feelings onto Holly? "She knows something's not right," she insisted.

"Well, maybe she's not so bad. Even if she does, like, tell whoppers. Her animals are cool."

Alex smiled. "I think you'd like your grandmother if you got to know her."

"Fat chance," Holly returned glumly.

At that moment, Grace Weston came into the room. Her face instantly grew pink with outrage as she recognized Alex. "What are *you* doing here?"

"Oh," said Alex. "Hello, Mrs. Weston. I was just visiting Holly. I'll go now."

The woman, dressed in a sleek black wool pantsuit, turned to her daughter. "What have you been talking about?"

Holly surprised Alex. "Why do you think I'd talk to anyone in this place? I've been telling her to cool it."

Grace Weston held herself stiffly. "That's right, Holly. She has no business here."

Taking her cue, Alex walked towards the door.

*   *   *

After relating the conversation to Briggie and her mother as they wound their way back to Winnetka, she mused aloud, "I think Grace Weston is scared. I think for some reason she's got Holly in the treatment center for Holly's own protection. And Grace was really freaked out over what I might have been talking to her daughter about."

"Hmm," Briggie answered. "What do you think they'd be scared of?"

"I think it must be some physical threat. They were driving her to and from school."

"But then why would she have worried about what you were talking to her about?" asked Amelia. "It must be something to do with the genogram."

Alex pondered her mother's contribution. "Why would she be worried I'd tell Holly about the murder?"

"Scandal," her mother said. "She's worried about scandal all her life."

It was perhaps inevitable that her mother should come to this conclusion, but it didn't explain why the Westons had put Holly in the treatment center.

"Come to think of it," Amelia said thoughtfully, "maybe Grace

Weston knows her mother committed the murder. Maybe that's what she's afraid you'll find out."

Alex didn't know whether to be more shocked at the suggestion or at her mother's having made it. Amelia was entering into the case with a vengeance now.

"I never thought of that," she admitted.

"Stranger things have happened," her mother observed. "You never know what people are going to do when their backs are against the wall."

Alex had to agree with that sentiment.

"Maybe she is pulling the wool over our eyes," Briggie said. "Maybe she's not such a sweet old thing. Maybe Grace Weston knows it."

Alex pondered this. "That doesn't explain why she stuck Holly in the treatment center."

"Maybe she does have problems with drugs," her mother insisted.

Looking out the window at the temporarily serene lake that could blow up such sudden, treacherous storms, Alex said, "I believe Holly. But you're right. I guess we have to remember that everything isn't always what it seems."

*   *   *

That afternoon, Alex, her mother, and Briggie finally drew straws over the question of who was to prepare Sunday dinner for Charles. Briggie was the unfortunate winner and decided the meal was to be stew. Alex, having relinquished all control when she agreed to the draw, winced inwardly. Charles was a gourmet. Oh, well.

"I don't think I've made a good stew since the kids left," Briggie said.

"Well, don't make it for eleven," Alex reminded her. "Isn't there a bakery in town where I can buy some yummy little pastries or something?" she asked her mother.

"Ashley's, of course. We've gone there since you were a baby," Amelia reminded her.

So they went together to Ashley's, leaving Briggie to do her shopping in the Bronco.

"Just how do you feel about this young man, Alex?" her mother asked.

Suddenly reduced to teenager status by her mother's question, Alex replied with an edge. "First of all, Charles is not a kid, Mother. He's forty-six."

"Divorced?"

"No. Bachelor. He was in love with his first cousin, and of course they couldn't marry. Anyway, they had a strange relationship."

"What do you mean, strange?" Her mother was looking at her with interest.

Alex swallowed her indignation. After all, her mother had never been around when she'd dated Stewart. They'd never talked about men together. "He dated other women but never wanted to marry anyone but her. He was afraid if he did marry, he couldn't go on loving Philippa."

"You sound like it's all in the past."

"She was the one who was murdered at Oxford."

"Oh." Amelia contemplated this for a moment, looking as though she had been given a bitter pill. Then she drew a breath and said, "Well, I'm looking forward to meeting him. But you still haven't answered my question."

Alex felt as though she were being pinned in a verbal wrestling match. Had her mother always been like this? "You've never met Daniel," she said flatly.

"Richard's son?" She had had contact with Daniel's father, an estate lawyer, over the problematic settlement of her husband's estate. "Are you dating him?"

"Sort of."

"And this Charles?" she persisted.

"Well, let's just say I find him a little overwhelming. It's hard to believe he's for real sometimes."

"What do you mean, 'for real'?"

Alex squirmed. After all, she had put herself in this position. Didn't she want to get closer to her mother? But she didn't discuss these things even with Briggie. "Well, he's so British and so good-looking and has obviously had so much experience with women, I find it hard to believe he could really be interested in me."

"That sounds like an inferiority complex. Why shouldn't he be?"

She made a face. "I'm hardly Princess Diana."

They had reached the bakery. Her mother patted Alex's arm before beginning to maneuver her walker, and they went inside.

The yeasty, sugary smell struck Alex, getting under her defenses and taking her back to what she knew instantly had been a happier time. The warmth and sweetness of the bakery did what no amount of therapy had been able to do. It made her feel safe.

"I think I remember this place, Mother. Did we come here often?"

"Every week," Amelia answered. "The baker gave you a free cookie. Don't you remember?"

Chapter Nine

Just as Briggie and Alex were leaving the next morning, they encountered Amelia coming into the kitchen.

"I suppose you're going to church," she said, eyeing Alex's turquoise sheath and Briggie's all-purpose navy polyester suit.

"Yes, Mother. We'll be back around noon. Briggie has just put the stew in the slow cooker."

"Noon? Three hours?" Amelia asked, her eyes clearly suspicious. Did she think they were going to go investigating without her?

"Yes," Briggie said stoutly. "We have a block of three meetings, back to back."

"That's a lot of church," Amelia replied, awed.

Alex laughed. "That's just what I told Briggie the first time I went. But now I find that it takes a full three hours to start seeing life the right way up."

"What do you mean?"

"You're welcome to come with us sometime if you want," Alex told her, spontaneously hugging her mother to her side.

As they drove south to the chapel in Wilmette in Alex's CRX, Briggie looked out the back window. "I thought so," she said.

"What?"

"There was a black Taurus parked down the street from your house. It's following us."

Alex's heart thudded. "Are you sure?"

"Yeah. Slow down. Let's see if he passes us."

She did as her friend requested, watching the speedometer drop to fifteen miles per hour. After a few miles, the car finally pulled out to pass. "Take a look, Briggie," she said. "What does he look like?"

"Well, he's not the same guy we saw in Ernie's. This guy is bald. And he has kind of a beak nose."

"Oh. Good. It must have been a coincidence then."

Briggie didn't say anything.

*   *   *

Charles knew better than to come offering wine. Instead, he carried a bottle of sparkling nonalcoholic cider and a bouquet of mixed hothouse flowers. As he took off his long black wool overcoat and white silk scarf, Alex could tell her mother was immediately smitten. To her surprise, she found this made her slightly defensive on Daniel's behalf. He had good taste, but he would never cut such a dashing figure.

"Briggie is the cook tonight," Alex announced. "We're having Mormon stew. It's a little bit of everything. I hope you're hungry."

"I could eat the Sears Tower," he replied with a grin. "I don't eat too well, living alone."

"But you lived alone in Oxford," Briggie objected.

"Not really. I'd lived there all my life. There were always friends

81

and family to have me round. Not to mention my club, when I felt like it."

Soon he had put them all at ease, and Alex forgot her self-consciousness, even ceasing to worry what he thought of Briggie's stew. In fact, he appeared to relish it, asking for several helpings. Under his probing, Briggie revealed the bare bones of their current investigation, after which Charles entertained them with his impressions of Chicago.

"I find it very amusing the things they consider old. Like the water tower, for instance."

"That's the only building that survived the Great Chicago Fire," Alex told him with a grin.

"I've been examining your American poets a bit. Found some Carl Sandburg that I thought was particularly appropriate . . . 'Chicago: Hog Butcher for the World.'"

"Stop!" Alex implored, laughing. "That's turn-of-the-century Chicago you're talking about."

"I find it very refreshing, however, all that raw power. Chicago has broad shoulders. Oxford, by comparison, is effete and turned in on itself. What good does it really do?"

"Charles, is it possible you're discovering the voices in your blood?" Briggie asked. Alex's third cousin had, to his delight, recently learned he was one-quarter American. The second great-grandfather he shared with Alex was from Chicago.

"Well . . . there is something very appealing about all this muscle and vigor. A meatpacking plant, for instance. Who would ever have dreamed I would be co-owner of a meatpacking plant?"

"Wouldn't you rather be writing amusing reviews of London plays?" asked Alex, unable to associate the elegant Charles with anything plebian.

"You know, I wonder," her cousin mused. "I'm finding parts of me I didn't know were there. It's oddly revitalizing."

Alex thought about her own love of Oxford and its golden towers and plethora of intellectual entertainments. Would it have been as appealing to her if it hadn't been some kind of escape from the real world?

Charles leaned back in his chair, apparently replete. "I had no idea you were such a good cook, Briggie. This is an excellent stew. Very American."

Her friend grinned. "Glad to see you're learning to appreciate your roots, Charles."

Something was certainly having a thawing effect on him, Alex realized. He was as handsome as ever, but his smile tonight was kinder, more genuine.

After dinner, Charles and her mother sat at the butcher block in the kitchen while Briggie and Alex put the dishes in the dishwasher.

Amelia said, "It must be pretty lonely for you. Do you have to be downtown? Couldn't you stay up here, closer to us? Then you'd have some family, at least."

He laughed. "You don't need a bachelor planted on your doorstep."

"It would do me good to have someone to look after," Amelia objected. "Alex and Briggie are only here temporarily. When they leave, I'll be just as lonely as you are."

Alex turned around to look at her mother in surprise. Charles was surveying Amelia with a twinkle in his eye. "I believe you really mean it."

"Of course I do."

Alarms went off in Alex's head. What was her mother trying to do? Adopt the man?

"I don't know of any apartments close around here," Alex objected.

"Oh," Amelia waved an airy hand, "people are always going off and wanting someone reliable to sit their houses."

Charles looked at Alex and grinned charmingly. "I might just do it. I know Alex would feel better if she had someone to keep an eye on you."

She had to admit that was true. But Charles? And Mother? She couldn't put them together in her mind. They belonged to completely separate parts of her life. She didn't know if she wanted them coming together.

"That's settled, then," Amelia said. "Excuse me. I've just thought of a call I can make right now. I think the Lawsons are going on a cruise to Australia this next week. I don't know if they've gotten anyone yet or not. They were frantic. They didn't want a student or anyone like that." She left the room, completely forgetting to take her walker for safety.

Next week? Alex bit her bottom lip and turned back to her dishwashing. Briggie was shaking with silent laughter.

"You should see your face, Alex."

"It's just . . ."

"Yes?" Charles prompted. She turned to see that he had an eyebrow raised.

"Mother doesn't usually act like this."

"Perhaps Charles has swept her off her feet," Briggie suggested. "It wouldn't be surprising."

His face sobered a bit. "I really think she's lonely, Alex. I know I am. And I find her perfectly charming. You don't really mind, do you?"

"I never would have believed you'd act so precipitately. It's not like you. You like to be settled."

"Remember, it was you who told me I needed to reinvent myself, allow a little more unpredictability into my life."

Amelia reentered the room. "You're to go over to the Lawsons' right now. Alex, you remember the way? You can take him."

Alex stared.

"I'll get our coats," Charles said.

Her mother's confidence in herself was growing by the minute, she reflected sourly. She was beginning to have stirrings in her memory of a house run by a benevolent dictator. What was that her father used to say? "Your mother knows her own mind, Alex. It's a quality I admire. I hope you grow up to be just like her."

Now where did that thought come from? she wondered, untying her apron. How old had she been? She had a vague memory of her father, not the stooped, gray-haired old man she had confronted last year, but a vigorous man with wavy black hair and a tan. They had played tennis together. Amazing. The memory came without any attached pain.

Walking into the hall after Charles, she watched him delve into the small coat closet next to the new elevator while she grasped at the memory. She had it now. Because her father had worked so hard, they hadn't played often, but they had sometimes had a match at the club. It was over post-match lemonade that he had said those words to her. Upset because her mother was taking her shopping that afternoon in Chicago, she had been complaining to her father that she wanted to play longer.

Yes. Shopping trips to Marshall Field had been a regular part of her life. Every spring and every fall. Her mother had purchased new wardrobes for her. Everything from dresses to jeans and sweaters, shoes, and bags. And they had lunched in the tearoom. She had had Frango mint pie.

Smiling vaguely at her cousin, she held the vision close. Amelia

Borden had not always been an alcoholic. She had been a normal mother.

In America, Charles evidently drove a Range Rover. In Oxford, he drove a Jag. As they pulled away from the house, he grinned in evident amusement. "Anyone would think you didn't like me."

"I just feel outmaneuvered, that's all." Alex struggled to express herself. "You haven't seen my mother before tonight. I'm afraid she's recovering at a rate I'm finding difficult to keep up with, now that she's started. And you . . ."

"Mmm?"

"Well. I just hope you realize she's a lousy cook."

"But I'm a good one. When I have someone to cook for." He started the car.

A picture of her mother and Charles cozily enjoying a gourmet dinner for two cooked by him amused her. She gave a short laugh.

They had pulled into the Lawsons' driveway now. He took her chin and pulled it towards him. "You know, in England you gave me the idea that you felt more for me than cousinly affection."

For a moment she was held by his gaze, and then she moved away suddenly, opening the door. She *had* been powerfully attracted to him at Oxford. But this was America. This was real life. "Oh, Charles. You can't help charming every woman you meet, can you?"

As he came around to help her alight, she could see that his lips were pressed tightly together. "Is that what you think?" he asked. "You were different at Oxford."

"I know," she said solemnly. "I'm sorry. Maybe I just resent that you take so much for granted."

"We'll continue this conversation later," he said as he approached the Lawsons' front door.

Of course, the Lawsons were delighted with him, and it was

arranged that he would move into their house Tuesday. They were to be gone six weeks. Alex witnessed his charm with mixed feelings.

"What do I take for granted?" he demanded on the way back to her house.

"Charles," she said tentatively, "are you just flirting with me as a matter of course?"

"No!" he exploded. "Why do you think I came over here? I could have hired legal representation to clear up the estate. I'm thinking of settling here. I thought you wanted me to."

"Really?" Alex heard his words with amazement. Charles had left his comfortable life in Oxford for *her*? How could she believe that this elegant, sophisticated man of the world wanted to be with her?

"Remember? How can you have forgotten our talk on the river that day? We discussed your religious beliefs." His hands were gripping the steering wheel, and there was a note of exasperation in his voice. "You offered me hope, Alex. Hope for a better life."

A memory of that day was photo clear in her mind. It had been a gorgeous summer afternoon, and they had been punting on the Cherwell. In Charles's presence, her heart had begun to thaw for the first time since Stewart's death. But when she returned home to Kansas City, it had seemed like some sort of dream. She had convinced herself, over time, that it was nothing more to Charles than a pleasant afternoon.

They had reached the house. Her cousin pulled up and turned off his car.

"I haven't forgotten, Charles," she said slowly. "That was a wonderful day. I didn't know it meant so much to you."

Turning to face her, he said, "You're not just another woman, Alex. And I took what you said seriously."

"You really are interested in the LDS Church?"

"Yes. I've been reading your Book of Mormon, as a matter of fact."

Her heart leapt in her breast. This *was* big news. She remembered when Briggie had convinced her to read the Book of Mormon. It had been like drinking sweet water after years of bitter thirst. Its deliciousness had begun to fill the emptiness left by Stewart's death and her parents' abandonment. But it had been a very private healing. Then she had seen a like need in Charles's eyes after Philippa's death. And she had shared. "What do you think of it?" she asked cautiously.

"I think I'd have to be pretty arrogant not to take it seriously. I'm in Alma now. I've been wanting to talk to you about it. Why are you so distant, Alex?"

She looked away from him. Why *wasn't* she allowing herself to feel? Maybe because this was not the Cherwell. This was winter in Chicago. Chicago hurt. There was the whole thing with her mother and father. And, of course, Daniel, who had waited so patiently. "We don't really know each other very well," she temporized.

"That can be remedied."

For Charles there seemed to be no obstacles. By his very nature, he just saw what he wanted and took it. The only time he hadn't been able to do that was with Philippa. Looking into his eyes, she read impatience. "It's not quite as straightforward as that," she said. "I've been seeing someone else for a long time."

"Are you going to marry him?"

The blunt question barreled into her heart, forcing her to look away again. "He hasn't asked. And he's not a Church member."

"This was a great idea of your mother's, having me move up here," he said, suddenly cheerful. He opened his car door.

After inviting them all for dinner on Wednesday night, Charles left. Alex turned to her mother. "Well, I take it you like him?"

She just smiled, a new triumphant smile. "I do. And he liked me.

We're going to get along very well together, Alex, no matter what you decide to do with the man."

Rolling her eyes, she turned to Briggie. "What do you think?" Briggie had not always been a fan of Charles's. She had thought him too smooth, too handsome, and too likely to lead Alex from the straight and narrow.

"It's none of my business," her colleague said. "But he's not a member of the Church."

Alex forbore mentioning that Daniel wasn't either. She went to bed that night pondering Charles's surprising words. Gratified that he was enjoying the Book of Mormon, she tried to read her heart and failed. There was just too much going on. It wasn't just her mother's emerging personality and her own uncertainty about Daniel. There was this crazy case and her returning memories to deal with. And Charles's revelations had taken her by surprise. Burrowing under the quilt, she realized she couldn't possibly handle this now.

Chapter Ten

Monday began with a call to Gladys Harrison.

"Briggie and I are trying to fill out all the remaining places on your chart, Gladys. Can you tell me your niece's name and birth and death dates?"

"Oh dear," the woman said, fretfulness sounding in her usually serene voice. "I'm afraid I've had some very bad news over the weekend. One of my friends died. It happens at my age, you know."

"I'm so sorry," Alex said truthfully. Listening to the woman, her conscience pricked her. How in the world could she have supposed for one second that this woman was a murderer?

"It's shaken me up, I'm afraid. I can't decide whether to go to the funeral or not. It's in Minneapolis, you see, and I haven't traveled by myself in such a long time. I'm afraid I'm not too confident about finding gates and things. And O'Hare's so overwhelming."

She sounded bewildered, and this was so unlike the Gladys Harrison Alex knew that she asked, "Don't you have someone who could take you to the airport and see you settled?"

"I could ask Grace, I suppose." She seemed to be considering. "Yes, I'll ask Grace. That's a good idea. Now what was it you wanted to know?"

"Your niece. Could you give me her name?"

"Oh, yes. Sonia. I'm afraid I can't remember when she died exactly except that it was some time last April."

"Did she have a family?"

"No. Not Sonia. She had some sort of career. Let's see—real estate, I think."

So. The money must have reverted to Gladys. Interesting.

"Was there ever any investigation of the accident or anything?"

There was a pause. "You mean . . . are you wondering . . . was it intentional?" Gladys Harrison's voice quivered.

"How did it happen, Gladys?"

"She lives—lived—out in the country and had to drive into Austin every day on the highway. One of the witnesses was kind enough to call me." She stopped, and Alex could hear her blowing her nose. "I guess Sonia listed me as next of kin on her application at work. Bless her heart. I suppose I *was* her next of kin."

"What did the witness say?"

"Well, he told me a big semi just ran her off the road as if he hadn't even seen her." She sniffed, and Alex could hear a little sob. "His plates were covered with mud. He'll never be caught. It just made me sick!"

Was this another murder? Alex clenched the receiver, her stomach tight. "Do you know of anyone who would want to kill Sonia?"

"You don't think it was done on purpose?"

The woman sounded close to hysteria. Like an insensitive bloodhound on the scent, Alex had forgotten Gladys was grieving. How could she be so horrid? Making an instantaneous decision, she asked,

"Would you like Briggie and me to come up, Gladys? It sounds like you could use some company."

"But you have your work . . ."

"Nothing that can't wait. Besides, you can give us more information on the family, I'm sure. While we're at it, we might as well find out everything you know about your Welsh relations."

Though Alex knew this probably wasn't necessary for the genogram, she thought it would be the perfect distraction for a woman who seemed to enjoy talking about her family. And maybe they could find out more about Sonia.

"Well, I'm a bit of a mess, but if you don't mind that, I'd love to see you. I do have the Williams family Bible."

Briggie heartily agreed with Alex's decision.

"Do you mind if I come along?" her mother asked. "I've been dying to meet this woman. And I might be able to help . . ."

"You think she's a murderer," Alex reminded her sharply.

"That's why I want to meet her," Amelia said, her face open and frank.

"Mother, she's upset. She's grieving, for heaven's sake."

Her mother bowed her head and said in a small voice, "You don't want me to come, do you?" Exasperated, Alex looked at Briggie, who winked at her.

"Oh, all right," Alex said without grace. "Only you're not an employee of the treatment center, so I don't know how we're going to explain you."

Amelia thought a moment. "Well, we're all widows. I'll just be a fellow widow come to condole."

"I don't think Gladys will mind," Briggie assured Alex. "She likes company."

Soon they were on their way up the Shore. Unfortunately, today they weren't as lucky with the weather. It had begun to snow. They had chosen to make the journey in the Bronco, and, unfamiliar with the road, Briggie made her way cautiously. Several cars passed them. Alex checked, but there was no black Taurus following them that she could see. Of course, the weather made it difficult.

Briggie remarked, "We need to find out who benefits from Sonia's death."

"Don't you think it would be insensitive to ask her if she inherited Sonia's money? After I've implied it might not be an accident?"

"Well, maybe," Briggie acknowledged. "I can't really picture Gladys driving a semi. Besides, I don't think she cares at all about the money. But the Westons might."

Alex considered this. "The Westons. You know, something's teasing me about the Westons, but I don't know what it is."

"They're the ones with motive," Briggie assured her.

"Yes, but it isn't that. Grace is scared of something, remember? This whole thing started because she put Holly in the treatment center . . . Briggie!"

"What?"

"Holly told me that her mother started getting 'paranoid,' as she put it, last April. That's when Sonia was killed!"

"Her cousin!"

"What?" Amelia demanded. "I'm all at sea here."

"Sonia's death was a hit-and-run, Mother. It may have been intentional. Around the time she was killed, Holly's mother started keeping strict tabs on her. She even drove her to and from school. Then she ended up putting her in the treatment center, and Holly says it wasn't because of drugs. It sounds like they must be frightened of someone they think killed Sonia."

"Oh, my goodness," her mother said. "This is getting a little dangerous. Do you think we should go ahead with it?"

"It's our business," Briggie told her briskly. "If it's an inheritance deal, then something's up with this genogram. You say Gladys has the family Bible?" she asked Alex.

"Yes."

"Maybe that will give us some kind of lead," Briggie said, squinting to peer through the falling snow. "Boy, this is getting interesting."

"But," Alex said, thoughtfully, "why last April? Sonia had had that fortune for years."

"Maybe someone has been doing their genealogy," Briggie suggested. "Or maybe she was about to get married or something."

"We need to ask Gladys," Alex said. "She was too shook up about her friend to tell me much. And we need to be tactful, Briggie. She's mourning. We're going to help her out, not distress her. I already did that over the phone."

"Poor woman," Amelia said.

"I gather you don't think she murdered her father anymore," Alex said, turning to look at her mother in the backseat.

Amelia sighed. "I'm afraid I really don't know what to think. It's getting awfully complicated. Are you sure that hit-and-run was intentional? I mean, it seems to me you're building an awful lot on it."

"I guess we shouldn't get carried away here," Briggie said. "We need to talk to Gladys and get all the facts."

Alex looked out the side window of the Bronco. The snow was falling in heavy, wet flakes. Behind the snowflakes, the scene looked like a Christmas card. But occasional glimpses of the lake showed that it was angry with white caps. This was likely to be a bad storm. She caught herself wishing her mother was still homebound and then reproached herself. Amelia really was showing unbelievable pluck. Her own reluctance to have her mother involved was no more than childish pique. That wasn't a very attractive quality.

Reflecting on this, she studied the scenery intently. Everything malevolent was covered in a pristine blanket of white outside.

Suddenly, displacing all thoughts of murders and hit-and-run accidents, a wave of nostalgia like the one she had experienced in the bakery overcame her. She had always loved snow. Sharply now, she recalled snowfalls of her childhood. Snow angels, sledding, snowmen. In spite of the circumstances of this journey, she could still feel a slight flicker of the safety a younger Alex had known in sitting and looking out the window, sipping hot chocolate. Maybe winter in Chicago hadn't always been so bad.

"I need to get new wiper blades," her colleague murmured, bringing her back to the present. "I wonder if that old murder fits in here anywhere."

"Someone did it," Alex said. "Maybe it was Lloyd Jr., after all."

"Then why didn't Grace Weston want you to know about it?" Amelia demanded. "I still think there's some sort of scandal she's afraid of."

"I thought you'd eliminated Gladys," Alex said, feeling her exasperation return.

"Maybe it would be best if we kept an open mind," her mother said.

"We're all over the map here," Briggie said thoughtfully. "But we have hardly started confirming this family tree, and already we've got a murder, Grace's paranoia, the money thing, a hit-and-run . . ." Taking her eyes off the road for a moment, she looked at Alex with a furrowed brow. "Alex, have you given much thought to that suicide?"

"What suicide, for heaven's sake?"

"Wasn't it Lloyd Sr.'s older brother? Wouldn't he have been the heir if he hadn't died?"

"Yes. What are you driving at?"

"What if that wasn't suicide but murder? Was he married? Did he have any kids?"

"I don't know. Good grief, Briggie. Don't you think it's complicated enough?"

"I'm just trying to get the whole picture," she replied. "I think we should ask Gladys about that."

"You know how she likes to dramatize things. It was probably an accident," Alex said.

"She didn't dramatize her father being murdered."

"Briggie, why do you always do this?"

"What?" her colleague growled as she pulled into the long driveway of the Williams estate. The hedges were frosted with snow, and the driveway was hidden under growing drifts.

"Make everything unbelievably complicated."

"Life's messy," Briggie said.

"That's for darned sure," Amelia agreed.

They were parked in front of the mansion now. Concern for Gladys made Alex suddenly annoyed with everyone and their theories. She opened her car door. Gladys would help fill in the blanks. Honestly, Briggie always took the most convoluted view of things.

Marching to the door, she knocked. There was no answer. The three women stood shivering in the stiff, cold wind that was blowing off the lake.

Chapter Eleven

After ten minutes of the three women standing in the freezing weather, it was obvious they weren't going to get any answer to their increasingly urgent tattoo with the brass knocker. They could hear Lord Peter and Tuppence attempting to greet them through the door.

Alex shivered in her pea coat. Wasn't Gladys expecting them? Would a seventy-three-year-old woman venture out in a snowstorm? Looking at her colleague, Alex could tell Briggie shared her concerns.

"She could just be out," Alex said.

"Or she could have fallen down the stairs, or had a heart attack, or . . ." Briggie didn't mention further possibilities. Instead, she began to march firmly through the snow around the house.

Alex followed Briggie instinctively. Amelia clutched Alex's arm, walking carefully through the snow in her leather pumps. A small garage covered with leafless ivy sat just behind the house on the south side. Set in its ancient walls (it had obviously started life as a carriage house) were tiny windows almost entirely covered with grime and cobwebs. Alex and Briggie peered through them, and Alex's alarm deepened. Something was wrong, for there sat a white Lincoln Town Car. Gladys Harrison had not gone anywhere unless someone had taken her.

"Wait." Briggie said. "What's that?" She indicated a small building almost hidden by the garage. The three of them approached it.

The door was unlocked. It appeared to be a playhouse—a miniature, half-timbered mansion with ivy growing up the sides, carefully trimmed around the diamond-paned windows. There were even window boxes, barren at this season.

Briggie, always intrepid, opened the door and turned on the light. The room was lovely. At one end was what looked to be a gas fireplace. It was flanked by child-sized, plaid wingback chairs. A child-sized table and chairs filled the other end of the room. Glass-fronted cabinets displayed a store of graham crackers, Goldfish crackers, and Oreo cookies.

Alex wondered if Holly had ever played here. Or Grace?

There was no one here now.

"She must be inside the house," Alex said. "She was expecting us. For some reason, she can't get to the door."

"I think we should call the police," Briggie said stoutly. "No doubt she has one of those fancy alarm systems."

Alex pulled out her cell phone and dialed 911.

The dispatcher promised to send a patrol car and an ambulance. Alex, Briggie, and Amelia went to wait in the Bronco. The snow continued to fall heavily, and Briggie ran the engine so they could have the benefit of the heater. Even so, Alex felt cold to the marrow. What could have happened to Gladys? Had her grief over her friend caused her to have a stroke? A heart attack?

By the time the authorities arrived, Alex's unease was burrowing its way through her intestines. Using special tools, they unlocked the door. As Briggie, Alex, and Amelia followed the officers into the foyer of the house, they were greeted by pets. Lord Peter growled and barked repeatedly at the two muscular men in blue and the youthful paramedics, but then, seeming to recognize Alex, scampered to her, wagging his whole body. Tuppence rubbed against Briggie until she picked her up and held her under one arm. In the background they could hear Professor Moriarty, "Feather your corners."

Urgently, Alex led them to the living room. It was deserted, a partially crocheted afghan lying in the needlepoint chair. No one was in the old-fashioned, fifties' style kitchen, or the perfect English library that smelled of dust and leather. There was a richly appointed ballroom behind closed double doors. Its mirrors reflected no one but their small party.

"I'm going to check upstairs," Briggie said briskly and bustled out of the room as the police and paramedics made for the conservatory. Alex followed Briggie. Maybe Gladys hadn't felt well and had decided to lie down. Lord Peter galloped after them as fast as his short legs would carry him.

But after half an hour's searching of the immense three-story mansion, they had discovered no sign of Gladys Harrison. Shaking their heads, the paramedics went back to their ambulance and drove away.

The tension within Alex screwed itself tighter. Though glad the woman wasn't ill, she knew something wasn't right. Gladys had been waiting for them to come. She was upset. She wanted to talk.

"Officer," she addressed herself to the tallest of the two. His red hair was buzzed flat. "I don't believe Mrs. Harrison left of her own free will. She was very upset. She'd just heard that a friend had died. She wanted to talk to us about it."

"Are you friends . . . relatives?" the officer asked.

"We're genealogists," Briggie told him. "We've been working on

Mrs. Harrison's family tree. She's an heiress. The Williams steel fortune."

The shorter officer, who looked like Alex's idea of Joe Hardy, pulled out a small notebook. "How about if we go into that room with the parrot?" Once they were all seated, he asked, "When did you talk to Mrs. Harrison last?"

Alex and her mother sat together on the Regency couch. Briggie sat next to the Professor's perch and tried to coax him onto her finger. Tuppence sat in her lap.

"This morning," Alex told him, stroking Lord Peter's velvety ears absently. "About nine o'clock. She was very upset about her friend. We'd gotten acquainted, and it seemed to me that she was kind of lonely. We offered to come up from Winnetka and talk to her."

The officer looked at his watch. "So you came right away?"

"Yes. The storm delayed us a little," she explained.

"So . . ." Joe Hardy scribbled. "If you're a genealogist, you must know her next of kin? Someone we could talk to?"

"Yes," Alex answered him. "Grace Weston. Her daughter. She lives in Wilmette."

"You have her number?"

Alex dug through her multicolored Guatemalan carryall and pulled out her case book. She read Grace's telephone number to the officer.

"Why don't you just give us your names and addresses, and we'll give you a call?" the redheaded officer asked, far more offhand than his colleague. "I'm sure she'll turn up soon."

"Just why are you doing her genealogy?" Joe Hardy asked. "Is she trying to get into the Daughters of the American Revolution or something?"

"No. Nothing like that," Alex told him. She explained about Holly and the genogram.

"And her daughter, Grace, didn't like it," Briggie interjected flatly. "Not one little bit."

The redhead smiled soothingly. "Just leave this to us, ma'am. I'm sure there's a simple explanation. We'll call you when we find her."

"Something has to be done about these pets in the meantime, officer," Briggie told him. "They can't be left here alone."

"This . . ." he glanced at his notes, "this Grace Weston will have to see to that."

"She has an aversion to pets," Alex said firmly. She turned to her mother, eyebrows raised in a question. Her mother had had, she remembered now, a Pekingese when Alex was younger. It had died of old age and broken Amelia's heart.

But now her mother spoke up gamely. "Mrs. Poulson is right. We can't possibly leave these poor things here alone. We'll take them with us for the time being."

"I'm sure Mrs. Harrison will turn up, ma'am."

"Well, I'm not," Amelia said firmly. "Her father was murdered, you know."

Joe Hardy raised his eyebrows but merely took their names and contact information. After that there was nothing to do but leave. They wrote a halfhearted note to Gladys, telling her that they had taken her pets. Then they searched kitchen cupboards for pet food and cat litter. Finding Lord Peter's L. L. Bean dog bed in Gladys's French provincial bedroom, they took it and, covering the Professor's cage, hurried the bewildered pets out to the Bronco through the snow. Frustrated and deeply uneasy, Alex climbed into the backseat of Briggie's red conveyance and held the Professor on her lap. He squawked, "I'm rolled up." Tuppence sat on Amelia's lap in the front seat, and Lord Peter walked unsteadily around in circles next to Alex, finally settling, his nose next to his tail. They headed south to Winnetka.

"Where could she be?" Alex's mother fretted.

Briggie said, "This doesn't look good. It's got me downright worried."

"Me, too," Alex said. "I sure wish the police would take it seriously."

When they arrived home, they shepherded Gladys's menagerie into the house and made a hearty wood fire in Amelia's sitting room. Alex set the Professor's cage there next to the desk. While Lord Peter scampered off gaily to inspect the house, Tuppence seemed lost. After looking around her, she climbed onto Briggie's lap.

"I think I'll try to lie down," Alex's mother said, her face weary.

Briggie, settled by the fireplace, said, "You do that, dear. I'll see to a litter box for Tuppence as soon as I'm warm."

Sitting down at her mother's desk, Alex pulled out the genogram. What if something had happened to Gladys? And what if it was her fault?

Twice she had embarked on cases that resulted in murder. Would this be the third time? Charles had tried to tell her that the evil was already there; she was just the catalyst. But she didn't like being a catalyst. It was a horrible, impersonal thing to be. Like the jet whose crash had killed Stewart. It had, of course been the terrorist who was the source of evil, but the jet had been his weapon of destruction. Even the bomb by itself couldn't have killed so many. It had been strategically placed. Then one thing had followed another until the jet became a flaming ball of fire.

Suddenly, she got up, unable to sit still. Anxiety was consuming her. What should she do?

Snatching up the telephone on her mother's desk, she called Grace Weston.

"Hello, Mrs. Weston? Have the police been in touch with you?"

"No!" The woman sounded alarmed.

Alex knew at once that her concern had led her into making a false step. What right had she to push her anxiety off onto others?

"It's probably nothing," she tried to reassure the other woman. "It's just that your mother made an appointment with us today, and when we turned up, she wasn't home, but her car was in the garage. The only reason we called the police was that we thought she might be ill."

"*You* called the police?"

"We thought she might have fallen . . ."

"Mrs. Campbell, I consider this most officious and interfering. I can take care of my mother. I absolutely forbid you to have anything more to do with my family's affairs, and I intend to telephone the hospital this moment to tell them so!"

Sudden anger with Grace Weston's misplaced concern prompted Alex to push the limits with this angry woman. "What about your cousin, Mrs. Weston? What about Sonia?"

There was a silence. "Sonia?" the woman said, her voice small and breathy. "What about Sonia?"

"Was her death accidental?"

More silence. Then finally, "I don't know what you're talking about, Mrs. Campbell." Grace Weston hung up.

Alex banged down the telephone, saying to Briggie, "I shouldn't have called her. She didn't even seem concerned about her mother. She's taking us off the case."

"Queer as Dick's hatband," the Professor responded.

"Can she do that?" Briggie asked.

"I don't know. She can certainly have Holly moved to a new treatment center. I don't imagine North Side wants to lose her business."

"Well, I'm not quitting," Briggie said stoutly, putting down her knitting. "There's nothing to prevent us doing a little genealogy. Get out your genogram. Let's start with the basics."

Alex handed the chart to her colleague. Briggie scanned it briefly. "Let's see here . . ." Alex joined her on the couch. The older woman continued, "Unless we find someone else we don't know about, the only ones with any motive for doing away with Gladys and Sonia are Grace and her husband. But, of course, there are other question marks. Lloyd Sr.'s murder. They couldn't have done that. And I'm still not easy in my mind about that suicide." She put her finger on the name of William Williams Jr. "When did he die?"

"I'm not sure. Gladys just said it was before her father. Too bad we didn't get that family Bible. What are you thinking, Briggie?"

"Just that his death was awfully convenient for Lloyd Sr. I'd sure like to get the details."

"Find yourself in Queer Street," Moriarty warned.

"Well, we're not going to get them today. Not in this weather. We were lucky to make it back from Lake Forest."

"Did Grace Weston seem anxious when you asked her about Sonia?"

"Grace is always anxious. She really came unglued when I mentioned the police."

"That's a little weird, don't you think? She didn't even wonder what happened to her mother?"

"No. She just heard the word *police* and freaked out."

"I wonder why?"

"Something's going on," Alex said. "Since last April, probably. "She's definitely scared."

"Well, there has to be a reason," Briggie said stubbornly. "I say we need to dig deeper into this family tree. There may be some renegade heir running around."

Lord Peter streaked into the room at this point, clearly delighted with his new domain. He stood looking expectantly at Alex. Remembering the pet's affection for his mistress, she pinched her brow between her eyes. "That would explain it if something has happened to Gladys."

"Yeah. This all ties together somehow. Offhand, I'd say we've made someone pretty uneasy by our poking and prying."

"Don't say that, Briggie. I've been trying to convince myself that it's not true."

"Honey, that murder and Sonia's hit-and-run happened long before we came on to the scene. This family's got serious problems. We've got to stop 'em."

"You sound like the Roto Rooter guy," Alex said with a sad smile.

"Isn't that just what we are? The Roto Rooters? We get down there and get those roots all squared away."

Amelia Borden, who had just come into the room, spoke with renewed vitality. "Briggie's right, Alex. You can't give up now. Hello, Professor."

"Top o' the trees!" the macaw answered.

The telephone rang, and Alex waited while her mother answered it. "Roto Rooter!"

Alex groaned inwardly.

"Oh, it's you. Don't worry. This is Amelia Borden, Alex's mother. We're just having a little fun. Alex will explain. Alex, it's Daniel Grinnell."

Alex signaled that she would take the call in the kitchen and walked out of the room.

"Daniel," she said, "she's getting out of hand. Now she's making jokes, and this is serious."

But her Kansas City swain was chuckling. "I suppose the joke is a pun on RootSearch . . ."

"Yes, Briggie put it in her head, which was only to be expected, but for Mother to answer the telephone . . . it could have been the police!"

His voice turned sharp. "The police? What's happened?"

Alex sat down at the butcher block. "Oh, Daniel, Holly's grand-mother's missing. And I'm feeling awfully responsible. What if my meddling caused something to happen to her?"

"First of all, Alex, you weren't meddling. You were doing your job."

She sighed heavily. "How come you're always so danged rational?"

"Okay. Maybe your presence on the scene precipitated something. Does that make you feel better?"

"No. Of course not. But I'm afraid it's the truth. My presence on the scene always precipitates something."

She could almost hear Daniel bite back a therapeutic retort. Something about all-or-nothing thinking. She amended her state-ment before he could speak. "Well, almost always. I have done a few cases where murder hasn't cropped up."

"More than a few," he said. "Tell me about your mother."

"If I weren't feeling so bad, I'd laugh," she said with a faint smile. "If that isn't a therapist's question, I don't know what is."

"I didn't mean it that way, and you know it. I can tell she's bug-ging you."

"Well, a little. But she's really the most amazing person, Daniel. I mean, she's gone into remission and sort of taken charge, and she's . . . she's turning into another Briggie."

"Now that *is* interesting. Do you suppose that's what she was like before she became an alcoholic?"

"I'm starting to have little flashes. Just now and then. I think she was a pretty down to earth personality."

"Exactly like Brighamina Poulson, in fact. I suppose it's occurred to you that that's why you took to Briggie?"

"It did. Just now. How weird. Do you think so?"

"Do you know, Alex, this is a landmark moment. Never before have you come to me with a 'psychological problem.' And just to show you my heart's in the right place, I'm not going to touch it with a ten-foot pole. As you so often remind me, I'm not your therapist. That sure as heck isn't why I called you."

"Daniel, I've specifically asked for your advice!"

"I don't give advice out of office hours. And I don't date my patients. Therefore, you're not going to get it."

"I can tell the weigh lifting must be having some effect." Alex felt her spirits begin to rise a little.

"It's working wonders. But there are limits. May I visit you this weekend?"

Alex came back down to earth with a jolt. Thoughts flashed through her mind. How on earth would she cope with Daniel and Charles in the same town? This thought was followed speedily by the idea that maybe that kind of friction would jolt something loose inside of her. Suddenly appalled at her cold-bloodedness, she wondered what kind of neurotic diva she had become. *Why does anyone want to have anything to do with me, anyway?*

"Yes," she said in a rush, running from her skittish self. "I'd like to see you. But you may have to ride shotgun. There's a lot going on. We're in the middle of a case, remember."

He affected a groan, presumably remembering the last case he'd been involved in. "Maybe I'll just stay in Winnetka and hold Mama's hand."

"She'll be with us," Alex replied.

When she returned to the sitting room, it was to see Briggie poring over the articles they'd copied at the Newberry. Alex realized that Gladys's cat was no longer glued to her lap.

"Where's Tuppence?" she asked.

"I think she's got a touch of post-traumatic stress," Briggie told her. "Who knows what she witnessed? She's disappeared."

"Oh, dear."

"Don't worry," Briggie reassured her. "Cat's are pretty good at taking care of themselves. She just needs to be by herself to figure things out."

Briggie looked up from the papers she was studying. "I wonder if the Newberry has anything on this so-called suicide," she said.

"Lake Forest has a local paper," Amelia offered.

Chapter Twelve

On Tuesday morning, all were dismayed to find that Amelia was feeling weak again. She could walk but not far.

"You've been doing too much, Mother," Alex told her. "It's my fault. I shouldn't have let you go out in that storm yesterday."

"But I *wanted* to come. And this just makes me so mad!"

"Well, I'm glad you're mad and not sad," Alex told her truthfully. "That's a good sign."

Her mother smiled a little crookedly. "I'm feeling more myself anyway. I think it's more like me to be mad than sad."

The phone rang. Amelia answered.

"Yes. My daughter's here, Dr. Goodwin. It's nice to hear your voice."

A pause.

"Yes. I'm doing really well, thanks. It's wonderful to have Alex here." She passed the phone to her daughter.

"I'm really sorry, Alex," Dr. Goodwin told her. "But Mrs. Weston was adamant. She'll move Holly if we don't stop this genogram business."

"Did you get any specific impression when you talked to her?" Alex asked, dismayed but not surprised.

"Yes. Outrage." Dr. Goodwin waited a second before adding, "But now that I think of it, I do believe it was put on. She sounded just a little bit like she was reading from a script."

"Do you think she's afraid?"

"She could be, I suppose. But why would she be?"

"I told you that she said her grandfather wasn't murdered, remember?"

"Of course."

"Well, we've confirmed that he was shot and that it was ruled murder."

"Really?" There was a short silence. "Then Mrs. Weston has been lying all these years. I wonder if Mr. Weston even knows the truth."

"I don't think he does. He wasn't worried about what we might find out. But," Alex took a deep breath, "now, just when we've begun investigating it, Mrs. Weston's mother has disappeared."

"No!"

"Yes. I'm really afraid of what might have happened to her."

"That's terrible, Alex."

"I called the police, and that's what got Mrs. Weston upset."

"She didn't tell me any of this. She just said you were violating her privacy."

"I don't know if she's involved in this or not. But my colleague and I decided that even if you took us off the case, we had to pursue it."

"Yes. I can see why. Perhaps you *have* uncovered the family secret. Good heavens! I hope I haven't put you in any danger."

Alex hadn't even considered this aspect. Unfortunately, she and Briggie never did until it was too late. "Why don't you call Mrs.

Weston back and say you've spoken to me and taken me off the case? We'll continue to pursue it, of course."

"Have you talked to the police about it?"

"We tried to. But they're not interested. However, if anything has happened to Gladys Harrison, they will be, I think."

She heard Dr. Goodwin sigh. "Well, I hope nothing happens to you. I would feel responsible."

"I'm doing this for Gladys's sake. One other thing. Holly told me her mother is scared of something. I don't think Holly's on drugs. I think her parents have put her in the treatment center for her own protection." Alex told Dr. Goodwin her theory concerning Sonia Williams's death and Grace Weston's paranoia.

There was silence while Dr. Goodwin considered this. "A hit-and-run? You really don't think Holly is on drugs?"

"No. And the times coincide exactly."

"That would imply that there's a lot more to the situation than we know right now." Dr. Goodwin pondered. "You've given me a lot to think about. I'm glad you're pursuing this. If you find out anything, be certain to let me know immediately. If Holly's really in danger, we need to know about it. We can no longer bill the Weston account for your time, of course, but I'll arrange for you to be paid on an ad hoc basis."

"Being paid is the last thing I'm worried about right now," Alex told her.

The snow had stopped, the roads were clear, and Briggie decided they should spend the day at the Newberry. "We need to start looking for hard evidence," she said.

"Well, we've barely started. I'm sure they'll have obits on some of these people."

Before they could leave, the telephone rang again. It was Lorna

Jean calling from California. She had succeeded in unearthing the marriage certificate the day before.

After hanging up, Briggie told Alex, "They were married in 1939, all right. Lorna Jean got the goods. She's sending a certified copy of the marriage certificate by FedEx, but this is what it says."

Alex read Briggie's large, loopy script: *Robert Harrison, attorney, aged 29, married Gladys Williams, spinster, aged 19, on 12 November 1939. Husband's birthplace: Pittsburgh, Pennsylvania. Husband's father: Walter Harrison. Husband's mother: Eliza Frueh. Wife's birthplace: Lake Forest, Illinois. Wife's father: Lloyd Williams. Wife's mother: Sarah Norman.*

"Well, that does it. Gladys's story was true. The certificate was signed by the county registrar in the County of Los Angeles," Briggie said.

"So Grace lied about that, too."

"Yeah. It looks like her mother was a 'drama queen' for real, doesn't it?"

* * *

This time they had no trouble being admitted to the select library collection. A kindly woman with streaked blonde hair was at the desk. She asked at once if there was any way she could help. Informing her they were only after obituaries, they made their way to the microfilmed index.

Briggie insisted on following her hunch about William Williams Jr.'s death. "We don't know when he died, right?"

"All I know is that it was before his father. But we don't know when his father died, and William Williams is a very common name. If you want to plow through that index, go ahead. I'm going to look up Robert Harrison's obit."

"Why?"

"It's probably clutching at straws, but you taught me never to miss any documentation. I know that he died in 1980."

Putting their respective spools of microfilm on machines, they both squinted over the indices. Alex was soon successful. Robert Harrison's obit was in the September 13, 1980, issue of the *Tribune*. As she went to the desk to order it from the stacks, she left Briggie muttering, "For crying out loud," as she scrolled through dozens of William Williamses.

When Alex received the correct microfilm spool, she loaded it onto the machine. Before she had a chance to look at it, she became aware that someone was watching her. She could just see him with her peripheral vision. Turning, she spotted a middle-aged man with gray, wavy hair and tortoiseshell glasses. He was studying a book intently and didn't seem to have the least interest in her.

Shrugging, she began scrolling through her film until she came to the issue she wanted. "Got it," she told Briggie.

Her friend stood up and read over her shoulder at the copy that was magnified on the microfilm screen.

"Robert Harrison, aged 70, died today of a heart attack at his residence in Lake Forest. He was survived by his wife, Gladys, daughter Grace Weston of Wilmette, and one grandaughter. Harrison was employed as chief counsel for the Williams Steel Foundry in Gary, Indiana. He authored a regular column in the Illinois Bar Journal and also published a book on the history of the Williams Foundry, a family concern. A private funeral is to be held Saturday. No flowers by request."

Briggie and Alex exchanged a significant look. "I'll go ask that nice librarian if they have the book. You'd better copy that," Briggie said.

Alex felt the man with the tortoiseshell glasses looking at her again. Turning quickly, she met his eye. He smiled suddenly. "Having fun?" he asked.

"Yes, thank you," Alex said. Genealogy library patrons were notoriously friendly.

Briggie's helper directed them to a small section of the library where Chicago-area company histories were shelved. Reference number in hand, they scanned the old books until they found it.

Alex's heart did one of the flip-flops that accompanied a really serendipitous genealogical find. There it was in gold-tooled maroon leather. Instinct told her it was going to be important. It looked as though it had hardly ever been read.

Finding a table behind the bookcases, they opened the book carefully. It had been written in 1940 for the ten-year anniversary of William Williams's death and was dedicated to the steel magnate himself. On the inside cover was a bookplate inscribed, "Donated to the Newberry Library by Angela Duncan Williams."

It began with a short biography of the founder. Briggie took down details for the genogram. William Williams had been born in Llanegryn, Wales, in 1850 and emigrated to the United States with his father and sister when he was fifteen years old. Beginning work in the coal mines of Pennsylvania, near Pittsburgh, he found favor with his boss early for his "robust and enterprising spirit" and at the age of eighteen was made foreman. Then fortune smiled upon him again.

He married the daughter of the mine owner; however, she died in childbirth. Her "nice dowry" was invested according to Williams's new father-in-law's advice. Soon he had enough to begin a business of his own but decided to go west. In Gary, he built the small concern that later grew to be the great Williams Steel Foundry. He married again at age forty to socialite Angela Duncan and began his family—William Jr., Lloyd, and Gwenyth. At his death in 1930, the ownership of the plant had passed into the hands of Lloyd Williams, his elder brother having predeceased his father.

"Wonderful," Alex said. "This fills us in on the details of his life."

"Yes. But we're not any more forward," Briggie mumbled as she filled in the genogram.

Briggie and Alex paged idly through the book, looking at the formal photographs protected by sheets of tissue paper set into the binding. There was a picture of William himself, just as Gladys had described him—fierce and white haired, with forbidding eyebrows and a challenging expression in his eye. There was a picture of the unfortunate William Jr., who had held the post of president of the company after his father's retirement until his own death in 1929. Then there was Lloyd, the next president until his death in 1936 (Alex noticed the word *murder* was not mentioned). At that time the presidency of the company apparently passed into the hands of a person outside the family, Joseph Collins, who still held the position at the time of publication.

Studying Lloyd's picture carefully, Alex was more than interested in the murder victim. He was a smoother, more polished version of his progenitor, with a mustache and pomaded hair. The look in his eye was quite different from his father's. It was evident that he didn't feel he had to prove anything to anyone. Other portraits followed of men who had been significant in starting the company.

One in particular puzzled Alex, and she pointed to it, saying, "He looks exactly like Lloyd Williams, but his name's been crossed out." Under the picture a line of heavy black ink obscured the caption. Written by hand were the words, "Lloyd Williams, President, 1930–1936."

"The book's Angela's, so she must have done that," Briggie said. "Do you think the printer made a mistake? It happens sometimes with these self-published histories."

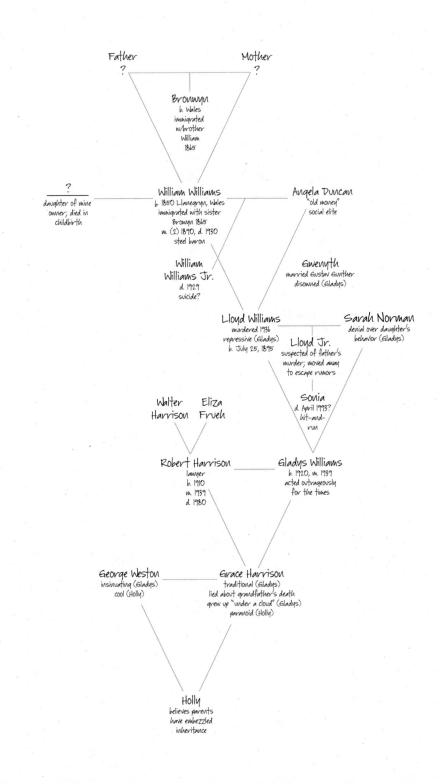

Father
?

Mother
?

Bronwyn
b. Wales
immigrated
w/brother
William
1865

?
daughter of mine
owner; died in
childbirth

William Williams
b. 1850 Llanegryn, Wales
immigrated with sister
Bronwyn 1865
m. (2) 1890, d. 1930
steel baron

Angela Duncan
"old money"
social elite

William
Williams Jr.
d. 1929
suicide?

Gwenyth
married Gustav Gunther
disowned (Gladys)

Lloyd Williams
murdered 1936
repressive (Gladys)
b. July 25, 1895

Sarah Norman
denial over daughter's
behavior (Gladys)

Lloyd Jr.
suspected of father's
murder; moved away
to escape rumors

Walter
Harrison

Eliza
Frueh

Sonia
d. April 1993?
hit-and-
run

Robert Harrison
lawyer
b. 1910
m. 1939
d. 1980

Gladys Williams
b. 1920, m. 1939
acted outrageously
for the times

George Weston
insinuating (Gladys)
cool (Holly)

Grace Harrison
traditional (Gladys)
lied about grandfather's death
grew up "under a cloud" (Gladys)
paranoid (Holly)

Holly
believes parents
have embezzled
inheritance

It did appear to be a duplicate photo of the profile of Lloyd. Alex studied it carefully and then looked back at Lloyd's picture. They had been taken at slightly different angles, and it was hard to tell if they were indeed the same person.

Then Briggie chortled. "The ears. You can always tell by the ears."

The ears were distinctly different. Lloyd had attached lobes. The unnamed man didn't. They turned back to William Jr.'s picture. His earlobes were unattached as well, but in general appearance he resembled his father less than either of the other two men.

"What in the world do you think this means, Briggs?"

"It looks like Lloyd and William had an illegitimate brother, if you ask me. Robert Harrison must not have known about it, and when he came across the man's picture, he put it in the book. The man must have had some important job at the foundry." Briggie raised her voice in excitement.

Alex mused, "Then Angela Duncan Williams for some reason accidentally drew attention to it by crossing out the man's name. Do you realize what this means?" She couldn't help her excitement. This was genealogist's gold.

Her friend in the tortoiseshell glasses leaned around the bookcase, grinning. "Find something?" he asked.

"Did we ever!" Briggie announced. She turned to Alex. "Now we've got to stop and think. If this illegitimate son was older than Lloyd, he was the heir. I'd have to ask Richard, but I'm pretty sure that since the money went to the oldest son and his issue *in trust*, that means it might never have been Lloyd's or Gladys's or anyone else we've talked to. There's a whole different set of heirs."

"Or how about this?" Alex interposed. "If he was younger than Lloyd, he could be the murderer. He could have known the money would come to him as the oldest surviving son under the trust," she

117

reflected and pinched the bridge of her nose. "But no, that doesn't work, because Gladys and Lloyd Jr. got the money."

"Gosh, we've really stirred up a hornet's nest," Briggie said, slumping back in her chair.

"How are we going to find out who this man is?"

"There must be another copy of that book somewhere."

As Alex and Briggie emerged from the stacks, their friend with the glasses was perusing a shelf of books behind them. He waved gaily.

Chapter Thirteen

O h, I'm so glad you're back," Amelia greeted them, her face puckered with worry, her eyes agitated. "A policeman from Lake Forest called. We were right. They found Gladys Harrison this afternoon. She's dead!"

Alex dropped her carryall in the black-and-white marble foyer. Lord Peter, oblivious to the tragedy in his life, was running circles around her, yapping happily. She instinctively embraced her mother, holding her close as her own heart fell. *Gladys. Dead.* She tightened her grip on her mother, who had begun to weep. Amelia's bones felt tiny and frail under her hands. A conviction that this death was all Alex's fault descended on her with a heaviness that rendered her mute. What had she done?

Visions of Gladys holding Tuppence in her lap, stroking Lord Peter's ears, and proudly displaying the portrait of her deceased husband all crowded together in her mind. Gladys Harrison had loved life. Her own death had been the furthest thing from her mind when she had called them about the death of her friend. Alex closed her eyes against the guilt that pounded in her heart.

"How did she die?" Briggie demanded.

"They found her in the lake," Amelia said, sniffling. "Her body washed up against one of the neighbor's piers this morning. The police were searching there, and they found her."

She pulled away from her daughter's embrace and wiped her eyes. "Oh, Alex! They think it was suicide. But it can't be, can it? Someone did it! It all has to do with that wretched genogram. It has to."

The little dachshund, aware of distress, began to whine. Briggie came over and rested a hand on Amelia's arm. "We'll find out who did this, honey. Don't worry. We're good at what we do."

Alex looked into Briggie's face, seeking, in her own shock, the reassurance she always found there. "Mother's right. It must have to do with the genogram. We have to talk to the police."

"They left their number," Alex's mother said.

The cause of death had not yet been determined, but suicide was not being ruled out, according to Lieutenant Laurie, a burly, brown-haired policeman with a surprisingly sensitive mouth and deep blue eyes. Those eyes were now fixed noncommittally upon Alex's own. Their interview was taking place in the cold formality of the Borden living room. Lord Peter, apparently aware that the occasion was a solemn one, stayed close to Alex. She could feel him quivering.

"I don't think it was suicide, lieutenant," she told him firmly. "She had just made a date to see us. She was expecting us. We were on our way."

"Just what was your business with Mrs. Harrison?"

Alex explained once more about the genogram.

"Genealogy, huh?" His eyes momentarily softened. "My grandma does genealogy." Then, seeming to recall himself, he said, "This Holly Weston. Her mother inherits Mrs. Harrison's estate?"

"Yes. But I don't think Grace Weston murdered her mother," Alex told him. "There's something strange going on, lieutenant. Mrs. Weston is terribly afraid. You see, last April her cousin who inherited half the original Williams fortune was killed in a hit-and-run accident."

Briggie was seated next to Alex on the couch but so far was allowing her to answer all the questions. She had issues with policemen.

Alex continued, praying Briggie would remain docile. "At that same time, Mrs. Weston started keeping a close watch on her daughter. I don't think it was a coincidence. Holly said her mother was 'paranoid.' Mrs. Weston took her to school and picked her up."

Alex studied the young Lake Forest policeman as she spoke. He was politely attentive. Just how sophisticated was he in dealing with murder investigations? "Holly says she's not on drugs but that her mother has put her in the treatment center for other reasons. I think her mother is afraid that the same thing that happened to her cousin will happen to her daughter."

"Kids on drugs always try to deny it," the lieutenant said dismissively. "But just out of curiosity, what tale did this Holly spin you?"

"Well," Alex realized suddenly that what she had to say would put Grace Weston under yet more suspicion. "She thinks her parents have embezzled her trust money."

The lieutenant raised his eyebrows and whistled.

"She's supposed to get it when she turns eighteen, but if there is a history of mental incompetence, she won't get it then."

Frowning, the policeman said, "Well, if this turns out to be murder, it looks like I might have to have a chat with this Holly's doctor. See what her opinion is. Where did you say she was?"

Alex told him.

Briggie broke in. "I think you need to tell him about the other murder, too, Alex."

Her mother, who was seated across from them on the love seat, nodded sharply.

"Murder? Look here, Mrs. Campbell," the lieutenant said indignantly, opening his notebook to a fresh page. "If these people are mixed up in something else, I need to know about it." His gentle mouth had firmed into a line, his heavy black brows drawn into a frown.

"Well, we don't know for certain if that murder has any bearing on this case, lieutenant. It might, but we haven't figured out a link yet." Alex frowned down at her hands and smoothed the scar on her thumb that was the result of an accident with a pocketknife when she was a Girl Scout. Girl Scout? *She* had been a Girl Scout?

"Mrs. Campbell?"

Alex pulled herself back to the case at hand. She realized the importance of her testimony, but her mind kept veering away from it, focusing on nonessentials, like the way Lieutenant Laurie had missed a spot on his chin when he shaved his heavy beard this morning. She didn't want to think about Gladys Harrison or how her own meddling could have caused her murder. But she must. "In 1936, Mrs. Harrison's father was killed. Shot in his bed. Mrs. Weston denied that it ever happened."

"And she didn't like it at all that Alex was doing the genogram," Amelia added. "I thought it was because of the scandal. I thought Mrs. Harrison might have committed the murder, you see. But obviously there's something else wrong."

"Badly wrong, I think," Briggie interjected. "Alex and I have just discovered that someone else may have been the heir to the Williams fortune. It may not ever have belonged to Gladys's father."

"Wait a minute, for Pete's sake." The young lieutenant held up his hand. "It sounds to me like you need to draw this geno . . . whatever it is . . . for me."

Briggie, who had planned from the beginning to thrust the police into this aspect of the matter, triumphantly pulled the family tree from her canvas briefcase.

"Here," she said, handing the chart to the policeman, pointing. "There's Gladys's father. And we just discovered this morning what looks like an illegitimate brother. We don't know if he was older or younger than Lloyd. We don't even know his name."

"What?" demanded Amelia. "You didn't tell me anything about that."

"Gladys's murder put it out of our heads," Briggie told her soothingly.

Alex took pity on the bewildered policeman and told him of the two portraits in the Williams's foundry history.

"And you say Mrs. Weston didn't want you looking into the family tree? I'd say this gives her more of a motive than ever," he said firmly, flicking a finger at the paper in his hand.

"The Westons are scared of someone, lieutenant," Alex said a little desperately. "It seems to me that a missing heir must have turned up and is threatening them."

"Well," the policeman remarked, surveying the three women. He looked faintly amused. "It sounds to me like something out of an old-time romance or something. My grandma would love this. Missing heirs, for crying out loud." He shook his head. "But I think you're stretching it, ladies. You've got a great motive staring you in the face. If, and I say if, this Holly Weston is telling the truth, her mother is scared to death her daughter's going to discover she's embezzled her fortune. She'd want to get her hands on that money ASAP. And even if Holly turns out to be making up stories, her mother and father still have the best motive. They inherit. Bingo." He stood up. "Provided it was murder, of course. And we should know that when we get the post mortem tomorrow."

"But the Westons couldn't have committed that other murder." Alex's mother said. "They weren't even born yet."

"I'm not in the business of solving a sixty-year-old murder," he told them. "I don't see that it comes into this at all."

"It may not," said Briggie belligerently. "But there's some reason Grace Weston lied about it."

"Sounds like that woman's nothing but trouble," the lieutenant said. "I believe I'll go have a little chat with her."

He walked to the door, the three women trailing behind him with Lord Peter. "Nice dog. But puny. If that wasn't a suicide up on the lake, you ladies could be in danger until we get this wrapped up." He handed them his card. "You stay together. And be sure you lock your doors."

"But, lieutenant," Briggie objected, "we are especially trained at this sort of thing. I still think the whole clue to these deaths could be genealogical."

"Well, you may be right, ma'am. The daughter or son-in-law kills Mrs. Harrison for the inheritance. Even I know that much genealogy." He smiled down at Briggie, his mouth gentle again. Alex knew he was humoring her colleague. "They may even have had a hand in that old hit-and-run, I'll admit." He darted a look at Alex. "You thought I'd forgotten about that, didn't you?"

"We think the Westons are being blackmailed," Briggie said, not to be defeated.

"I figure you're making this too complicated. Just let us do our job, okay?"

Lord Peter, evidently objecting to his tone of voice, barked adamantly at Lieutenant Laurie's departing back.

"Well!" Briggie said, obviously miffed. "He's nice, at least. But in some ways, he's almost as bad as Lieutenant O'Neill. He doesn't take us seriously."

"O'Neill?" Amelia asked.

"The Winnetka policeman who worked with us when . . . when . . ."

"When Daddy died," Alex finished. "He suspected me and thought Briggie was partially demented. He impounded her deer rifle."

Alex could feel her mother's eyes on her as she tried to keep her tone light.

"You musn't blame yourself for this, honey," Amelia said. "I know that old lady was your friend. But if her daughter killed her . . ."

Feeling an overwhelming sadness for the spunky woman in the bleak old house she had striven so hard to make cheerful, Alex thought also of the pets they had inherited. Thank heavens they hadn't left them for the neurotically tidy Grace. The cheerfulness of the afternoon tea they had shared with Gladys and the pride the woman had taken in her ancestry and even in her own youthful peccadilloes were much too clear in Alex's mind. And now Gladys was lying somewhere on a cold slab in a morgue. She wondered if Grace Weston would choose to bury her mother in her tweeds and pearls. In any case, Gladys would never see her beloved pets again.

The pathetic image made her suddenly angry. Who would kill such a vital being and put her in that freezing lake? "It wasn't Grace," she said defiantly. "Even though I don't like her, I know enough to know that she's scared something's going to happen to Holly. That's the key to the whole thing. We've got to find out who she's afraid of."

"Why was Gladys killed, then?" Amelia asked.

"Either she knew something or someone is systematically wiping out this family. Same goes for Sonia," Briggie answered.

"Let's get on with this," Alex said, pounding her right fist into her open left hand. "I've got to *do* something."

Amelia said practically, "We need to call Lake Forest and see when the library closes."

The two others looked at her questioningly.

"That history you found," she explained. "Don't you think they'll have a copy of it at the local library?"

Briggie smacked her forehead. "Why didn't I think of that? Gladys's death has put me off my stride. Good job, Amelia."

Reflecting with gratitude that her mother seemed to have recovered her spirits, Alex agreed. "Great, Mother. Why don't you call them?"

The library informed Amelia that they would be open until nine o'clock and that they did have the foundry history in their catalogue.

Refusing to be left out of the chase, Alex's mother treated them all to tacos at a drive-through, and they made the run up to Lake Forest. Briggie drove, and Amelia rode in the front seat, chattering about people she knew who lived in the houses they passed. Alex sat in the back, brooding, wishing Briggie would go faster.

The library proved to be a charming stone building nestled among carefully tended shrubs now frosted with snow. It smelled like a private gentleman's study should smell—of leather and dust and bookpaste.

The librarian, a stout matron with improbable red hair, looked to be near Gladys's age. Alex wondered if they had been friends. She had the book waiting behind her oak desk.

Hovering over the maroon leather volume, the three of them held their breath as Briggie turned the pages. The picture of the mysterious man appeared to have been sliced out with a razor.

* * *

"Alex, did you know we're being followed?" Amelia Borden asked from the backseat of the Bronco.

"It's night, Mother. How can you tell?"

"There was a black car in the library parking lot with a man sitting in it. As soon as we came out, he started up his car. But I watched, and he waited until we left to follow us. He's still right on our tail."

"Is it a Taurus, Briggie?"

Briggie studied her rearview mirror when the road straightened out. "Can't see anything but those doggoned headlights."

"A Taurus?" her mother repeated.

"A black Ford Taurus followed us the other day. And there may have been one behind us the day we went up to Waukegan," Briggie told her.

"You mean you've been followed before?" Amelia leaned forward in her seat anxiously, reaching back to touch Alex on the shoulder. "Why didn't you tell me?"

"I didn't want you to worry. And anyway, we weren't certain."

"I'm calling Charles as soon as we get home," Amelia said firmly. "He'll have moved in today. After this murder, I think we need a man in the house."

"Mother!" Alex protested. "If we are being observed, whoever it is will have seen the police at our house. They'll think twice about doing anything."

"No. They know you're researching this, Alex. That may be all the more reason for them to act," Amelia said ruefully. "They may think you know more than you do. Or maybe you already know more than you think you know. I'm calling Charles."

Chapter Fourteen

Charles turned up on their doorstep only fifteen minutes after Amelia called. A frown corrugated the marble smoothness of his forehead, and his eyes were anxious as Alex's mother led him into the sitting room where they were drinking cups of chamomile tea.

"And Bob's your uncle!" Moriarty greeted him.

He gave the parrot a somewhat frazzled glance. "Alex! Briggie! It's happened again, has it?"

"It's terrible, Charles," Alex told him. "We liked Gladys Harrison. A lot."

"So why was she killed?"

Briggie brought him up to date on their suspicions and on their discovery of the probable illegitimate son of William Williams.

"But could he inherit under the will?"

"It doesn't say anything about legitimate or illegitimate in the trust," Briggie told him. "It just says 'the oldest son and his children in perpetuity.'"

"Then why *didn't* he inherit?"

"Queer as Dick's hatband," the Professor interjected.

"I never thought of that," Briggie murmured, obviously abashed.

"Maybe *he* didn't think he could inherit," Alex suggested.

"And his heirs have consulted a lawyer," Amelia finished.

"Then why didn't they just take their case to court?" Charles asked reasonably. "Why murder people? What do they hope to accomplish?"

"You're right, Charles," Alex said. She sank into a fit of gloom. Someone had killed Gladys. Did their discovery of that day mean nothing, then?

"We're being followed," Amelia told him. "That's why I called you."

"I don't know what you thought he could do about it, Mother," Alex said ungraciously. It wasn't that she wasn't glad to see Charles in his camel's hair trousers and sky blue cashmere sweater. But she didn't like the inference that she was out of control. Besides, she really didn't want Charles taking up residence here. That was much too close for comfort.

"We're in danger," Amelia reasoned. "We need a man."

Charles grinned and looked at the obviously indignant Alex and Briggie. "I hate to tell you, Amelia, but it was Alex who got *me* out of a fix at Oxford."

Briggie nodded shortly. "Dang right."

"So where in the world did you come up with this parrot? He sounds like he was educated in Regency England."

"Gladys's," Briggie said shortly. "The cat and dog, too."

"Right." Charles apparently took this in stride, looking down at the inquisitive dachshund, who was regarding him hopefully. "So. What's the next step, gang?" he asked.

Alex didn't respond but sat quietly looking into the fire. First her mother, now Charles. And, of course, Lord Peter, Tuppence, and the macaw. This case was beginning to resemble a circus.

"We can only do what we're trained to do and hope that it turns up a murderer," Briggie told him. "I'm not saying that it *was* an unknown heir, but the fact is, Grace Weston is afraid of something, and I think that something has to do with the family tree." She filled Charles in on the hit-and-run death of Sonia Williams and Holly's subsequent treatment.

"Hmm," he said. "That puts a different complexion on the matter." Alex could feel his eyes on her. "What do *you* think?" he asked.

"That you should stay here and watch Mother, as she is obviously nervous. That would be very kind. And Lord Peter seems to have taken a shine to you."

"What will you and Briggie do?"

Briggie pulled out the genogram and studied it. Charles looked over her shoulder.

"It looks like you have some question marks," he said. "William Williams' first wife's name, the illegitimate son's identity, and the problem of William Jr.'s suicide."

Alex listened to them propounding their theories, feeling as though a scrim had suddenly fallen in front of her. To everyone else, it was just a puzzle. She was obscurely glad for that. She wouldn't want anyone else to feel things as she was feeling them. But she left the room and went upstairs. Someone had to put fresh sheets on her father's bed if Charles was to spend the night. Tuppence, appearing out of nowhere, trailed her, obviously disconsolate. She, at least, seemed to miss her mistress.

Alex thought of the gloomy mansion in Lake Forest, steeped in snow. Gladys's tall, plump body dead and wrapped around the pilings of the neighbor's pier. Then, suddenly, she was seeing Holly, sitting scrunched up against her postered wall at the treatment center.

Was she really in danger? Alex remembered Dr. Goodwin with a start. She must be put in the picture.

Running lightly back down the stairs, she went to the kitchen phone. Dr. Goodwin's emergency number was in her carryall.

"Dr. Goodwin? Alex Campbell."

"Oh, yes, Alex. Have you found something new?"

"You mean the police haven't been in touch with you?"

"Police?"

"Gladys Harrison was found," she explained. "In the lake. They're waiting for the post mortem, but I'm sure it was murder."

There was a silence. "The only alternative is suicide, I suppose?"

"Yes. She wouldn't have been walking by the lake in the middle of a snowstorm. And she was waiting for us to come. She wanted to talk to us. I'm sure it wasn't suicide. The police suspect Grace Weston or her husband."

"Poor Holly!" Dr. Goodwin said, obviously aghast. "What an awful shock it would be if her parents were arrested."

"That's why I called. I think the police are going to question you. I was trying to suggest that this murder was connected to the hit-and-run and Holly's parents' decision to put her in the center, and I told them about Holly's suspicions about her parents."

"What do you mean? I didn't know Holly had any suspicions."

"She thinks they've embezzled her inheritance and are trying to prove her mentally incompetent."

"Do you think there's any truth in that?" Dr. Goodwin was quick to ask.

"No, or I would have told you about it. I think she's just trying to account for their bizarre behavior."

"But Holly's idea does give them a motive."

"Yes. I didn't think about what I was saying until it was too late, I'm afraid. And now I think I've set the police off on the wrong track."

"You don't think they did it?"

"No," Alex said emphatically. "I still think they're being black-mailed or something. I really don't think Holly was on drugs, Dr. Goodwin. Will you please see that she gets some support? She needs to know that someone believes her. This whole thing is apt to throw her into a terrible tailspin."

"Yes, certainly," Dr. Goodwin said. "I can see that. Good heavens, it has all kinds of awful ramifications. Betrayal. Abandonment. I'll talk with her myself in the morning. I'll tell her that you've convinced me that she's telling the truth. But I don't think it would be wise to mention the murder just yet."

"I'd really appreciate that, Dr. Goodwin. I know what it feels like not to have anyone believe you."

In her prayers that night, Alex prayed earnestly for Holly. It was imperative that the girl not feel abandoned. Then she cried softly for Gladys and her beloved pets, suddenly unable to believe that the universe was not a random place where bad things happened to good people. Grief over Stewart, lulled these many months, fell upon her as it always did in times of nonsensical disaster. She saw the burning fireball that had been his plane plowing into the earth. The cold emptiness that that event had carved in her life yawned, threatening to suck her into its familiar black pit.

A soft knock sounded on her door. She ignored it, wiping her streaming eyes. The door opened quietly, and someone came in and gently knelt beside her. It was her mother. An arm went around her shoulders and held her tightly.

"I knew when you were quiet that something was wrong," Amelia said, observing her tears. "You always used to go quiet when you were a little girl and something was bothering you."

Alex couldn't answer.

"I hope you don't mind my interrupting your prayers, but I wanted you to know that I love you."

Where had her mother been when Stewart died? Alex's heart cried out from the depths where it had fallen. Remembering those long, achingly lonely months when Stewart's family, handling their grief with Scottish phlegm, had been aloof and reserved, she still said nothing.

Amelia kissed her softly on the cheek and rose. "I'll leave you now."

Alex slept badly.

*   *   *

She woke to turmoil. How could she have been so cruel to her mother? Obviously, her conversion to Jesus Christ was only skin-deep. It didn't reach that deep dark place in her heart where fear and resentment dwelt. Maybe she wasn't converted at all. Maybe there wasn't any sense to be made of things. Poor Gladys Harrison had been murdered. That was undoubtedly *her* fault. But couldn't God have prevented it?

Swinging her feet to the floor, she reflected that it was less than useless to reflect on such things. The world was a dark place. What had happened had happened. The thing was to go on from here. She sagged. Why? Why bother?

Looking around the room listlessly, she at last focused on the photograph she carried with her. She had found it in the attic last summer. It was of herself and her parents, taken when she was about nine or ten, she guessed. She was sitting on the back gate, squinting into the sun. Long legs dangling from her shorts, the young Alex took for granted the presence of the lanky man with the wavy black hair and the fragile blonde with the insouciant smile. A family. She could see it, but she couldn't remember it. In the Latter-day Saint faith, families were sacrosanct. The most vital unit of society.

And wasn't that what drew her to genealogy? The sense of family, the sense of belonging? Putting together units long rent by death was very satisfying to one whose own experience of family was so unsatisfying.

What about Gladys's family? What about Holly?

Alex sat up straighter. Holly. She would go on for Holly's sake. She had to find out the truth of Gladys's death for Holly.

The problem was, she had no idea where to go from here. As promising as it had seemed, the idea of the disinherited heir probably didn't have anything to do with the murder of Lloyd Sr., if one were to follow Charles's reasoning.

Then she remembered the black Taurus. *Someone* had been following them. Someone was nervous about what they were doing. Was it just the Westons? Getting up, she went into the bathroom and got ready for her shower. As Alex foamed the body wash over herself underneath the water spigot, she tried to remember what Briggie had said about the driver of the car on the way to church on Sunday. A bald man with a beaked nose. That was unusual. You didn't really think of a "tail" as being middle-aged or elderly. And Nike Man had been middle-aged, too.

It seemed unlikely that the Westons would hire anyone but a professional to follow them. A professional would be young and muscular, for heaven's sake. Wouldn't he?

She was missing a piece here, she thought as she towel-dried her mass of ringlets. It all came back to Grace Weston's refusal to let them tamper with the family tree. And Gladys, who had been all too willing to help them, was dead.

"We need to go forward with what we've got," she announced at breakfast. They were eating cornflakes with hothouse strawberries that Amelia had been out to purchase, presumably at the crack of dawn. She had also brought back croissants, which Charles was wolfing down with tremendous appreciation. "It's the only thing we can do."

"Let the police do their investigation," Briggie said darkly. "We'll do ours. We need to track down that book, if we can."

Tuppence, ignoring her dish of albacore, had found a perch on top of the refrigerator from which she regarded them balefully. Lord Peter ate dry dog food that her mother had apparently augmented with something that looked like yogurt. "Has anyone tried looking at the steel foundry itself?" Charles asked.

"No," Briggie said. "We just found out about the thing yesterday. But that's a good idea. We'll run down there today."

"I think I should be a party to any further expeditions," Charles said promptly. "Alex and I could go down. Isn't there something you and Amelia could do here, Briggie?"

"Wait a minute," Alex protested at this high-handedness. "I think you need to stay here with Mother, Charles. She's nervous."

"No," her mother said immediately. "If you go out, it's you who are in danger, not me. Charles needs to go with you."

Exasperated, Alex looked at Briggie, who shrugged her shoulders and grinned. "Good hunting, Alex."

"But what will you do?"

"I stayed awake last night thinking," Briggie told her. "Charles is right about our question marks. I think we should try to clear them up. Now that we know that William Williams Sr. died in 1930, we have an idea about when William Williams Jr. would have died." Her eyes danced. "How do you think Earlene would like to do a little detective work?"

"Earlene?" Alex asked blankly.

"Our waitress at Ernie's, remember?"

Alex's mind went back to the blonde woman with the western shirt and the bolo tie who had warned them about Nike Man. She gave a little laugh. "Briggie, you're a stitch. I bet she'd love it."

"I'm going to call her and see if she can come up with a death certificate for us. That way I can stay here with your mother."

"We'll make dinner, too," Amelia said virtuously. "I have some cookbooks I haven't used in years. We can't starve Charles."

Reflecting resignedly that Charles was very good at getting what he wanted, Alex agreed.

Chapter Fifteen

To get to Gary, Indiana, Charles and Alex had to travel what seemed like an enormous distance across space and time. They left behind the sparkling North Shore, the stately skyscrapers of a new Chicago, and traveled over the industrial wastes of the past, through the housing projects, and finally into the landscape of enormous manufacturing plants which made up Gary.

As far as Alex could tell, no black Taurus was on their tail. During the drive, they were not silent.

"I'm sorry about your Mrs. Harrison," Charles told her. "I know how much you liked her." Today he was dressed in gray flannel slacks and a navy sports coat. Alex had put on her sapphire pullover and black slacks. She was even now engaged in picking Tuppence's orange hairs off them.

"Yes, I did. Very much. She was charming, Charles. And even though she was lonely, she loved life. She shouldn't have died."

"I agree, of course. Is that why you're not yourself, Alex?" he asked. "You're so pensive and sad."

She attempted to perk up. Charles was used to a take-charge Alex, after all. "Sorry."

"You feel responsible, don't you?"

"Yes, I'm afraid so."

"Why don't you tell me why?" he asked earnestly.

A little flame of anger flared underneath her misery. "Isn't it obvious? I mean, the woman never sees a soul. She lives alone in that big old house for years, unmolested. Then along comes Alex with her deadly little genogram. Gladys is absolutely thrilled to talk about the past. No one else will listen to her, you see. But I do. And then she's killed."

"That niece of hers was killed last spring," Charles said reasonably. "And you didn't even know about Gladys then."

"I've got all these hang-ups, Charles," she said irritably. How had she expected that she could ever keep them from him? "You'd be bound to find out sooner or later."

"You mean you take the blame for everything?"

"Number one characteristic of a child of an alcoholic."

"Well, cheer up. It's better than what I do. I don't take the blame for anything. Number one characteristic of an Oxford man, son of the liberal establishment. Everything is someone else's fault."

"You're not really like that, though." Alex looked at him. His words had been said with some bitterness.

"I've lived like your classic narcissist, Alex. You're the first woman I've ever met besides Philippa who didn't fall all over herself to please me. That tends to have a disastrous effect on one's character."

She laughed at this piece of self-description that tallied so closely with her initial impression of him. "You're not irredeemable, you know."

"No. That's what Alma says. I feel quite in charity with Alma, you know. He was like the scion of a noble house. And a total rotter. But he changed."

"It took an angel to do it, remember."

Taking his eyes from the road, he gave her a warm glance. "Maybe you're my angel, Alex."

Uncomfortable, she said gruffly, "I'm no one's angel, Charles. You've got it all wrong." Struggling to keep her own nose above water, she was certainly ill qualified to be a member missionary to Charles.

"My saving grace, then. Doesn't your church have missionaries or something? I seem to remember them causing some sort of ruckus at Oxford once."

Here was irony. He was *asking* for the missionaries, for Pete's sake. It was *she* who was wallowing in doubt. "What kind of ruckus?"

"Rather like Daniel in the lion's den," he said. "They were just young kids, and they apparently said something that absolutely enraged one of the dons at Christ Church." He laughed. "But as I recall they held their own. Just like Daniel. Anyway, do they have missionaries in the States?"

"You would be willing to be taught by nineteen-year-olds?"

"Who taught you?"

Alex gave a little smile at the memory. "A farm boy from Tabiona, Utah. His companion was a college freshman. They baptized me a little over a year ago."

"So. They must have known what they were doing."

Alex took a deep breath. Impossible to imagine Charles with two earnest young men teaching him about the true nature of God and man. Charles? But she had believed the missionaries who had taught her, hadn't she? The story of the First Vision had seemed outrageous, but she had been more humble then. Absolutely leveled. And it had been what Briggie believed. Could she still believe it?

Closing her eyes, she leaned her head back on the seat. She traced her testimony back to its genesis. Going carefully over in her mind what the missionaries had told her, she weighed everything against her doubts.

There *had* been gold plates, she concluded. There was absolutely no other explanation for the Book of Mormon. Joseph Smith couldn't have written it. He could hardly write his name, for heaven's sake. And, besides that, she knew it was the word of God. It really was indisputable. So he had to have been a prophet, had to have translated it by divine power. And therefore, all of its teachings about Jesus Christ *had* to be true. There *was* another life after this one. Death *wasn't* the ultimate tragedy, murder and terrorism notwithstanding. Why couldn't she just remember that?

"Alex?" Charles's voice came to her from a long way off.

"Yes," she answered. "It's not the missionaries who teach you but the Spirit. The secret is to get the humblest missionaries you can find. My missionary from Tabiona was as humble as they come."

The universe had righted itself. How odd that Charles, with his new humility, should be God's instrument. But Heavenly Father never seemed to grow tired of her doubts, even when she was so consistently willing to question His existence. Though she, Alex Campbell, couldn't see it, God must know what He was doing. And maybe if she focused more on His will and less on her own need to be in control, He would give her the grace to change her heart. That was going to be an uphill battle.

Right now I'm in His hands. The thought startled her and made her sit up straight. She would see that Charles met the missionaries, and she would find out who killed Gladys. Yes, and Lloyd Williams, too.

* * *

The factory, an enormous grasshopper-green mass of buildings with steam rising from it, was clearly still functioning. With some difficulty, they found the foreman's office. He directed them to an address downtown where the management offices were.

Downtown Gary was depressing after Chicago. The terra-cotta brick building that housed the managing directorship of the Williams Steel Foundry was on a street that was no longer in the best part of town. If Gary could be said to have a good part of town. Weeds grew up through cracks in the sidewalk, and spray paint adorned the light posts and the backs of stop signs. Alex spared a moment to be glad that Charles was with her.

An extremely thin, middle-aged woman greeted them in the office with a tight smile. She looked startled. Guessing at once that the woman was not used to visitors, Alex realized she had given no thought as to what she would say. But she had reckoned without Charles.

"I say, I'm a journalist from Great Britain, and we're interested in writing up a biography of William Williams for inclusion in a book we're doing on the great Welsh emigration to America." Charles took out his press card. He was a legitimate member of that corps as theater critic of the *Times*. "I would be interested in any information, books and so forth, that you might have about the foundry and particularly about Mr. Williams."

The thin woman looked from Charles to Alex and back again. "We have a little library with cuttings and that kind of thing. I've never heard of any book. But I don't suppose there's any harm in your looking. Won't you follow me?"

The "library" was a dim little room on the second floor containing horsehair and leather furniture. It was lit only by two standard lamps.

"There are some very outdated books on steel production there."

She pointed to a bookcase. "And then we have years of trade journals. I think the clippings are all in a folder." She produced this out of the top drawer of a filing cabinet and handed it to Charles. "I must ask you not to remove anything, because those are our only copies, but I'll run a photocopy of anything you need."

It was a grim little room, evidence that the glory of the Williams Steel Foundry was no longer celebrated. While Charles browsed through the clippings, Alex combed the dusty shelves looking for the maroon binding of the foundry history. She found it wedged between two old trade journals. Quickly opening to the page where she knew the picture would be, she found it. This time the name wasn't crossed out.

"May I help you with something?"

Alex and Charles, startled, looked up. Mr. Weston with his neat goatee and three-piece suit was regarding them dryly. Alex, crouched on the ground in front of the bookshelves, nearly fell on her face. *George Weston! Here!*

Charles moved forward, his hand extended. "Charles Lamb, *London Times*."

"George Weston," the man replied.

Closing the book, Alex stood quickly and said, "Hello, Mr. Weston. Do you remember me?"

"I thought my wife removed you from Holly's case," he said blandly. His face gave absolutely no clue to any displeasure he might feel. He went on. "I find it rather amusing that you got in here with that absurd story. You could have asked me for anything you needed, you know. I'm not quite as unreasonable as Grace."

Alex let out her breath. "The North Side Treatment Center did take me off the case," she told him. "But my cousin Charles was really interested in William Williams. He *does* want to write an article on him."

"Oh, come now." The little man laughed. "Do you really expect me to believe that? Doing it much too brown, as they say in Mr. Lamb's country. If I were to hazard a guess, I'd say that you were here because of Gladys."

Putting the book back on the shelf, Alex asked steadily, "Gladys? You mean Mrs. Harrison?"

For the first time he showed irritation. "You know very well my wife's mother is dead."

"Oh, how horrible!" Alex said, putting her hands to her mouth. She knew she wasn't a very good actress.

But Charles was superb. He put his arm around her shoulders. "You liked the old woman, didn't you? Made her come alive for me. I could swear I knew her, too." He looked at George Weston. "You have my condolences, sir. This must seem like an unpardonable breach of manners."

"Was it a heart attack?" Alex asked.

"You know as well as I do she was found in the lake. You're the one who called the police!" She had completely forgotten until that moment that she had spoken to Grace Weston. The small man was looking at her in that insinuating way she found so irritating. What could she say?

Charles put down the folder he was holding and shepherded her out the door. "Come, darling. I think it's time we were going."

George Weston's voice followed them. "Trying your hand at being a detective, eh? What I'd like to know is what in the world you think William Williams has to do with anything!"

* * *

Once they were in the car, Alex drew a long breath, "Thank you, Charles. I had no idea he worked there. What an impossible situation. I wonder what he thinks!"

143

"The worst, undoubtedly. You heard him."

"Well, we got the goods, anyway."

"Did we?"

"Yes. I got the name under the picture just before he walked in."

"What was it?"

"Jonathan Crowell, Senior Vice President."

"Not a Williams?"

"Not a Williams in name but clearly a Williams genetically."

Chapter Sixteen

B riggie was thrilled with the news.

"And George Weston? What did you tell him?"

"We fell back on the old journalist's credo," Charles said. "'Never apologize.'"

"He guessed we were doing detective work," Alex conceded. "But by then there was nothing he could do, because I'd already seen the picture."

Amelia had made chicken divan. "I got the recipe out of my Junior League cookbook," she confided. "I remember now that it was one of Joe's favorite dishes." She looked at Alex as she referred to her father. "He would have been so proud of you, honey."

Alex teared up, much to her embarrassment. Her mother rarely spoke of her father. Briggie gave her a brief hug. "I vote for an early dinner and then a council of war," she said.

"So, what do we do next?" Charles asked as he put the last dish in the dishwasher. Lord Peter had his front paws on the door and was licking water dripping from the dishes. Tuppence remained ensconced on the top of the refrigerator.

"Well," Briggie said, once they were all settled around the dining room table, "what we really need to do is find out when this man was born. If he is the older brother of Lloyd, then his issue are the heirs to the Williams money under the trust. If he's the younger brother, then the money would only come to them if the older branch of the family were wiped out. Right now, the only people who stand in their way are Holly and Grace Weston."

"I wonder if they know that," Charles said, taking notes on a legal pad. "I wonder if these people have been threatening the Westons."

"But surely, if they had, the Westons would have gone to the police, wouldn't they?" Alex objected. "If this Jonathan were the younger brother, they have absolutely no legal claim to the money. Any threats would amount to extortion."

Amelia sat up very straight and said just one word, "Scandal."

"Not again," Alex said.

"I truly think you'll find that's the key. Whatever is going on, there's a scandal at the back of it. I've said so all along. There's a real compost heap of issues here. Speaking of which, your waitress came through for us, Alex."

"Earlene?"

"Yeah," said Briggie. "William Williams's cause of death was listed as accidental drowning. He died in July 1929. I think we need to get an obit or the local newspaper story on him."

"And speaking of accidental drowning, that policeman called, too," Amelia interrupted again.

Alex looked at her mother. "What did he want?"

"He says Gladys Harrison drowned. There was no evidence of violence or anything. Just drowning. The idiot is treating it as suicide, believe it or not."

"Suicide!" Alex protested. "But we told him . . ."

"I know," Briggie interrupted briskly. "If I had been on the phone,

I would have given him a piece of my mind. But now it's up to us. I say that we go to the Newberry tomorrow to see what we can dig up on Jonathan Crowell."

Charles, the genogram in front of him, asked, "Where do we start?"

"If we're very lucky, the *Tribune* will have his obituary. We can also try the 1920 census." Briggie pulled her folder with the case's supporting documents out of her battered denim briefcase. "From Lloyd Williams's obituary, we know that he was born on July 25, 1895. If Jonathan was around his age, he would have been near twenty-five in 1920. He should be old enough to show up by himself somewhere."

"We'll want to find him on the 1910, too," Alex added, "so we can get his mother's name. That's the only way we're going to get a birth certificate."

"Okay." Charles added to his notes. "This is fun. Do you need another business partner?"

Alex made a face at him. "This isn't exactly lucrative. I'm counting on coming into some money, if you ever get that estate settled."

He sighed elaborately. "This is far more amusing."

*   *   *

To everyone's surprise, Amelia decided not to accompany them the next morning.

"It's nothing," she reassured them. "Just a bit of a headache. The pets will keep me company. You can report everything when you return."

This was so unlike her new mother that Alex looked at her suspiciously, but she just held up a bottle of Motrin and waved them out the door.

Jonathan Crowell proved elusive. They could find no obituary listed for him in the *Tribune* index.

"Is it possible he lived in Indiana?" Alex asked.

"A senior V.P. of the company?" Briggie refuted. "Undoubtedly, he lived on the North Shore. I think we're going to have to go for a death certificate. If he died after Social Security records started, maybe he'll be on the Social Security Death Index. That'll give us a death date. Then, the Cook County Clerk's office is right on Clark Street, I think. How about if I take that on and leave you two here to check out the census? I asked, and they have the Soundex for 1920, 1910, and 1900."

"What's a Soundex?" Charles inquired.

"It's a sort of index by the way a name sounds," Alex told him. "They replace sounds with numbers. Everything that sounds like Crowell will be together on the same roll. Then it gives you the actual page in the census where you can find the original entry."

She showed him as Briggie moved off to the computers to find the death index. "The Soundex code will start with *C* for Crowell. Then you use three numbers for the rest. *R* is a 6. You skip vowel sounds. So the next sound is *L*, which is a 4. You don't use double consonants, so you round off your three digit code with a 0. That means our Crowells will be under the C-640s. We'll start in Cook County. If we don't turn anything up there, we'll go to Lake County, where Lloyd lived."

In the census area of the library, Alex located the Soundex reel they were looking for, found an empty machine, and threaded it. They looked very carefully through the 640s for a Jonathan Crowell but found none.

"Wait a minute," Charles said. "I notice these are listed alphabetically by the head of the household. What if he was living with someone else, like his mother?"

"Brilliant, Charles. I didn't even think of checking all the Crowells to see who their children were."

It began to look as though they weren't going to find anything until at long last they reached the W's. A Wilma Crowell, age fifty, was listed as living with two children: Jonathan, aged twenty-five, and Portia, aged twenty-three.

"How can we tell they are the right ones?" Charles wanted to know.

"Well, we get the actual census, first of all. It's this roll number in the upper righthand corner."

Charles was a quick study. Once he had the roll in his hands, he threaded the machine easily.

"Then we turn to this enumeration district"—Alex indicated the number 175—"and look for page 3. He should be somewhere on that page."

The writing was faint, but at last they located Wilma and her family on Surf Street in Chicago. "That's a good neighborhood— Lincoln Park." Alex's eyes quickly went down to Jonathan's name. "Look!" she said. "It gives his father's birthplace. It's Wales!"

"And Bob's your uncle, as Professor Moriarty would say. Now, let's see what it has to say about his age." Charles consulted the genogram. "If he was twenty-five, it's going to be a close thing between him and his half brother."

The census showed his month of birth to be July 1895.

"Oh, my gosh! Can you believe it? It's going to be a matter of days between them."

Catching on, Charles examined the page further. "The daughter evidently had the same father. Born in Wales, anyway. The affair must have been a long-standing one," he said.

Alex added, "If Jonathan worked at the plant, it's as though

William really had two families. He seems to have taken care of them, at least. I wonder what happened to them when he died."

"If the resemblance to his brother was so clear, surely everyone must have known who Jonathan was," Charles reasoned. "I wouldn't be surprised if he got the sack once his half brother was at the helm. When did his father die?"

"In 1930. Jonathan and Lloyd would have been thirty-five."

Briggie joined Charles and Alex triumphantly. "Sorry that took so long. I had to wait for a computer, but I got it! The Social Security death record for Jonathan Crowell. He died in 1965. At least I think it's the right one. Did you find him on the census?"

Charles brought Briggie quickly up to speed. "So does that document give a birthdate?"

"It sure does. July 20, 1895."

"Well," said Alex on a deep breath. "That takes care of it. Jonathan was the elder. Lloyd was born July 25th. Good grief! What a mess."

"It would be interesting to get this Jonathan Crowell's birth certificate, just to make certain," Briggie cautioned. "I want to see if his mother listed his father on it. The Cook County Clerk's Office is downtown on Clark Street."

Leaving the now friendly environs of the Newberry, they got back into Charles's car and headed downtown. Traffic was bumper to bumper.

"My gosh," said Alex suddenly, looking out the back window of Charles's Range Rover. "I completely forgot to see if we were being followed."

Briggie likewise craned her neck. "Geez, Louise. I can't see anything in that mess."

Cars clogged behind them, all shapes and sizes, threading their way through the deep canyon between Chicago's buildings.

"Don't worry, ladies," Charles said. "Remember, you have me."

Briggie snorted. Alex was pensive. "I didn't notice anybody in particular at the library, but I can't say that I was paying much attention."

"No," Charles agreed. "We were engaged in high drama. I can see how this gets to be addictive. Who needs caffeine?"

"You're right," Briggie said with a smug grin. "We've taken our vice and managed to turn it into a respectable business."

When they arrived at the county clerk's office, they put in their request for the birth certificate and then went in search of vending machines for lunch. Standing on the cement floor of an unfriendly basement, Alex ate a Snickers, Charles a pineapple Danish, and Briggie a pair of Reese's peanut butter cups.

"I think I'll check on Mother," Alex said, pulling out her cell phone. She dialed the number. There was no answer. "That's odd," she reflected. "But maybe the Motrin knocked her out, and she's asleep."

"I hate to think of her missing this," Briggie said. "What a day."

Alex was silent. She was suddenly remembering all those years when her mother hadn't answered the phone because she had been passed out on the bed. Had she relapsed? Was it possible? She had seemed so normal this morning. Suddenly convinced that her mother had been lying about the headache, Alex felt a worm of worry. Had her mother taken that rejection of hers the other night to heart? Was Amelia more wounded than she had imagined?

Charles was looking at her. "What's wrong, Alex?"

"Probably nothing." She shrugged. "Let's go upstairs. Maybe they have those things ready for us."

"There!" Briggie crowed twenty minutes later, birth certificate in hand. "Jonathan's father is listed as William Williams. I knew I never liked that Lloyd. He never had any right to that money at all."

"But what a close thing it was, Briggie," Alex said. "What a scoundrel William Willams must have been. His wife and his mistress were pregnant at the exact same time."

"I wonder if he knew just what he was doing when he made that will," Charles pondered as they walked out into the harsh winter wind blowing off the Chicago River.

"I don't suppose we'll ever know," Alex answered. "But one thing we have to surmise, and that is that Jonathan probably never knew he could inherit as an illegitimate son. He might not even have known his half brother's birthdate. And to give him his due, Lloyd may not have known his, either."

"Well," said Charles, "unless I miss my mark, someone's figured it out." He unlocked the car and held the doors open for Alex and Briggie.

"But that doesn't make sense. As you said the other day, why would they have to murder anyone? They could just come forward with the documentation and say that the money was theirs," Alex protested, climbing into the Range Rover.

"Not if there's no proof," Briggie objected once they were under way. "They didn't have DNA testing back in 1930, you know. Jonathan Crowell could claim to be the illegitimate son and his birth certificate might list William Williams as his father, but would that be considered real proof in a court of law? His parents weren't married. His mother could have been making it all up. I'd say it gives the Crowells more of a motive than ever and gives the Westons more to lose than ever."

Charles nosed carefully out into the traffic.

"I don't know," Alex said thoughtfully. "Something still isn't right somehow. It doesn't hang together. Would someone really wait all these years to embark on a murder spree? And if they had no solid proof then, what makes them think they have it now?"

* * *

"Mother?" Alex called, as they entered the house. Lord Peter made a mad dash for the bushes. There was no answer to her hail except an ominous emptiness. Alex's former worry assaulted her, and she bit her lip. "Mother, we're back."

It was four o'clock in the afternoon. Leaving her friends in the hall, Alex sprinted up the stairs and ran to her mother's bedroom. Entering, she stared at the empty bed in relief. Amelia wasn't passed out. She hadn't relapsed.

"Alex?" Briggie called from the bottom of the stairs. "Is she up there?"

"No, thank heavens. I was afraid . . ." She let her sentence trail off. If her mother wasn't here, where in the world was she?

Walking slowly down the stairs, Alex reflected back on that morning. "I think she was up to something," she said slowly. "I'm still getting to know her, but I think she thought she could pull a fast one on us."

"Like what?" Briggie asked, intrigued.

"First we need to see if her car's here," Charles said, his face grave.

Alex looked up at the tone in his voice. "What are you thinking?"

"Would she have gone off alone? She was so worried about being followed."

Staring at him for a moment, she suddenly comprehended his concern. Then she bolted from his side, running to every room in the house, dreading what she might see. She found nothing but the Professor sitting innocently on his perch, grooming himself. Her mother wasn't anywhere.

Briggie was just coming in from the garage. "I can't tell if her car is gone. The garage is locked."

"I have a spare opener," Alex said, rummaging through her

carryall. She ran out the kitchen's back door and, facing the garage, pressed the button. As the door raised slowly, she saw that only her little red CRX was parked there. She felt a surge of relief.

"She's gone somewhere to scoop us," she said as she reentered the house. "But what does she know about this case that we don't know?"

Charles went into the dining room with a purposeful air. Following him, Alex and Briggie saw his notes from the night before spread out on the maple dining room table. He was reading them: "Earlene. The death of William Williams Jr., July 1929. Check local newspaper."

"For Pete's sake." Briggie smote her forehead. "I completely forgot about that. I wonder if she went back up to the Lake Forest library."

Alex smiled. "She'll probably walk in any minute now, pleased as punch."

But she didn't.

Chapter Seventeen

By 5:30 Alex had become anxious once more. She called the Lake Forest Library.

"Hello. This is Alex Campbell calling. We were up there a few days ago, doing research on the Williams family."

"Oh, yes. I remember." Alex had no trouble identifying the voice of the elderly redhead who had reminded her of Gladys. "Your charming mother was up here today, you know. We even went out to lunch together. I didn't know she was a detective! It was so exciting. We found just what she was looking for and then we had a comfortable gossip about Lloyd Williams and his father. But surely you know all this."

Alex's reaction to this was mixed. Her mother had been to Lake Forest, that was certain now. But then what? "Actually, no. She hasn't come home yet, and we're a little worried. Can you tell us what time she left?"

"Oh, let's see. My lunch hour was over at two. She just dropped me off here and then went on her way."

Two o'clock? Where in the world was she? "Thank you very much," Alex managed to say before she hung up. Alarm stampeded through her body, speeding her pulse and causing sweat to start on her brow.

Briggie and Charles were seated on the stools at the kitchen island. "What is it, Alex?" Briggie demanded, small brown eyes suddenly alert.

"She left there at two o'clock. What can have happened to her?"

"Does she have a cell phone?" Charles asked.

"No!" Alex said, hitting her forehead with the heel of her hand. "But she has a car phone. Let's see. Where did I put that number?" Unlike her racing body, her mind seemed frozen and sluggish, fixed on a picture of her mother as she had last seen her, gaily holding up the bottle of Motrin.

Finally locating the number in the address book in her carryall, she dialed. There was the bleak, impersonal message that her mother's car phone was turned off or out of the service area. She bit her lower lip hard, trying to stop it from trembling. "No good. The car must be stopped somewhere."

"I don't want to alarm you, Alex," Briggie said, standing four-square and solid in her cherry-red sweats. "But she did just go into remission. She knows we never would have let her drive that far alone. What if her legs got weak again and she had an accident?"

"I should have checked the answering machine first thing," Alex said, running back to her mother's sitting room. There were no messages.

"Rum go," the macaw echoed her thoughts.

Collapsing into her mother's desk chair, she forced herself to think, clutching fistfuls of hair in her hands. Hospitals. They needed to check the hospitals.

Charles came into the room and stood in the doorway. "I'll call the hospitals if you like," he volunteered. "Give me the telephone directory."

"Do you have your cell phone, Alex?" Briggie asked over his shoulder. "I can help."

"No," Alex said, drawing a deep breath. "I can do it."

But after a half an hour of calling, they were assured that no Amelia Borden or anyone answering her description was at any of the hospitals on the North Shore.

Alex's sweating had turned to a deep chill. Gladys Harrison. The cold, malevolent lake. Had someone, one of their watchers, forced her mother off the road, knocked her senseless, and put her in the lake? Visions crowded her mind. Closing her eyes against them, she clutched her middle.

"What is it, darling?" Charles asked, leaning across the desk. "What are you thinking?"

"We have to call the police," Briggie said stoutly.

"Someone must have followed Mother," Alex murmured. "She was probably feeling on top of the world and never even thought of checking her rearview mirror."

"I think calling the police is the right idea," Charles said, beginning to pace the small room. "But you don't have any Scotland Yard or anything like that. Who do we call?"

"Lieutenant Laurie," Alex decided, forcing herself to think constructively. "He's the one who was called in on Gladys's death. He already knows the background."

"Right!" said Briggie. "Though whether we can get him to take us seriously is another matter."

Lieutenant Laurie, as soon as he had heard about the black Taurus that had been following them for days, took it very seriously. He reprimanded her for not mentioning their tail before. "I know what it's like with you root diggers. You lose all your ideas about what's really important."

Alex sank back into her mother's desk chair, accepting the reproach and giving the necessary details. "She has a white '93 Mercedes Coupe."

"License?"

She racked her brain, trying to picture the plate. "I'm not sure. Something starting AEE. When you met us, she was the one with the strawberry blonde hair. Petite." Tears stung her eyes. "The thing is, lieutenant, she isn't strong. She's got multiple sclerosis."

"And she drove all the way to Lake Forest alone?"

"We didn't know she was going," Alex said, acutely aware of her seeming lack of responsibility. "She told us she had a headache, and we left her at home. But we should have known . . ."

"If she's anything like my grandma, she's hard to keep in one place. When that woman gets on a trail, I never know where she's going to take herself off to. But we'll put an APB out on her car, pronto. You just stay there, close to the phone."

They waited in strained silence for him to call back, Alex trying to control her anxiety and the pressure of tears just behind her eyes. Every muscle was tense, and she felt as though a storm were threatening to break inside her head. Lord Peter sat at her feet, looking mournfully up at her.

"I just got her back," she said tightly. "She seemed so in charge. I was beginning to remember what it was like to be a little girl again." Alex pulled the dog up into her lap for comfort.

Charles looked at her quizzically and too late she remembered that he didn't know of this part of her struggle. She had a fleeting longing for Daniel, who would have understood without any explanation.

"It was her decision to go today, Alex," Briggie said, her voice down to earth. "No sense in blaming yourself."

Alex moved to the couch, and Charles seated himself on its arm, putting a steadying hand on her shoulder. He refrained from saying anything. She continued to hold Lord Peter's sausage-shaped body against her.

"She was just coming into her own," she said, remembering with painful clarity her mother's joy at being able to walk without her walker.

"Don't talk like she's dead," Briggie said shortly. "It isn't like you to give way like this."

When the telephone finally shrilled, it was Alex who answered. "Yes?"

"Mrs. Campbell?"

"Yes."

"I haven't had any answer from any of the patrol cars in Lake County. I'm wondering, do you think we ought to extend the search into Cook County or maybe into Wisconsin?"

Alex swallowed with difficulty. "Have you looked in the lake, lieutenant?"

"We have a patrol of deputies searching the lakefront. But it's dark, so I don't know how much they can see tonight."

Once again the image was there. Her mother's frail body awash in the freezing lake. As though she could feel the water, Alex was trembling all over. "Okay, lieutenant. Extend the search as far as you think necessary. Only find her. Please find her."

Briggie came across to her and put her arms around her. "I'm ashamed of myself, Alex. There's one thing we've forgotten. We've got to pray."

Alex looked into her friend's solemn face, recognizing each familiar seam. Mostly there were smile lines. But after raising nine children, her friend had known worry, and those lines were there, too. Her usually bright eyes were soft with tenderness; however, her mouth was firm.

"On our knees," her friend continued. "Charles can join us."

Briggie knelt in the middle of Amelia's sitting room. Looking slightly uncomfortable, Charles followed suit. Alex sank down between them. "You say it, Briggs," she said in a low voice. "I'm afraid I'm in too much of a turmoil."

Briggie said a brisk, heartfelt prayer, asking that the officers be guided and that Amelia might be found unharmed. All Alex could think of was the last time she had knelt in prayer, when her mother had knelt beside her and told her that she loved her. And she, Alex, had been still and silent as stone. She didn't deserve for the Lord to listen to her.

But her mother didn't deserve to die! She cast that thought heavenward, pleading in her heart.

Charles stayed awkwardly on his knees, his arms dangling helplessly while her friend embraced her. Alex held herself rigidly in check, continuing to exert every effort to hold back her tears.

"Well, then," Charles said, rising and seating himself on the couch, "let's try to think of something constructive. I don't think anyone had anything to gain from killing your mother. It's not like she knew anything the rest of you didn't know."

"No," Alex said, "but she did go to Lake Forest on her own. She was pretty vulnerable."

The lieutenant was right. How could they ever have failed to take the watcher or watchers seriously? She remembered with lucidity sharpened by fear Nike Man and the man with the tortoiseshell glasses in the Newberry. Or was she seeing conspiracy everywhere? But someone had killed Gladys.

As though her thoughts were traveling along similar lines, Briggie went out to the Bronco and returned with her deer rifle.

"What's this, Briggie?" Charles inquired.

"My self-protection. I've had it bore-sighted since the last time I tried to go after someone, so I think it'll be okay."

"Briggie, I don't want you firing guns around here if my mother's involved," Alex protested with a fleeting memory of her friend, dressed in nothing but her white Royals nightie, firing at a departing car from the front lawn of this house last summer. She was momentarily diverted.

"It doesn't hurt to have a little intimidation value. We have Charles, and we have me. And, of course, your karate. So I think we're all set." Lord Peter was eyeing Briggie's rifle with respect.

At 8:30 the telephone rang again. Expecting Lieutenant Laurie, Alex answered it with a feeling of mingled anticipation and dread. A strange plummy voice enquired for "Alexandra Campbell."

She identified herself, hands damp, heart free-falling into her middle.

"Mrs. Campbell. Your mother is a very nice lady. We've had a good chat, I think. She understands the situation. I'm leaving her in her car in the Jewel grocery store parking lot in Wilmette. Her hands and feet are tied, unfortunately, so she can't go anywhere, but if you come and get her, she'll explain the situation to you, and we'll have no more of these unfortunate happenings."

The man hung up.

Alex sank into the desk chair, limp, her heart galloping so fast she found difficulty speaking. Relief finally released her tears. They swelled instantly into her eyes, rolling down her cheeks.

"What is it?" Briggie demanded in alarm.

Through her tears, she could see that Charles's face was turned to her, pale as a Greek statue.

"She's not dead," Alex said, forcing the words out through chok-
ing sobs. "She's tied up in a parking lot in Wilmette. Oh, thank
heaven!" She held herself tightly as emotion lashed through her.
Until that instant, she had not known how certain she had been that
her mother was dead.

Instantly, Briggie took over, calling Lieutenant Laurie. She thrust
the telephone into Alex's hands, who took it and haltingly explained
the kidnapper's message.

"Well, if that don't beat all!" he exclaimed. "Your mother was just
plain lucky, I'd say. Someone on high must have been watchin' out
for her. I'll get in touch with the Wilmette police and have them and
an ambulance meet you at the scene. The Jewel is down near the train
tracks, I think. I'll join you as soon as I can get there." Then he added,
"I'll have my siren on, don't you worry."

Charles drove them in the Range Rover. Alex sat silent, still hugging herself, hoping and praying that her mother would be okay.
Briggie, inexplicably, rode with her deer rifle across her knees.

*　　*　　*

"Mother!"

When Alex arrived at the parking lot, a crew of paramedics was
just preparing to load Amelia into an ambulance. The scene was
unexpectedly grim—a dirty parking lot with the blue and red lights
of the emergency vehicles strobing through the night, bleaching all
color out of the flesh of the gathered policemen and medical
personnel.

"She's been knocked on the head, but it wasn't serious, and she
was conscious when we found her. We had to give her a sedative after
the police questioned her, though. She was pretty upset," the short,
squat EMT worker told her, his voice flat and matter-of-fact. "Maybe

you can follow along after us to the hospital. We think she's basically fine, but we want to do a thorough work-up because of the trauma she experienced."

"She has MS," Alex told them. "Her doctor is Dr. Towby in Winnetka. Could you radio in to have him come to the hospital? He'll want to check her, too, if I know him."

"Will do." The paramedic stepped aside to make the call.

"May I ride in the back?" she asked the very young blonde girl who was strapping her mother onto the stretcher.

"If you like."

Her mother's white flesh seemed papery thin, crushed, as it lay across its fragile bones. She looked near death. Alex could barely refrain from embracing her. How pleased she must have been with herself that morning, deceiving them all, planning to surprise them with her own investigations. How intrepid she was now that she was free of all the worries and the addiction that had bound her for the past twenty years.

Alex suddenly knew that this mother, lying on the stretcher, who had started the day with such high hopes, was the same mother she had lost when she was sixteen. That was the year Alex had been battling Algebra II and there had been no one to help her because her mother was mysteriously ill and insensible. Her father had come home from work only in time to tell her good night. Now as she looked into the vulnerable face on the thin pillow, she was stripped of all her fear of her mother, and her resentment drained out of her until it lay like a puddle at her feet. It was as though the intervening twenty years had never been.

Alcohol. Her mother had needed it to deaden her pain enough so that she could live. Alex knew about pain. Into her mind came the image of a gray winter day long ago when the sky had merged into the bleak landscape of the Scottish hills. The gray pain inside her after

Stewart's death was like bitter ash, a smoldering remnant of the fragile peace that she had found in her marriage. Walking off into the black winter hills on that morning, she had intended to find some remote crevice where she could lie down and just fall asleep and freeze away her existence and her anguish forever. Stewart's enormous Akita, Providence, had found her before that could happen, barking and pulling her back into this world. And then, shortly afterward, there had been Briggie.

Her mother had had no Briggie. No gospel of Jesus Christ to help her make sense of a world where she had been paralyzed by fear.

At that moment, Alex pictured her Savior, dressed in rough red homespun, stumbling up a sharp, rocky slope. Across his broad, carpenter's shoulders he was carrying a lamb with a damaged foreleg. His eyes reflected deep suffering, an infinite experience with every human pain and fear, and out of it a love so intense she would give her soul to be in His presence. Then she knew that the lamb was her mother. Her mother had been found, redeemed. Looking down at Amelia's defenseless face, it wasn't hard to imagine that.

Alex felt a rush of love for that found lamb. How could she not love someone that Jesus loved so much? The past was in the past. Because she hadn't been able to trust her parents, she had found it difficult to continue to trust the Lord after her initial conversion. Now, she knew she had had it backwards all this time. The key was in remembering. Her parents might have seemed to fail her, but the Lord *had* rescued her. She, too, had been a found lamb. *Was* a found lamb, in fact. The pain that could never be healed had been healed. She had come far from the frightened young woman she had been when Stewart died. She had walked into the darkness, tentatively at first, and found a brilliant light, illuminating all the blackest corners of her fear-filled world. At her baptism, she had exchanged ashes for beauty. It was only she who chose reflexively to shut her eyes against it, she who retreated into darkness when the past overwhelmed her.

But that past was taking a different shape now. Looking at this woman, her mother, lying in an induced sleep, Alex felt stirrings deep inside her of a different kind of love than she had known before. It wasn't protective, as it had been. Instead, she saw a different Amelia Borden. Her mother, tenderly buttoning up her cardigan sweater before she left for a birthday party. Her mother, pushing her skyward on the backyard swing, squealing, "Higher, Alex, higher!" Her mother, taking her hand as she led her across the street on the first day of fourth grade when she was scared because her new teacher was Mr. Evans, a notorious grouch. These fragments of memory emerged through a heavy mist. Amelia Borden had loved Alex fiercely. She hadn't let her down intentionally. By sending her away, she had been trying to save Alex's life, and in so doing, she had nearly ruined her own.

Alex felt a new certainty, a bridge over that twenty-year gap. Because she could trust her Savior to love her, she could trust her mother to love her, even if that love had not always been perfect. Maybe love sometimes appeared in disguise, maybe it sometimes became distorted by circumstances, but her mother's desire to love her did exist and it could be redeemed. The Savior could put her life and her mother's back together, healing the deep wounds with His eternal balm of compassion for them both.

The recognition filled her with a helium-like elation. Tears flowed freely down the cheek that she pressed to her mother's, thankful for the Savior of all those who loved imperfectly.

Chapter Eighteen

Once they got to the squat, brick hospital, she wouldn't allow anyone to separate her from her mother. Lieutenant Laurie had arrived and was talking with Briggie, Charles, and the Wilmette police. Dr. Towby, a roly-poly red-faced man with a row of neat white-capped teeth, sat with Alex in the curtained cubicle of the ER. The patient was hooked up to a saline IV and examined gently for broken bones. The bump on her head was swollen and tender but not dangerous. Her wrists and ankles bore ugly red chaffings where the ropes had bound them, and her feet were still purplish from lack of circulation.

"How is this likely to affect her, doctor?" Alex asked anxiously. "Mother was doing so well."

Patting her gently on the shoulder, he said, "Wouldn't have had something like this happen to her for the world. Told me about her remission over the phone the other day. No sense worrying, though. Taking this a step at a time. MS is tricky. Thing is, her attitude's changed. Best thing. Got you to thank for that, I think."

"I haven't done anything but get her involved in this crazy case and nearly get her killed!"

"Any idea who did this?" he asked, his white tufted eyebrows raised.

"No. We don't even have any leads. But we'll make sure she's never alone again, I can tell you that."

By this time, Amelia began to revive, and the doctor soothed her and examined her eyes for concussion. Alex hung anxiously over the pair of them.

"They took my notebook," her mother groaned.

"Don't worry about that now, Mother. At least they didn't kill you!"

"No. It was a warning, they said." With that she closed her eyes and seemed to go back to sleep.

"Let her rest," Dr. Towby advised. "Not going to try to get her up 'til she's slept off the sedative. May not be for a couple of hours."

"I want to be here when she wakes up."

"Take a break," he advised. "Think she's going to be in and out. Going to do a few little tests of my own here."

Taking the hint, Alex unwillingly left and joined the others.

"How is she?" Charles asked, concern creasing his white brow. He moved towards her.

"She's a little banged up, but basically fine, the doctors say. I wasn't able really to talk to her." Alex felt suddenly weary and sank into a plastic chair.

"The car was clean," Briggie informed her briskly. "No prints. Amelia apparently told the Wilmette police the guy was waiting behind a bush in the library parking lot. He knocked her out from behind."

Alex winced.

"Yeah," Briggie sympathized, running her hands through her

upstanding white hair. "Lucky he didn't hit her harder. Next thing she knew he had driven her down to a park somewhere by the lake."

"Do you think he meant to throw her in?" Alex remembered her horrible visions.

"I don't think so," Briggie soothed her. "He had a stocking over his face to disguise himself. But she could still tell that he was bald, I guess."

Bald. Like the guy in the Taurus. "What else did she say?"

"He left her there, bound up and alone for hours. If it hadn't been above freezing today, she might have died of hypothermia. Fortunately, she had on her thermals and her fur coat."

"He might have meant to leave her there. Why did he come back?"

Briggie's voice got the oddly gruff quality that masked her stronger emotions. "Well, personally, I think it was because of our prayer. He told her to give us all the word to leave the case alone and no one would get hurt." Briggie ruminated for a moment.

"Mother must have been frightened out of her mind." Alex could too easily picture her mother in the circumstances Briggie described. Just how resilient was her mother?

"I have a feeling she's made of pretty tough stuff anymore, Alex." Briggie, as usual, read her thoughts. "She's come through a lot."

Charles stood to the side, arms folded across his chest, regarding them both. "I wonder why he followed her today and not us?" he mused. "How could he even know she was working on the case?"

"Maybe he's sensitive to anything to do with Lake Forest," Briggie surmised. "Or maybe it's because she was alone and there were three of us."

He put an arm around Alex, who had begun quivering at the thought of how close her mother had been to death. "What do

Mormons use instead of coffee or brandy or an old-fashioned cup of tea?" he inquired.

"Love and common sense," Briggie told him bluntly. "Plus food. None of us have eaten properly since breakfast. Let's see if the cafeteria's open."

It wasn't, so they had vending machine ham sandwiches on white bread and pop in the lounge.

"They could so easily have killed her, Briggs," Alex said dully, crumbling the half-eaten sandwich in its wrappings.

"They're a funny bunch of villains, though," Briggie said thoughtfully. "I wonder if Gladys's death *was* accidental. I think I'll see what Lieutenant Laurie says."

When she had gone, Charles took Alex's hand in his own and squeezed it. "Buck up, old girl. Your mum's going to be fine. And this isn't your fault. She was game. And she's over twenty-one."

"It's just that . . . oh, you wouldn't understand, Charles." Once again she longed for Daniel, wanted to feel his sturdy frame next to her as she confided the fright she had felt and the consequent euphoria of her breakthrough.

"I don't suppose you could try me?"

She hesitated. It was impossible to let Charles into this lacerated part of her psyche. "It all has to do with this other side of me, I'm afraid. It's a part of me I hoped you'd never see."

His face, which had been all tenderness, seemed to shut down.

"Try to understand," she pleaded. "There are things I've been through with my mother that I couldn't possibly explain in a few moments. Stewart didn't even know."

He patted her shoulder and attempted a normal grin. "I'm behaving in a shockingly un-British manner, trying to force a confidence. Forgive me, Alex. I suppose I'd feel better if I were allowed to offer you a cup of tea."

"Then I'd be off your conscience." She smiled a little. "Never mind. I'll be fine. This has just been kind of a watershed experience for me, that's all."

Briggie returned with the news that Lieutenant Laurie now intended to take another look at Gladys's death.

"And I think it was murder," Briggie pronounced.

"But maybe unintentional," Alex mused, trying to look at it in light of her mother's experience. "There may have been a struggle, and she may have fainted or something. They could have thought she was dead. They could have panicked and dumped her in the lake. They might have done the same to my mother if she hadn't come around."

"It might have happened that way," Charles agreed, a muscle flexing in his cheek as he clenched his jaw. "But I don't like the sound of it one bit."

Without thought, Alex put out her hand and touched his arm. "Thank you."

"For what?"

"For not coming over the heavy male and forbidding us to go on with it."

"It's taking considerable effort, I want you to know."

Alex's mother awoke more fully near midnight and was allowed to get out of bed to test her legs. With her daughter sitting in a chair a couple of feet away, she stood uncertainly on the floor next to her bed and then carefully stepped with first one foot and then the other.

"They still work!" she said with awe.

Jumping up, Alex embraced her mother's thin body and hugged her as she never had. "Oh, Mother, I love you so much. I've been so worried about you. I'm never leaving you alone again! What on earth possessed you to go out by yourself?"

Disengaging herself gently, Amelia held her daughter at arm's length. She must have read something new in Alex's face, for she asked, "What is it, Alex?"

"Just that I finally think I understand. Forgive me for the other night."

Amelia looked up at her daughter's welling eyes, and her own began to tear up. "Life has been awfully hard, honey. But maybe now it will get better."

"I guess it's never too late," Alex said, clasping her mother to her once again.

Amelia was discharged from the hospital at 1 A.M., with instructions to stay quiet for a few days and not to drive. There was, miraculously, no concussion. They adjourned wearily home, Alex driving Amelia in her car, and Briggie, her rifle across her lap, following with Charles in the Range Rover.

When they arrived at the Winnetka house, Charles helped Alex to get Amelia up the stairs. After he had left the room, Alex assisted her mother in donning her lavender-scented nightgown and getting between her lavender-scented sheets. It gave her a feeling of comfort and normalcy. Recalling her feelings earlier at the hospital, she wished she could just curl in a ball next to Mother and go to sleep here in this peaceful room.

But she had to content herself with kissing her mother's cheek. "Just get some rest. You're done with your heroics."

"But I have so much to tell you, and I'm afraid I'll forget!" There was a determined glitter in her eyes. Alex recognized it.

"Mother, you've got it really bad. I suppose you found out something today?"

"Yes. Remember the older brother, the one who died before his father?"

"William Jr.?"

"Yes. He was accidentally drowned over the Fourth of July

171

weekend near where his yacht was moored. He was apparently giving a party. Lloyd was there and two other women, neither of whom was his wife." She put three fingers to her forehead as though trying to force her memory. "Oh, and I read the story on Lloyd, too. I have the feeling he was a womanizer. The librarian said he wasn't liked." She wrinkled her brow. "Oh! I wish they hadn't taken my notebook. There's something I'm forgetting. Something to do with the prime minister."

Alex looked at her mother, startled. Perhaps the experience had affected her more than she had thought. "The prime minister of Great Britain?"

"Yes," Amelia said and suddenly yawned hugely. "I took Mrs. Simmons out to lunch. She's a very nice woman." She chuckled. "I told her I was a detective. She believed me. Can you imagine that?"

Alex pulled the sheet up under her mother's chin. "You've had quite a day. Rest now."

Obediently closing her eyes, Alex's mother seemed to fall asleep instantly.

Alex went downstairs where Charles was opening a can of chili and Briggie was belatedly feeding Lord Peter. She tried, in vain, to coax Tuppence off the refrigerator with a bowl of freshly opened albacore.

"I think everything was a little too much for Mother," Alex confided. "She went to sleep babbling about the prime minister."

"Of Britain?" Charles asked, holding the chili lid between his thumb and forefinger.

Alex nodded.

*　　*　　*

On Friday morning, Lieutenant Laurie visited them, as fresh as though he hadn't been up until the wee hours of the morning. Alex had slept more soundly than she had in years. She couldn't remember when she hadn't slept scrunched up, clinging to the edge of the bed as though she might fall off. Last night she had slept blissfully on her back. Briggie was her usual self, toting her deer rifle down to the breakfast table. Basking in the love of her daughter and friends, Amelia, amazingly enough, seemed no worse for her experience. She was cheerfully making banana pancakes, a recipe she had unearthed in *The Joy of Cooking,* remarking that her husband used to make them for her and Alex on Sunday mornings. Charles was the only one who did not appear to advantage. Clearly missing his morning coffee, he sat hollow-eyed at the counter, drumming impatient fingers on the butcher block. Lord Peter scampered through the house, delighted that everyone was awake, while Tuppence lay on top of the refrigerator, oblivious to everyone, mourning her mistress.

Just before Lieutenant Laurie's knock, Amelia was exclaiming mutinously at the suggestion put forth by Alex that she needed to take it easy. "I'm just getting my teeth into this. I know the man that took me was bald, for heaven's sake. I don't think he'd be a match for Charles." She grinned wickedly at Alex. "Not to mention Briggie's deer rifle."

Ignoring Lord Peter's furious yapping, Lieutenant Laurie greeted them with a request to see the genogram.

Lieutenant Laurie repeated back their original hypothesis. "So you believe that the killing of Mrs. Harrison and the kidnapping of Mrs. Borden are tied to one of these lines you're investigating?"

"Yes," Alex said. "Either the illegitimate heirs, the original murder, or possibly even a scandal over the death of the intended heir, William Jr., although that seems unlikely. We feel the Williams money and some kind of scandal attached to it are behind all of this."

Lieutenant Laurie shook his head. "If it weren't for what happened last night to Mrs. Borden, I would find this all really

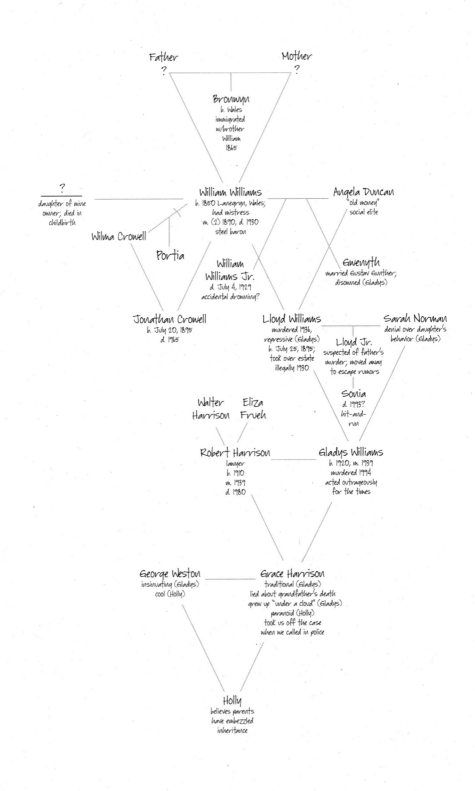

Father
?

Mother
?

Bronwyn
b. Wales
immigrated
w/brother
William
1865

?
daughter of mine
owner; died in
childbirth

William Williams
b. 1850 Lanegrym, Wales;
had mistress
m. (2) 1890, d. 1930
steel baron

Angela Duncan
"old money"
social elite

Wilma Crowell

Portia

William
Williams Jr.
d. July 4, 1929
accidental drowning?

Gwenyth
married Gustav Gunther;
disowned (Gladys)

Jonathan Crowell
b. July 20, 1895
d. 1965

Lloyd Williams
murdered 1936,
repressive (Gladys)
b. July 25, 1895;
took over estate
illegally 1930

Sarah Norman
denial over daughter's
behavior (Gladys)

Lloyd Jr.
suspected of father's
murder; moved away
to escape rumors

Sonia
d. 1993?
hit-and-
run

Walter
Harrison

Eliza
Frueh

Robert Harrison
lawyer
b. 1910
m. 1939
d. 1980

Gladys Williams
b. 1920, m. 1939
murdered 1994
acted outrageously
for the times

George Weston
insinuating (Gladys)
cool (Holly)

Grace Harrison
traditional (Gladys)
lied about grandfather's death
grew up "under a cloud" (Gladys)
paranoid (Holly)
took us off the case
when we called in police

Holly
believes parents
have embezzled
inheritance

far-fetched. Maybe we *should* get my grandma involved, after all. This is just her kind of deal. What're all these question marks?"

Briggie answered him, "Just things a good genealogist would uncover. I don't know if they're really important to the case or not, but old habits die hard."

"I wish I could remember that thing I forgot," complained Amelia. "I have a feeling it's important."

"What's that, ma'am?" the lieutenant asked, his eyes gentling as he looked at Alex's mother.

Embarrassed at the prospect that her mother might make rambling remarks about seeming irrelevancies, Alex interjected, "I think you got all the main points, Mother." She turned to the policeman. "Mother read a newspaper story about William Williams Jr. yesterday in the Lake Forest paper. It said it was an accidental drowning. But his brother Lloyd was present. William was the heir, so I don't really think we can rule out murder . . ."

"But there were witnesses!" exclaimed her mother. "And that's part of what's bugging me."

"Well," the lieutenant said, studying the genogram. "All that was a really long time ago—1929, after all. What do you have on these illegitimate heirs? That seems the surest line of inquiry to me."

"We have the death record of Jonathan Crowell. He died in 1965 in Chicago. The obituary wasn't in the *Tribune,* so I guess he must have been pretty obscure at the time he died," Briggie reasoned. "The next step, I suppose, would be to start combing cemeteries until we find where he's buried. The records there would show who paid for the burial, and that might give us the next of kin."

Alex interjected, "The Newberry Library should have a list of all the cemeteries in Chicago. If the four of us divide them up and start calling, it shouldn't take us too long to find him, even though there are a lot of cemeteries in the city."

Lieutenant Laurie's mouth firmed into an implacable line, and he became all business. "Time for a reality check, ladies. Mrs. Borden was almost killed. This is a police show."

Briggie looked back at him, a martial light in her eye. "Well, unless you mean to deputize your grandma, you'll never solve it. RootSearch, Inc., has solved two murders, lieutenant. One right here in Winnetka."

"Maybe you could contact the Newberry for us," Alex suggested peaceably. "You could get the list of cemeteries over the telephone. Then we wouldn't have to drive down there."

Amelia spoke up. "Do your files go back to the thirties?"

"Are you still going on about that old murder?" the lieutenant demanded, clearly exasperated.

"Yes," Amelia said, unperturbed.

"Begging your pardon, but I got better things to do with my time." He stood, facing them, and Alex was reminded of John Wayne as he placed hands on hips and looked her square in the eye. "If you insist on staying involved with this, you just keep working on those Crowells. But no more risks. I want you all staying together. No going out at night. And I want a full report of anything you find out." He turned his gaze on Charles. "Mr. Lamb, I assume you're staying with the ladies?"

"Yes, sir."

"Good."

"And we have another gentleman arriving tonight," Amelia assured him. "So we'll be quite safe."

Alex's eyes went to Charles's face. She had completely forgotten to tell him of Daniel's impending arrival. He looked at her in question.

As soon as the lieutenant had gone, Alex reminded Charles that it might be a good idea if he checked on the Lawsons' house. "I'll go with you," she told him.

He nodded his assent, and after getting into their coats and gloves, they went out to the Range Rover. The day was sunny but deceptively cold in the marrow-chilling way of the lake shore in the winter.

"I meant to tell you Daniel was coming," she told him as soon as they drove away. "With everything that's happened, it's not surprising it slipped my mind."

"I think it would be good, all things considered, if you told me just how things stand between the two of you."

The muscle jumped in his smooth cheek, and Alex was surprised to realize his jaw was clenched. *How could I bring out such emotions in a man a worldly as Charles?* she wondered, stunned. While struggling with this thought, she said tentatively, "I guess you might say we're in a state of suspended animation." She paused, tugging at her glove. "You see, my relationship with Daniel is a little strained."

Charles waited for her to go on.

"He's a therapist, you know, and, well, he doesn't intend it, but his profession gets in the way sometimes. He knows me almost too well. It's not always comfortable."

"Can one person know another person too well?" Charles asked, turning his light blue eyes on her. "You won't let me within a yard of you. Do you have some deep, dark secret or something?"

His voice was accusatory, and Alex bridled. Charles was actually angry.

"Why don't you go in and check on the house while you cool off?" she said. "I'm not going to talk to you when you're in this frame of mind."

He jerked open the car door and, unlocking the house, went inside. Alex reflected that in addition to Daniel, there was the whole issue of temple marriage to explain, but she wasn't about to introduce that subject now. How had she gotten herself into this mess? It wasn't what she had intended at all. And how on earth was she going to explain Charles to Daniel?

When her cousin exited the house and locked it, he stood on the doorstep for a moment, squinting into the sun. He was a magnificent specimen, standing there in his blue cashmere turtleneck and black overcoat. So British. So Oxford. He could have absolutely any woman he wanted. *What does he see in me, for heaven's sake?* Alex wondered. *And how on earth do I feel about him?* She didn't begin to know. It was like trying to cozy up to a Michelangelo or something. And then he smiled. The statue cracked and became the warm, interesting human being who grieved over his dead cousin, had punted with her on the Cherwell, and identified with Alma the Younger. Striding over to the car, he opened the door and got in.

"Sorry, Alex," he said with obvious contrition. His eyes looked confidingly into hers. "I guess I've never felt jealousy before. It's beastly."

She didn't know what to say to that. Charles started the car, and they went home.

Chapter Nineteen

ieutenant Laurie had expedited things with the Newberry, and the library telephoned with a list of cemeteries and telephone numbers. After an hour of calling, Briggie and Alex finally found that Jonathan Crowell had been buried in a small cemetery in the community of Roger's Park on the north side of Chicago. It was a working class neighborhood. Quite a comedown for the former vice president of Williams Steel Foundry. The records showed that Fredericks Funeral Home had handled the burial.

Calling the home, Briggie boldly gave Lieutenant Laurie's name and requested the names of the next of kin for the dead man. When she hung up, she turned to her eager audience, little brown eyes alight. "The bills were paid by one James Crowell and one Elizabeth Jacks. Now all we have to do is hit the phone books, praying that they're still alive, of course. Jacks is an unusual name."

"And Bob's your uncle," said the Professor with uncanny perspicacity.

The telephone rang. Alex answered and heard Daniel's warm,

familiar voice announcing his arrival time. "I'll rent a car and be with you by about seven or so. Is that okay?"

Something tight inside Alex relaxed. "We've already got three cars here, Daniel. Let me meet you. Then I can bring you up to date on everything that's been happening. What's your flight number?"

When she hung up, she found Charles had diplomatically left the room with Briggie and her mother.

"I'm going to pick Daniel up at six," she told them. They were assembling pastrami sandwiches in the kitchen for a late snack. Lunch had been canned clam chowder from mugs. "How about going to the Winnetka library after we eat and seeing if they have the Chicago directories there? If we don't find their names, we can go down to the Church family history library in Wilmette and look up the Social Security death records."

The Winnetka library welcomed them with an air of suppressed excitement. Story hour had just ended, and a line of women with toddlers clutching stacks of books wound through the lobby. The mothers were trying to convince their children to use their "library voices."

Alex, Briggie, Charles, and Amelia found, in the rear of the stacks, a row of telephone books for Chicago and its surrounding suburbs. Roger's Park was in the Chicago North directory. There were only two listings for the name Jacks. One was an F. Jacks and another was Joseph. There were no James Crowells in any of the Chicago or suburban directories.

Alex said, "I'm going to try these Jacks numbers. They may be children."

"They may be murderers," Charles interjected. "Don't you think you'd better let the police handle it from here?"

Looking at Briggie, Alex asked, "What do you think?"

"I'd go for it. But I'd do what Charles says, too. How about if I use the pay phone for the lieutenant and you use your cell phone for the Jacks calls?"

"What is it with you two?" Charles demanded, obviously nettled. "Haven't you got any common sense? Do you know what's likely to happen if these people find out you know their identity?"

"You're assuming they're guilty," Amelia said calmly.

"How can you be so dispassionate about it?" Charles exploded. "*You* were coshed yesterday!"

The three women looked at one another and shook their heads. "He doesn't get it," Briggie said sadly.

"You haven't got the passion yet," Amelia sighed.

"If you mean the genealogy passion, I can see that what we've found is pretty tantalizing, but I can also see that it has the potential to be awfully dangerous," he said, scowling at them.

"You're right," Alex said with a mock sigh. "But you *haven't* got the true genealogist's passion. Or should I say dementia?" She gave a little laugh at the sight of Briggie, her white hair standing on end and her little brown eyes fired with enthusiasm, and her sophisticated mother, looking the complete antithesis of Briggie but with a like expression in her eyes. "We're all three riddled with it. I'm glad you're not, actually. It's safer that way."

"Well, if I'm not to be allowed to put my foot down, at least let me be the one to call the lieutenant. I want to let him know what a bunch of lunatics I'm attempting to restrain."

As Charles put through his call to Lake Forest, Alex punched in the number of F. Jacks on her cell phone.

"Hello?" It sounded like a young woman's voice.

"Hello. This is Mrs. Alexandra Campbell speaking. I realize this is going to sound strange, but there isn't any subtle way to put it. I'm looking for the heirs of Mr. Jonathan Crowell. Would you happen to be one of them?"

There was a long silence on the other end of the line.

Finally, "Who did you say you were?"

"Mrs. Alexandra Campbell. I'm a professional genealogist."

"Why do you want to know about my great-grandfather?"

Alex's blood raced. *Paydirt!* She gave a thumbs-up sign to Briggie and Amelia. Briggie punched the air with her fist.

"It's a long story. Do you know anything about a family called Williams?"

"There are a lot of families named Williams," the young woman said, her voice slightly impatient.

"Did your great-grandfather ever speak of a William Williams and the Williams Steel Foundry?" Her mother and Briggie had moved closer, and Alex turned the little phone slightly so they could hear.

"Well, I've heard of it. My great-grandfather died before I was born." She hesitated and then said, her young voice hardening, "But I know about the foundry because Uncle Joey says that's where my great-grandfather worked before they laid him off. He says he was a wreck after that. I don't want anything to do with any of that family, if you don't mind. I don't see what kind of connection they can have to me." There was defiance in her tone.

"There is a connection, though," Alex told her gently. "Can you tell me what other descendants of your great-grandfather are still living?"

"I'd rather not until I find out what this is all about."

Alex looked in the telephone book and saw that the address given was in a borderline neighborhood of Chicago near Roger's Park.

"Can you meet with my partners and me tomorrow?" she asked. "You can name the place." She waited while the girl considered this question, holding up crossed fingers to her mother and colleague.

"How about Nate and Al's Deli at one o'clock?" the young woman suggested.

"How will I know you?" Alex inquired, forcing her voice into calm as she gave Briggie a high five.

"I've got flaming red hair to my waist. A gift from Nana."

"And your name is . . ."

"Frances."

"Thanks, Frances. I really appreciate this. Okay. I'll actually be with a group of people. I'm not sure how many of us will come, but I'll be wearing a navy blue pea coat, and I have black curly hair."

Charles received her news impassively and reported that Lieutenant Laurie was going to do background checks on each of the Jacks. "And I think it would be a good idea if he had people undercover at the deli, too."

"Charles, she's just a kid, for Pete's sake," Alex protested.

"Do you think she's going to keep this to herself? I'll bet you anything you like that she calls the rest of her family." Charles seemed incredulous at her naiveté. "A murderer may show up at that deli tomorrow, for crying out loud!"

Alex reluctantly agreed with this reasoning and surrendered her cell phone so that Charles could call the lieutenant.

As they walked out of the library afterwards, she said, "As much as it goes against the grain, I guess the prudent thing *would* be not to call this Joseph just yet." Alex twisted a ringlet around her finger. "Frances talked about an Uncle Joey and, from what she said, he *was* pretty steamed about the Williams Steel Foundry. He could be our man."

"Then you can bet your last pound that's who she's on the telephone with right this minute," Charles said grimly. "I'm getting you home, and we're going to lock all the doors and set that little yapping dachshund on guard."

"I've got to go pick up Daniel," Alex said stubbornly. "And I'm going alone."

Charles's face assumed its blandest expression. "You won't even take Briggie with you?"

"No."

The atmosphere somewhat strained, they drove to the house, where they had some Camembert on cocktail crackers that Charles had bought. Briggie fed Lord Peter and finally yielding to the inevitable, placed Tuppence's dish of albacore on top of the refrigerator. Then, after many admonitions to check her rearview mirror, Briggie, Charles, and Amelia went to the family history library to see if they could find a Social Security death record for James Crowell, whose name had not been in the Chicago phone book. Alex went to the airport to meet Daniel, trying to drag her mind away from the case and decide what she was going to tell him about Charles.

How could I have become involved with two such different men? she asked herself as she negotiated the onramp to the freeway. Friday afternoon rush hour had reduced traffic to a crawl.

At first glance, Charles was like a devastating hero out of a novel. But he had this spiritual side that took her by surprise and disarmed her. Daniel was much more prosaic, but it was with Daniel that she was at her most vulnerable. Partly because of his profession and partly because of the things they had been through together, he knew her inside out. But could he ever see the strong and capable side of her? If he chose to leave her, he could hurt her deeply, and she knew it. Charles only knew the part of her she let him see. In many ways that was more comfortable. But would it, in the long run, be as satisfying? Just how capable of intimacy was she?

She was selfish, that was certain. Stingy with her affections. Didn't she want to be loved? Didn't she want to remarry and have a family?

Maybe that wasn't the right question, she thought. Maybe what she needed to decide was who she wanted to be. Daniel's Alex or Charles's Alex? But why was she trying to define herself in terms of

184

another person? Neither one was the complete Alexandra Borden Campbell. Stewart hadn't known her totally, either. He had never known the truth about her family. She had, she saw now, grafted herself onto his life, content to become part of him and his passions, family, and experiences. She had seen through his photographer's eye, feasting with his vision on the grandeur of the Old World. Her poverty of spirit had remained hidden in a closed part of her as she tried to quench it with a gondolier's song in Venice, decadent chocolate *Sachertorte* in Vienna, and the clear, white heat of the summer sun on the Grecian isles. Had she ever been truly intimate with Stewart?

Alex shrugged as she turned into the immensely complicated terminal area of Chicago's O'Hare Airport. This was now. And Charles and Daniel were about to meet each other for the first time. Who would she be when both of them were present? The question brought her up short. What was she, anyway? Some kind of actress deciding which role to take? Maybe she should just try to be herself, whoever that was.

Amelia Borden's daughter. A daughter of her Heavenly Father. Loved. Wanted. Sweetness flooded her like one of Briggie's chocolate milkshakes. She was more whole now than she had been in twenty years. Surely that fact would affect her in her relationships. Her life had changed irrevocably in the last twenty-four hours.

Daniel was standing on the curb as she threaded her way through the tangle of traffic. The sight of him standing there with an incipient ginger beard made her smile. Unlike the elegant Charles, he wore an all-weather khaki trenchcoat. Reaching him at last, she got out of the car and accepted a light kiss on the cheek.

"You're growing a beard!" she exclaimed, rubbing her cheek where his bristles had scratched her.

"Yes. I've decided I don't look Freudian enough. Here, can you pop the trunk? I just have one bag. I'm relieved to see you don't have any black eyes yet."

"No. But Mother was mugged yesterday."

Appalled, Daniel stood dumbstruck on the curb.

"She's all right. Get in. I can't stand all these diesel fumes. I'll tell you about it."

With some foresight, she had brought Briggie's chart with her so that Daniel could get the gist of the case while they were driving. Allowing herself to bask in the comfort of long familiarity, she narrated their exploits as faithfully as possible while leaving out the two most vital things—her own personal renaissance and Charles.

As they approached Winnetka, she was glad of the darkness lit only by streetlights. Dr. Grinnell couldn't scrutinize her too closely. "And now I have to tell you something, Daniel. Before we get back."

"You sound funereal."

"I don't mean to. It's just that, well, it's going to be a little awkward. You see, my cousin's staying with us, too."

"Which cousin? I can't keep track of all your new family members."

"Well, this one's Charles. Your father's probably told you about him. Richard met him at Oxford. He's here to help settle my father's estate, and he's gotten rather involved in this case . . ."

"And rather involved with you," Daniel finished, defeat clear in his voice.

Alex threw him a glance. He looked dispirited and surprisingly resigned. Her heart opened, and she felt a sudden rush of contrition. He wasn't jealous, as Charles had been. Daniel was hurt.

"I told you it was awkward. I don't really know how I feel about it, Daniel. I mean I didn't come up to Chicago expecting . . . what I mean is . . . oh, please don't feel bad!"

He turned to face her. "Why didn't you just tell me, Alex? I wouldn't have come." His voice had an edge now.

"But I *wanted* you to come! I wanted to see you!"

"Why? So you could compare us side by side?" Now his face was implacable.

This was so near the truth that she faltered. "Daniel, please. Try to understand . . . you see, I'm a different person when I'm with you than I am with him. He thinks I'm strong and competent . . ."

"So you're going to throw my profession in my face again, are you?"

They had pulled into the driveway. Alex shut off the car and sat slumped at the wheel. She really was a horrid person. Why did anyone want to have anything to do with her? Putting her forehead against the wheel, she didn't say anything.

Daniel pulled out his cell phone and called a cab.

"You're not leaving?" she asked, incredulous.

"I'm not going to spend the weekend being compared to some Oxford Lothario."

Too late she remembered what he'd confided to her on the telephone—the chip on his shoulder and the fact that he was only five foot ten. "Daniel, you're jumping to conclusions. You haven't even met Charles."

"I don't need to," he told her shortly. "My father told me all about him. He thought that with my Rhodes scholarship I should have been much more like your precious Charles. He warned me that he was coming on to you. Pop the trunk, will you, Alex?"

"You can't leave!"

"I'm not staying. You can see me if you ever decide to come back to Kansas City."

"If? Of course I'm coming back!"

He just looked at her, his eyes hard. He was a stranger. "Pop the trunk, Alex."

She obeyed, biting her lip. The change in him was so sudden. From a warm confidant he had become stiff, unyielding, and clinical. She had never seen him this way. "You can't stand out here in the cold," she protested as he opened his car door.

"Give Briggie my regards," he said. "Sorry I won't get to meet your mother." Slamming the door, he left her sitting in the driver's seat. Then she heard the trunk lid slam shut. She craned her neck and looked out into the black cold of the Chicago night. Daniel was walking away, suitcase in hand, his light-colored trenchcoat outlining his sturdy frame as he disappeared down the street.

Chapter Twenty

W here's Daniel?" Briggie demanded as Alex walked in the door. "We're going to Hackney's."

Alex looked her straight in the eye and lied. "He couldn't come. Last-minute emergency. He called me on my cell phone." Inside, she felt as though part of her were broken. She didn't want any dinner. "You all go on without me."

Charles was looking at her strangely, his eyes penetrating. He wore his navy dinner jacket and a maroon silk cravat knotted at his throat. He'd never looked more dashing. Without another word, Alex went up the stairs.

Hollow and hurting, she cried desperately into her pillow, clinging to the edge of her bed as though it were the edge of a cliff. Daniel was a stranger now. Someone she'd never glimpsed before. He had shut her out, gone somewhere beyond her reach and left her alone and aching. Guilt swamped her. She'd done this. Her narcissistic indecision had cost her the love of the one person who knew her at her very worst and still accepted her. And she hadn't even been able to tell him about her healing, hadn't been able to share with the one person who would understand the miracle of her breakthrough with her mother. She couldn't tell him that some time in the last couple of months she had decided not to be sealed by proxy to Stewart.

Her short Superman. Only he wasn't Superman. He was all too human, and with her relationship to Charles, she had played to every one of his weaknesses. Alex wept harder, and the night stretched out in the hollow house where she had spent so many lonely nights so long ago.

*   *   *

"That James Crowell from the funeral home records wasn't in the Social Security Death Index," Briggie told her the next morning over breakfast. "He must still be alive."

Alex tried to summon up her enthusiasm. Briggie had been eying her with a diagnostic air ever since she had come down the stairs, dressed and showered but sleepless.

"What's that?" Charles asked, coming into the kitchen after accompanying Lord Peter on his morning outing. He was dressed in his gray flannel slacks with a black silk turtleneck. Daniel would have been wearing khakis and his tweed "therapist's" jacket with the leather elbow patches. Alex looked away from her cousin, who had gone straight to the refrigerator, greeting Tuppence with an absent pat.

"Just reporting our big zero last night," Briggie told him.

Alex's cousin sat down next to her at the butcher block island. He had a glass of orange juice and a carton of yogurt. Daniel would be eating Wheaties.

"How are you this morning, Alex?" Charles asked casually.

"Fine."

"Sleep well?"

Although she knew the purple circles under her eyes belied her words, she answered, "Of course. And you?"

"Thank you," he said. "I slept splendidly. Did you know that Briggie snores?"

"I do not!" Briggie asserted, hands on her hips. Today, in honor of meeting Frances, she was wearing her Royals' sweatshirt and matching sweatpants.

"I could hear you through the door," Charles told her with a grin.

Looking decidedly huffy, Briggie carried her dishes to the sink. "I must have allergies to something in this house. Mold or something."

Alex felt herself smile. Really, Briggie's sameness was a comfort. Charles might be here today and gone tomorrow, but Briggie would be there in her big, white house in Kansas City with her tiger-striped cat, her stacks of Agatha Christie novels, and her economy-sized bags of Hershey's Kisses. As for Daniel . . . well, hadn't she cried enough over him? Her momentary feeling of well-being faded.

Her mother walked in, dressed in an apricot gabardine pantsuit with a ruffled chiffon blouse. "Are we all ready for the day?"

Nate and Al's Deli was a wonderful Chicago institution that Alex hadn't visited in far too long. Noisy, packed, and redolent with the delicious smells of pastrami, sauerkraut, and rye bread, it was run by rude waiters in long white aprons.

A girl in blue jeans and a white man-sized T-shirt with the legend "White Girls get the Blues" stood waiting by the cigarette machine. She had long, curly red hair to her waist.

"Frances?" Alex inquired.

"You must be Alexandra Campbell." The girl held out her hand confidently. Its short fingernails were bare of polish, and Alex felt the calluses of someone who worked with her hands. She had large green eyes fringed with black lashes, and her complexion was heavily, but not unattractively, freckled. Though she wore no makeup, she had a nice smile and white, even teeth.

"Call me Alex. And this is my business partner, Briggie, my cousin Charles, and my mother, Amelia."

Everyone exchanged appropriate greetings. "A guy I know works here," the girl told them, lifting her shoulders and spreading her hands as though offering them the restaurant. "He's holding a table for us, or we wouldn't have a prayer of getting one."

"Great," Briggie said. "I love deli food, and I'm starved."

"A real Chicago deli will be a new experience for you, Charles," Alex told him as they made their way amidst the chaos to their booth in the back. It was the first time she had spoken to him since breakfast.

"I recommend the blintzes," Frances told them as they looked at their grease-stained menus while an impatient waiter in a dirty white apron hovered.

"I'm a pastrami-on-rye gal," Briggie said.

"What's a blintz?" Charles wanted to know.

Frances explained, showing him a tiny space between her fingers. "They're like little thin pancakes wrapped up with sour cream. You can have all different kinds of fruit on top."

In the end, Charles experimented with blueberry blintzes, Briggie and Alex went with pastrami sandwiches, Amelia requested a Kosher hot dog, and Frances ordered apple blintzes with extra apples.

"Now," the girl said, leaning forward eagerly on crossed arms. "I could hardly sleep last night. Tell me what all this is about."

"Well, how much do you know about your great-grandfather, first of all?" Alex asked. "Did you ever hear anything about his family?"

She sat up straight, looking, oddly enough, directly at Briggie. The older woman's presence seemed to bring her reassurance. "I was thinking about it last night. I think he died about five years before I was born. All I know is that he was brought up by his mother, who was a widow, and that he got laid off from the foundry right at the beginning of the Depression, when he was still young. He couldn't get another job because they blacklisted him. I don't know why."

"Beastly," said Charles.

Amelia took out her new steno pad and began making notes. Clearing her throat, Alex looked Frances in the eye and said, "We have pretty firm evidence that his mother wasn't a widow. At least, she wasn't widowed by Jonathan Crowell's father." The girl wrinkled her brow and leaned forward again. Alex didn't know how to put it delicately. "Your great-grandfather's birth certificate states that he was the illegitimate son of William Williams, the head of Williams Steel Foundry."

Frances's green eyes grew very wide, and she put a hand to her mouth. Alex rushed on, "I don't know if you know it or not, but you had a Great-Great-Aunt Portia, and he was her father, too."

The girl just stared at her for a moment. Suddenly she threw up her hands in an extravagant gesture and broke into a peal of laughter. "No possible way! I mean, someone would have known, wouldn't they?"

"I think your great-grandfather knew. He looked like the twin of his half brother, who took over the business," Alex told her. "I don't suppose you know when your great-great-grandmother died? Whether it was before your great-grandfather was laid off?"

"You really think this is true, don't you?" Frances said, incredulously, her eyes round once more. Alex didn't know when she had seen a more open countenance.

"Briggie, did you bring the birth certificate?"

Briggie nodded and produced the document from her black plastic handbag. "Here it is, child. In black and white."

The girl studied it intently.

"It happens, you know," Charles said, a gentleness in his voice that was new to Alex.

"But, not . . . not in *my* family," she said unsteadily.

"It's rather refreshing to find that someone in your generation can be shocked by such a thing," Charles said.

Anger flickered in Frances's green eyes. "*My* generation?" she said. "Aren't you a little holier than thou? Anyway, it's not *your* family."

"No," he agreed. "My family's even more of a mess."

"Hush, Charles," Amelia pleaded. "Can't you see she's upset?"

"Not upset, actually," Frances said. "I'm not sure what I feel."

"Family secrets are always a shock," Briggie told her.

"Uncle Joey would know the answer to your question," she said, looking up from the paper in her hands. "I called him last night to see if he knew what this was about. He didn't have a clue, of course."

Alex exchanged a glance with Charles. He had been right. Her heart beat an accelerated tattoo. Was Uncle Joey their murderer? She wetted her lips. "Well, I think she probably was dead," she said. "She wouldn't have let her son be turned out of the factory the way he was by his half brother."

Their orders arrived, and for a few moments everyone did justice to Nate and Al's cuisine. Alex had hoped the pastrami would sharpen her appetite, but she could hardly taste it. She looked around the crowded restaurant where the long-aproned waiters dodged each other neatly, their trays held high above their shoulders. Were there some Chicago policemen undercover somewhere?

"Why has this come up now, after all these years, and why do you care about it?" Frances asked finally, cutting her blintz deliberately into tiny wedges.

Alex decided after a quick look at Briggie that she had better meet Uncle Joey before telling the whole story.

"We were hired by a branch of the Williams family to do their genealogy," she hedged. "We got hold of a book about the foundry, and there was your great-grandfather's picture. It was so much like his half brother's, we guessed the truth. All we had to do was get a birth certificate to prove it. We are trying to identify all the Williams descendants and thought you could help us."

"How did you get my name?" Her air of excitement had diminished, and the girl was clearly wary again. She was looking back and forth between Briggie and Alex.

Briggie explained the process they had gone through, showing Frances a rough diagram of the family tree she had prepared.

"I say," Charles said at length, "thank you for recommending the blintzes. They're lovely."

The suspicious young woman was not proof against Charles's charm. Tossing her red hair over her shoulder, she looked at him boldly. "You're an Englishman."

Doing his part, Charles proceeded to put Frances at ease with the tale of how Alex and Briggie had found him.

"Well, that's quite a story," she said. "So you really are cousins."

"Third cousins," he modified. "We share a great-great-grandfather."

Heaving a sigh, Frances said, "Well, actually, I'm afraid you'll be disappointed after having done all your wonderful research. My parents were killed in a car crash when I was ten." She studied Briggie's sketch. "My father was Henry Jacks. It was his mother, Elizabeth Crowell Jacks, you found in the mortuary records. She's dead, too." Her voice was bleak. "I was brought up by my Uncle Joey. He's my father's brother. He doesn't have any kids or a wife. Just me and his music." Pausing, she took a bite of blintz, squinting her eyes as though concentrating. "I do have some cousins, I think. My grandmother had a brother, Jim, as I recall. He and his wife were divorced. They had a couple of kids who would have been . . . let's see . . . in my parents' generation." She shrugged elaborately. "But our families lost touch a long time ago. I probably have cousins my own age kicking around somewhere. Uncle Joey and I really should look into it."

Amelia had been sketching a descendancy chart in her steno pad. She showed it to Frances.

Alex, who was sitting next to Frances, admired her mother's neat, small handwriting, so different from her own large scrawl. Pointing to the place on the family tree where Jonathan Crowell, Frances's great-grandfather, appeared, Amelia said, "This is where you fit in. Your great-great-grandfather came from Wales. Just think. He began in the coal mines in Pittsburgh, and then he ended up starting the steel foundry and made his fortune. He built a huge mansion on the North Shore."

Frances sighed again. "It's all really romantic, isn't it? Like a book, or something. To be honest, I was hoping you were going to tell me that I was a lost heiress or something like that." She stirred the sour cream into the cinnamon syrup on her plate. "It sure would come in handy about now."

Alex looked at her sympathetically, hoping for further confidences. Amelia wasn't so subtle. "Are you having difficulties, dear?"

"Uncle Joey needs surgery. Actually, he needs a liver transplant." She frowned, looking down at her plate, still stirring her brownish mixture. "He works in a nightclub as a musician, part time, because he's so sick. No insurance. I don't have anything put away. I work as a waitress part time while I go to school."

Willing herself not to look at either her mother or Briggie, Alex trod firmly on Briggie's foot.

Charles smiled sunnily. "May I give you some advice? Say your prayers."

Alex could have kicked him. "Is there any way we can arrange to meet your Uncle Joey?"

Crowell Descendancy Chart

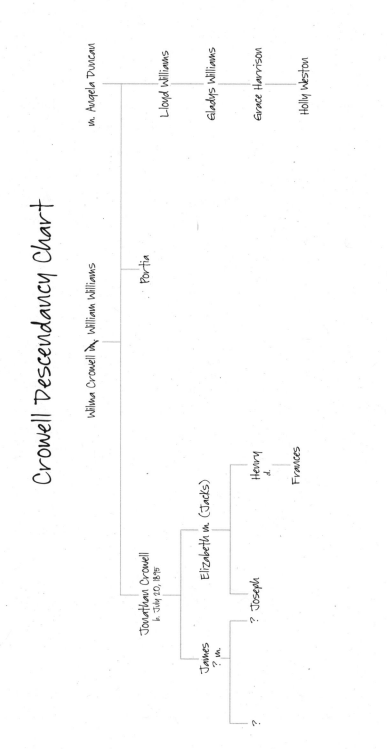

Wilma Crowell m. William Williams

m. Angela Duncan

Portia

Lloyd Williams

Gladys Williams

Grace Harrison

Holly Weston

Jonathan Crowell
b. July 20, 1895

Elizabeth m. (Jacks)

James
? m.

? Joseph

Henry
d.

Frances

?

Suddenly, mischief glinted in Frances's green eyes. "Sure. He's at another table. He's been watching after me all this time."

Alex looked around her sharply. Frances was beckoning to a large man with a yellowish complexion in the next booth. Charles glanced up, frowning, and then relaxed at a sight he saw over her shoulder. Turning around briefly, Alex saw the tall frame of Lieutenant Laurie dressed in black cords and a black leather jacket. He still looked exactly like what he was. In his vicinity was another man with an oddly vacant face who looked vaguely familiar, but she couldn't place him. Probably one of the throng of police who had surrounded them after her mother's mugging.

Frances was introducing her uncle to everyone. "Uncle Joey, these people are genealogists. They've been telling me some interesting things."

Charles rose and offered a hand to the man whom Alex was relieved to see bore no resemblance to any of the men she had noticed around her this past week. This man was so big, he would have stood out in any crowd. His hair was a magnificent white Elvis-style pompadour. He took Charles's outstretched hand as her cousin said, "Charles Lamb. This is Alex Campbell and her business partner, Brighamina Poulson. They're RootSearch, Inc. This is Amelia Borden, Alex's mother."

The older man smiled down at them and said, "Good afternoon. I guess you're not going to run off with my Francie."

"Won't you join us?" Amelia invited. "The booth will take one more, I think."

"Not someone my size. I'll just pull up a chair. They allow me certain privileges around here."

As soon as he had accomplished this, Briggie was able to put to him her question about his great-grandmother Wilma Crowell. "Do you know if she died before your grandfather was turned out of his job?"

He put both sets of fingers on the table as though he were going to play the piano. Then he drummed his fingernails in a little flourish. "I guess we're kind of a missing piece, me and Francie, aren't we? I've been listening to you. It's downright fantastic, what you're saying." Swaying like a blues player, he executed another flourish, thoughtfully, his mind clearly elsewhere. "Yes. She died of cancer when he was still making good money. He had her in a nice home up on the North Shore until she passed on."

Frances said, "Amazing! That fits right in with your story, doesn't it, Alex?"

Uncle Joey started playing a dramatic funeral march. "Pray for the dead, and the dead will pray for you," he intoned in a deep bass voice. "Is there likely to be any money in this?"

Alex looked at Briggie. Could this seemingly innocuous man be behind Gladys's murder? She bit her lip. It would be best not to take any chances. "Why would you think so?" she asked.

The man sagged and took his hands off the table. "I guess it was too much to hope for."

"Frances says you're sick," Charles said. "We're sorry to hear that."

"We sure are," Briggie added, squirming a little. "What else can you tell us about the family?"

Almost in a trance, Uncle Joey began playing the blues again. "Francie and I have never known a lot about the family. She told you there's another branch—my Uncle Jim got divorced, and I lost touch with my cousins." He swayed and closed his eyes. "Last I heard, they were living in Florida."

There was real pain in the man's face. Lines were etched in his yellowing forehead and from his nose down to the corners of his mouth. Alex stared at Briggie, who gave her a short nod. Her colleague was usually a good judge of character. "Mr. Jacks . . ."

"Joey. Call me Joey."

"Joey, then, there is some danger involved here, and I think it's probably best if you and Frances know the whole story."

Charles stood abruptly and motioned toward the back of the restaurant. "Why don't we let Lieutenant Laurie tell him, Alex?" he asked smoothly. "I think it would come better from him."

Chapter Twenty-One

Lieutenant Laurie joined them at Charles's signal. The other, blank-faced man who was dressed in khakis and a black turtleneck took the table that was emptying behind them. So Lieutenant Laurie thought there might be trouble, Alex surmised.

"These guests of ours are Frances and Joseph Jacks," Charles told the policeman. Alex felt a spurt of annoyance at the way he had taken control of the situation as though it were his right. Daniel would never have done that. "They are direct descendants of Jonathan Crowell." He reached out his hand for the descendancy chart. "Here. Mrs. Borden has drawn it out for you."

The lieutenant rubbed his upper lip while studying the chart. "No children, Mr. Jacks?" he asked.

The yellow-faced man was looking bewildered. "Look here, what's this all about? Who are you?"

"Sorry. I forgot I was out of uniform. I'm Lieutenant Laurie, with the police." Pulling out his wallet, he showed his badge. "There's been a suspicious death in connection with this case, Mr. Jacks. Can you tell us where you were on Monday morning?"

"Why should he?" Frances demanded, stiff with outrage, looking from Alex to Briggie as though they had betrayed her.

"Now, now, Francie, just keep your hair on, and we'll get this figured out," her uncle advised calmly. "As a matter of fact, I spent the morning at my doctor's office. Dr. Vince Jamieson. Pine Street."

The lieutenant looked crestfallen, and it occurred suddenly to Alex that he was actually, for all his swagger, very young. "And you, young lady?" he asked without much hope.

"I was at school," she told him shortly. "Roosevelt University. I have my jazz percussion class on Monday morning."

"There's this other branch, lieutenant," Briggie said, putting a comforting hand on Frances's stiff arm. "Joey says that Jim Crowell moved to Florida, and that's the last he heard of him."

Consulting the chart, the lieutenant passed the back of his hand across his forehead in a gesture that conveyed weariness with the whole business. "Where in Florida?"

"Don't remember," Joey said, narrowing his chocolate brown eyes. "But I may have an old postcard or letter or something. I have a few of my mother's things still. She was his sister."

"Uncle Joey's a pack-rat," Frances confirmed, relaxing a little. "He even has my old report cards. But what is this suspicious death you're talking about?"

The lieutenant shifted from one foot to the other. "Woman by the name of Gladys Harrison." He looked at Amelia's sketch of the Williams family tree and then, handing it to Frances, pointed at Lloyd's name. "This man's daughter. I'll leave it to Mrs. Poulson here to explain it to you."

"She would be your grandmother's cousin, dear. That makes her your first cousin twice removed," Briggie said.

"But why would you suspect us of having killed her?" Frances asked, her belligerence returning.

Alex and Briggie exchanged looks. Briggie gave her a nod.

Turning to face the girl, Alex looked straight into Frances's green eyes. "We believe you and your uncle and James Crowell are the legal heirs to the Williams steel fortune."

Frances's eyes grew enormous. "No way!" she said.

Uncle Joey slapped the table and then began vigorously to play "What do you do with a drunken sailor?" "Our ship's come in, Francie, honey!"

"But you just said my great-grandfather was illegitimate!" Frances protested.

"The will just stipulates the eldest son and all his children as the heirs. It doesn't say anything about legitimate or illegitimate," Alex told the girl.

She looked at her uncle. "I can't believe it! How big is this fortune?"

"I'm not really sure," Alex said. "But it's considerable."

Uncle Joey stopped his ditty suddenly. "But why would we want to kill this Gladys whatever-her-name-is if we were the legitimate heirs?"

Lieutenant Laurie looked uneasy. "Well, we thought maybe you'd just discovered it and maybe . . . well, maybe you thought you might have a hard time proving it. It looks like somebody is killing off the other heirs."

"I don't think that makes much sense," Frances said, looking squarely at the lieutenant. While he shuffled his feet, she frowned into her plate. "It would make much more sense for someone to kill us."

"You're right, of course," Briggie told her. "That's why we said there was danger. Like the lieutenant told you, someone may be killing off all the heirs. There was another death last year, Gladys's niece." She paused and gave Frances a reassuring look. "But don't worry. I don't think anyone knows about you except us."

"Let's hope not," Charles said fervently.

The dirty-aproned waiter came up to them then. "Look, you guys. I don't want to put a damper on your party or anything, but there's people waitin' for this table. You finished?"

Charles took the bill in the man's outstretched hand. Glancing at it, he removed a credit card from his wallet.

"You pay up front."

They separated at the front door, Lieutenant Laurie taking Joey's and Frances's addresses and telephone numbers and Amelia giving Frances the Borden telephone number. "We'll be in touch, dear."

"Call us if you find anything about those cousins," Briggie reminded Joey.

"What do we do about claiming this fortune?" Joey asked.

"Get a good lawyer," Charles advised.

"Richard might take it on," Briggie said. "He belongs to the Illinois bar."

At the mention of Daniel's father's name, Alex felt as though she had been sucker punched. She'd managed not to think about Daniel for the past hour.

"Actually, I think it might be better to get someone local," she said, trying to sound matter-of-fact.

"Nonsense!" Briggie answered. "Richard loves messes like this. And he's used to working with us. I'll call him for you today, Joey. He works out of Kansas City, but he would love a trip up here."

"That would be real helpful," Joey told her out on the busy Chicago street. "We'll be in touch." He waved his hand in farewell and moved slowly away.

"I have to go to work in a few hours," Frances said in parting, her arms hugging her thin body. "How am I going to keep my orders straight?" The excited question hung on the cold air as she rushed away towards the bus stop.

Lieutenant Laurie followed the RootSearch contingent to their car.

"Where's your henchman?" Alex asked.

"Who?"

"The man who was with you in the deli."

"I was by myself," he said ruefully. "Couldn't get the Chicago P.D. to take me seriously. All this genealogy stuff is too far-fetched. Turns out maybe they were right. We've got to look somewhere else for this perp." He leaned against the side of the Range Rover, seemingly oblivious to the sharp wind that was making Alex's ears sting.

"I still think it has to do with the family tree," Briggie maintained. "Gladys was talking to us about it. There was no other reason for her to be killed. And remember the joker who kidnapped Amelia. He warned us to stop our research."

"Maybe he was afraid you'd find the Crowells," the lieutenant reasoned, irreverently kicking the sidewall of Charles's tire. "That seems to me to point to the Westons. I guess I'm going to have to check up on their alibis. Should have done it before now."

Alex stubbornly maintained that the Westons were frightened of something themselves and then got in the front seat of the car beside Charles.

"What a nice girl," said Amelia from the backseat. "So wholesome."

"I'll call Richard as soon as we get home," Briggie said.

Alex remained silent, looking at the city street full of dry cleaners, Chinese take-out, and "pay-day loan" establishments. The gutters were dirty, and salt-begrimed cars were parallel parked bumper to bumper. Would Richard know about what had happened between her and Daniel? Probably not. Their relationship was somewhat strained.

When they got home, Charles suggested that Alex go with him to check the Lawsons' house. She declined, saying she wanted to go over the case notes with Briggie. Staring at her, his eyes grim and probing, Charles turned away and walked out the door, taking a delirious Lord Peter with him. Amelia declared that she would make hot chocolate for everyone. Briggie tried to lift Tuppence from the refrigerator and received a scratch for her pains.

"She's becoming more and more antisocial," Briggie said. "Frankly, I'm worried about her."

"She's grieving," Amelia told her. "Give her time."

As Alex and Briggie sat on stools at the butcher block going over the genogram, adding their recent discoveries, Briggie was inclined to blame herself. "That illegitimate line was so tempting, I'm afraid we got carried away. We've got to look at some of these other question marks."

Alex studied the chart, relieved that Briggie had apparently forgotten her intention of calling Richard. "Let's see," she said, tapping her forehead with the eraser of her pencil. "We've got the question mark about William Jr.'s death. Mother said there were witnesses, so it probably wasn't murder."

"She also said there was something she couldn't remember about the witnesses. Something she thought was important," Briggie supplied.

"Okay. So we'll check on that." Alex made a note. "Now, why did we have a question mark here?" She indicated William Williams's first marriage.

"Oh," Briggie said, placing a stubby finger on the question mark. "That was just kind of a genealogist's reflex. The book said his wife died in childbirth. It didn't give her name."

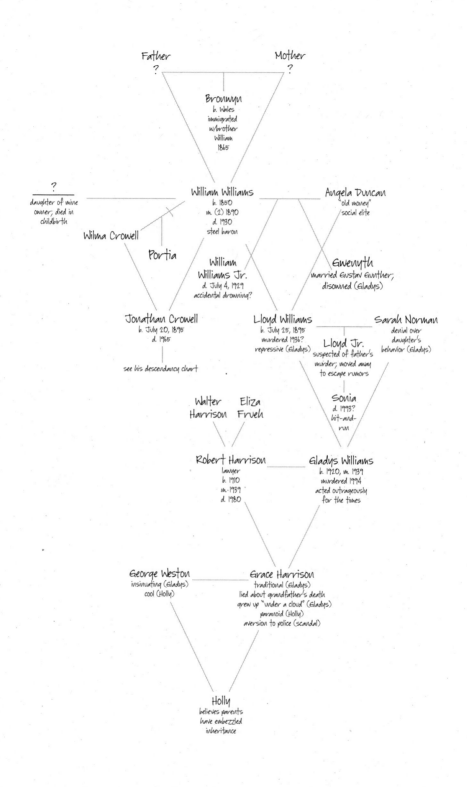

Alex reflected on this for a moment and then an idea bolted into her head like lightning. "Briggie!"

Briggie looked at her, white brows raised in question. Then together they said, "The child!"

At that moment, the telephone rang. Amelia answered, "Oh, yes, Joey. That's terrific. Here, I'll let you talk to Alex."

Amelia handed her daughter the telephone, an excited gleam in her eye. "Joey?" Alex queried, "What have you found?"

"Hi, Alex. Look, I was going through my mother's stuff, and I came across a postcard from her brother, Jim. It was after the divorce when they moved to Florida."

"Yes?"

"Well, the postmark says Sarasota. He just says he and Zach and Erin—those are my cousins, I guess—are getting settled and they like it there. He says he'll let her know their address, but I can't find anything except this one postcard."

"Well, that's a good start, Joey. We'll see if the police can find your Uncle Jim and Zach. Do you think Zach's around your age?"

"I don't remember. This postcard is dated 1942. I was about seven years old then. The only thing I can remember about my cousin is something vague about camping out in the backyard. I think he was real little and he was scared."

Alex thought. "Do you know if your Uncle Jim was older or younger than your mother?"

"He was Mother's little brother, I know that. She was born in 1915, if that helps."

"Uh-huh. It gives us a ballpark figure." Doing some rudimentary math, Alex said, "If Jim was born two years after your mother, that would make his birth year about 1917. Then, if he got married when he was about twenty-one or so, that would be about . . . 1938."

"We know he had his kids before '42 when he got the divorce,"

Joey said eagerly. "So that means they were probably born around '39 and '41."

"Zach would have been *really* young to have gone camping," Alex said with a little laugh. "No wonder he was scared."

"I'm fifty-nine, so he must be in his early or mid fifties."

Alex's mind flew at once to the bald-headed man who had kidnapped her mother. Middle-aged. But you'd think he'd *want* to be found. Joey was right. What motive would Zach have for murdering Gladys or Sonia or threatening her mother? "Well, Lieutenant Laurie will probably need this information. And you'll want to get in touch with him and your Uncle Jim anyway to tell them about the will. Maybe they can help foot the legal bill."

Then suddenly she remembered her recent discovery. *The child! What if it was a boy?*

"Uh, Joey," she said, wetting her lips and feeling like a traitor, "on second thought, you might want to wait on the legal front. Briggie and I just found what might be another line of investigation."

There was a little silence on the line. "What do you mean?"

She hated to tell him. "William Williams was married young. His first wife died in childbirth. We have absolutely no idea if the child lived and, if it did, whether it was a girl or a boy or what happened to it."

Chapter Twenty-Two

D ang! I knew there had to be a catch. How soon will you know?" Joey asked.

"Well, if there was a child, it grew up in Pittsburgh, I think. There was no mention of it in the company history compiled by your ancestor's grandson-in-law, Robert Harrison. We'll have to hire a local researcher, I think. And today's Saturday. But we'll see what we can do. Tell Frances not to quit her day job."

"She's a real talented little drummer. Going to go to New Orleans when she graduates. If I live that long, maybe I'll go with her. These Chicago winters and my ol' liver 'll be the death of me."

"Well, don't give up hope. Right now we don't know anything for sure."

Amelia had been listening, and Charles had come in midway through her conversation, the dachshund gamboling at his feet.

Her mother put a mug of cocoa in front of her. "Another line? In Pittsburgh? Show me." There were frown lines on her forehead. "I so liked that little Frances."

"What's going on?" Charles wanted to know. "It sounds like you've been pulling rabbits out of hats."

Alex and Briggie explained.

"We've got to call Lieutenant Laurie," Alex said. "He needs to know about Jim and Zach and Erin."

*   *   *

For Saturday night entertainment, Briggie proposed Scrabble and popcorn. Lieutenant Laurie had inquiries in hand for James and Zachariah Crowell in Sarasota, and they couldn't begin their Pittsburgh inquiries until Monday. It was a lively game, particularly when Charles tried to spell *color* with a *u*.

"That's the way they spell it in my country. Can I help it if you colonials are illiterate?"

"You also spell *checque* with a *que*," Alex said. "There's no way we're letting you get away with that. The prescribed dictionary for this game is *Webster's Collegiate Dictionary*, right here. If you have any questions, you can look them up."

"I think I'm being discriminated against," he murmured.

Alex gave a mock pout. "Poor Charles." Then she felt immediately uncomfortable, as this might be construed to be flirtatious behavior. To put herself back on course, she said crossly, "Like it or lump it."

She felt his eyes on her, assessing. She knew he couldn't mistake the change in her behavior towards him and was speculating about the cause. She wasn't ready to discuss it. At 10:30, exhausted from her sleepless night and the effort of keeping Charles at bay, she said good night.

But once in bed, she tossed and turned. Thrusting thoughts of Daniel out of her head, she thought of Frances and Joey. They obviously shared a strong bond. Though they had clearly struggled, they were doing what they loved. She smiled as she thought of Frances as a jazz drummer and Joey, strumming the blues. Did he sing, too? Compared to their cousin, Holly Weston, who was cooped up in a lockdown facility by parents she could neither trust nor admire, they had a good life. Of course, there was Joey's liver disease. Money did have its uses. Certainly someone, somewhere, was willing to do murder after murder to secure a fortune for himself. She ruminated on that. Who in the world could it be?

Sitting up straight in her bed, she suddenly remembered where she had seen the man at Nate and Al's who had been standing next to the lieutenant. *He was the man in the tortoiseshell glasses from the Newberry.* He hadn't been wearing his glasses today! That's why his face had looked so blank. And he had sat down at the table behind them. *He had heard every word they said!*

Leaping out of bed, she drew on her thick navy terry cloth robe and ran barefoot downstairs to her mother's study. She found Charles sitting there, looking at Stewart's book of photographs, the only evidence of her husband that existed in this house. Lord Peter was curled up at his feet. At her entrance, the little dog became instantly alert.

"Alex! What's wrong!"

"The Jackses. They're in danger. I've got to call Lieutenant Laurie!"

"Not much in his brain box," the parrot warned her.

Charles set the book down carefully on the coffee table. It was open to a picture of a young hiker in the blooming Scottish heather looking into the sunset, a ruin looming up behind him. "What gave you that idea?"

"The man at the library when Briggie and I discovered Jonathan Crowell's picture. He was at Nate and Al's today! He was sitting in the booth next to us. I thought he was with Lieutenant Laurie at the time, but later the lieutenant said he wasn't. The man heard everything we said."

Charles swore and reached for the telephone. "What's the lieutenant's pager number?"

"It's written there. On the blotter. In that corner. Oh, my gosh, I hope we're not too late!"

They woke Lieutenant Laurie out of a sound sleep.

"What?" He asked Charles to repeat the story.

Hanging up the telephone a moment later, Charles said, "He's going to have Chicago police check on the addresses they gave. I wish we knew where Joey or Frances worked. It's Saturday night. I'm certain they're both at work."

"All rolled up," the Professor told them.

"That man probably followed them. Oh, Charles! We've got to *do* something."

"What do you suggest?" He consulted his watch.

"What time is it?"

"A few minutes before midnight."

"Let's go down to Frances's place in Roger's Park. I have the address."

"Couldn't we just call?"

"Oh . . . well, I guess. Wait. I'll get the number." Alex's carryall was on the floor by the desk. She pulled out her notebook and gave him the number she had copied down at the library.

Charles dialed. The telephone rang several times, and then to Alex's relief, her cousin said, "Frances?"

When she replied, he handed Alex the telephone. "Frances, I'm sorry but I'm afraid I've put you and your uncle in danger. The police are on their way. Did you have any trouble tonight?"

"Danger? What do you mean?"

"I think someone was following you. I just realized it. There was a man next to us at the deli . . . never mind, I'll explain later. Anyway, someone knows who you are."

"You mean about the will?"

"Yes. I was stupidly careless. I didn't recognize him at the time. But nothing happened to you tonight?"

"No. But my boyfriend took me to work and brought me home. Bobby is a big guy. No one would mess with him."

"Is your uncle still at work?"

"Yeah. He sings blues at a little club in Old Town. He's on till one."

"What's the name of the club? What's the address?"

"It's called Casablanca. It's on Clark Street. I'm not exactly sure of the address."

"The police will know," Alex assured her. "I'm calling them right now. I'm sorry about this."

"I'll never sleep until I know he's okay. I'm calling Bobby. I'm going down there."

"Can you call us when you find out if he's okay?" Alex asked.

"Sure. I've got your number."

Alex quickly relayed Frances's information to the lieutenant. He promised to give it to the Chicago police immediately. It was twelve-twenty.

Then Charles and Alex sat and waited.

Chapter Twenty-Three

These are remarkable photographs," Charles said. "I used to go to Scotland for the long vacation when I was an undergraduate. I took photos. But I can tell your husband really had an eye for significant detail."

"Yes," Alex said, staring at the book in Charles's hands, surprised at his insight. How long ago those days seemed. Stewart had published his photo essay of Scotland shortly before his death. It had been a work of love. An expatriate draft dodger from America, he had embraced the land of his ancestors, where he still had considerable family. In Scotland they had been married in the village kirk, and they had lived among all of Stewart's Campbell cousins. "Stewart loved the country. Especially the Highlands. We would go there every year for the summer solstice. They still have feasts and all sorts of festivities. And, of course, the Highland games."

"Yes. I love his photographs of the contestants in their tartans. This one is especially good." He indicated a picture of an elderly discus thrower whose naked arm muscles still bulged above his full

Highland kit. In his eyes was a look of warlike determination that Stewart had claimed to be the hallmark of his countrymen.

"He loved that man," Alex remembered. "They spent hours in the pub together. I could hardly understand him, his Highland burr was so thick, but Stewart never had any problem."

"You loved him very much." It was a statement, but there was a question in Charles's eyes.

Perhaps it was the strain they were under. Perhaps it was the fact that she had been without sleep for a day and a half, but she found herself saying, "Yes, but not enough."

"Not enough for what?" Charles was suddenly alert, a light flickering in his eyes.

"Oh . . ." Embarrassed at her disclosure, she turned to the side. "Just not enough. I can't explain."

"Can't or won't?"

"Look, Charles," she said, feeling as though her back were against the wall, "it's late and I'm tired and worried. I shouldn't have said that."

"I'm sorry. I shouldn't have pressed. You're right. It's not the right time." He continued paging through the book. They were silent.

At length, the telephone rang. It was 1:15 A.M. Lord Peter awoke out of a sound snooze. Moriarty remarked, "Flummoxed, by gad."

"Oh, Alex! It's Frances! I just got here, and the police are everywhere. Uncle Joey . . ."

"What is it, Frances?"

"The police got here just in time! There was a man . . . Uncle Joey is hurt real bad . . ."

"Is he going to make it?" Alex asked, feeling guilt smash her heart.

"I don't know."

"Where are they taking him?"

"Northwestern University Hospital."

"Charles and I will meet you there."

*   *   *

The emergency room was teeming with people of all colors and ages as Charles and Alex stepped through the doors at two o'clock. An African-American doctor and his team of nurses hustled beside a gurney where a bloodstained victim was being rushed towards the elevators. A little girl with blonde ringlets and a tear-stained face was sucking her thumb and holding on to her anxious mother's hand as they stood at the admitting desk. Beside the swinging doors that led to the regions beyond, an Asian family huddled on Naugahyde chairs, staring with unblinking stoicism into space. The gray-haired grandfather was bundled in an enormous overcoat, his face as smooth as onion skin. His sons, dressed in expensive overcoats, wore Gucci loafers. In a corner, an anxious father-to-be coached his wife on her breathing. She was obviously in labor. Alex took in all these details as she searched frantically for a redhead.

Finally, a bony young man of about six foot six inches approached them, his dark brown hair cut close to his scalp. He was accompanied by a uniformed police officer who looked like a choir- boy with sharply planed pink cheeks and springy brown curls.

"Alex? Charles?" the tall young man asked.

"You must be Bobby," Alex guessed. "And this is?" She turned to the policeman.

"Officer Hambleton." The curly-haired man identified himself, showing his badge. He glanced a little nervously at Bobby. Alex drew the immediate assumption that he was a raw recruit who had drawn the assignment of dealing with "the wacky genealogists."

"Frances is with her uncle," Bobby said. "She wanted me to wait and meet you." She felt herself being assessed by the tall young man.

"How could you get a nice kid like Frances involved in something like this?" he demanded. "Her uncle is all she's got."

"How bad is it?" Alex asked, her head hammering with fatigue and worry. She didn't blame him for his aggressiveness.

"They're doing a CAT scan of his head. He was hit pretty hard. The police got there just as he went down." He kicked a tiny Dixie cup lying by his feet. It sailed across the room into the corner by the Asian family. They didn't even blink.

"Did they catch the guy?" Alex turned to Officer Hambleton.

"No." Bobby socked one huge fist into an open palm, replying before the officer had a chance. He was clearly in the grip of a testosterone overload. "Joey was coming out of the back door of the club. The dude just ducked inside when he saw the police and mixed with the customers. It's Saturday night. It was full."

"You didn't get a description?" She directed her question once more to the seemingly hapless policeman.

"No," he said, shrugging. "It was too dark to see. The alley spotlight was out."

"Dang!" Alex said. "How's Frances?"

"Mad as you know what," Bobby told her. His massive forehead loomed over concerned deep brown eyes. "She's a redhead, y'know. Plus she's really protective of her uncle."

"Thank heavens you were with her tonight." Alex impulsively gripped his black leather sleeve. "I don't blame you for being upset with me. I feel really guilty about all of this. I didn't know . . ."

"I have a few questions for you, ma'am," the police officer said diffidently.

This was Chicago's finest? Alex mused.

Charles was now moving forward and shook Bobby's hand. "I don't believe there're many who would mix it up with you. You look like a rugger blue."

Bobby grinned suddenly, showing large white teeth with a slight gap in front. "Hey! I don't know about the blue part, but I am a rugby player. Down in Grant's Park. Have a match tomorrow, as a matter of fact."

A middle-height, slight Asian doctor with *Nguyen* stitched on his white coat went over to the anxious Asian family, chart in hand. Whatever he told them evidently wasn't good news. Closing ranks, they bowed their heads. A nurse came out and held a wheelchair for the mother in labor.

Lieutenant Laurie strode in, breathless and harassed. He'd obviously traveled at top speed from Lake Forest. "Did they get a description?" he asked Alex.

"No," she said. "The alley light was out. He went back into the club and disappeared in the crowd. This is Officer Hambleton. He was about to question me."

Lieutenant Laurie gave the junior officer a curt nod. "Of all the luck!" He looked like he wanted to spit out something bitter. "How is the old guy?" he asked.

"This is Bobby, Frances's friend," Alex informed him. "He says Joey was hit pretty hard. They're doing a CAT scan." Turning to the young man who loomed over them all, she added, "Bobby, this is Lieutenant Laurie. He's been investigating a death up in Lake Forest. Also my mother's kidnapping."

"Kidnapping? For crying out loud! I didn't hear about that part. Frances told me about the murder and the steel money." He looked belligerent. "And now, Joey. Seems to me like this money isn't worth it. Francis and Joey were perfectly fine the way they were."

"Joey does need a liver transplant," Alex reminded him patiently. Bobby probably resented the change that wealth would bring into his girlfriend's life.

Officer Hambleton shuffled his feet on the gray tile floor. "Ma'am, would you mind stepping over to the corner with me for a moment?" He indicated a corner of the lobby occupied by the coffee vending machine. "I understand you're the one who called in the police?"

"Certainly, officer," Alex said, and leaving Bobby, Charles, and Lieutenant Laurie behind, she walked a short distance away with the cherubic policeman. "Lieutenant Laurie has all the details of the case, you know," she told him. "It's quite complex."

"I understand you never met the victim until this afternoon?" The officer's eyes were pleading, as though he were begging her to give him a chance.

"No. If you don't know, my colleague and I have been hired by North Side Treatment Center to look into the family of William Williams . . ." As she went on to describe the details of the case to the young man, he scribbled frantically in his notebook, looking more and more bewildered. Finally, she took pity on him. "As I said, Officer Laurie has all the details. We really appreciate your department's coming to the rescue tonight."

"Do you really expect any further attempts will be made on Mr. Jacks's life?" The man looked up from his notebook, his pale green eyes dazed with all the information she had given him.

Alex realized that she would have to say she did. "I'm afraid so. Do you think you could post a police guard outside his door?"

"I'll recommend it." The officer puffed out his chest with a sudden gesture of self-importance. Rummaging in his shirt pocket he pulled out a card and presented it to her. Alex read, "Otis Hambleton, Officer, Chicago Police Department, 534–9871."

"Thank you, officer. I'll be sure to call you if anything comes up that you need to know about." She tucked the card down into her carryall, which she wore slung over her shoulder. "Now perhaps I can get back to my friends?"

"Yes, ma'am. Our department will be in touch with Lieutenant

Laurie about this." With that he snapped his notebook shut and bade her good night.

"What in the world does your mother have to do with this, anyway?" Bobby demanded as she returned. "She's not another heir, is she?"

The lieutenant shook his head, sighing. "She went out by herself to do some investigating on this family tree. Seems someone didn't like it." He turned to Alex. "You saw this person in the deli. Why didn't you tell me you recognized him?"

Alex returned his sigh. "I'm sorry, lieutenant. At first, I thought he was with you. When you said he wasn't, I just sort of forgot about him." She hung her head. Could she have prevented this? She had been asking herself that question all the time she and Charles had been hurtling down Lakeshore Drive to the hospital. As though reading her mind, her cousin put an arm around her shoulders and gave her a reassuring pat. He had been trying to get her to see that Joey actually owed his life to her intervention. But she felt as though she had been too slow off the mark. "I didn't remember him until tonight when I was lying in bed, going over the case in my mind, trying to think of who could possibly be behind all of this."

"Where did you see him before?" Lieutenant Laurie asked, his eyes bloodshot but alert. "And what did he look like?"

Scrunching up her eyes, she exerted an effort to picture the man in the deli. "I saw him at the Newberry Library the day we discovered Jonathan Crowell's picture. I think now he must have been eavesdropping on Briggie and me. The main thing I noticed about him was his tortoiseshell glasses." She shook her head. "There isn't anything really distinguished about him. I'd say he was in his mid-fifties. Graying hair. Medium height. He just looked like your typical genealogist. He was even friendly."

"Hmm." The policeman hooked his thumbs in the belt loops of

his uniform pants. "The guy who kidnapped your mother was bald. It looks like we're dealing with more than one person."

His words jogged Alex's memory. "In Waukegan," she said quickly, "there was another man. He was at the courthouse when we got the will and then at the restaurant. Earlene said he asked for the table next to us."

"Earlene?"

"The waitress. She was suspicious of him. She told him the table hadn't been cleaned yet."

"Criminy," the lieutenant muttered. "Could there be three of them in this?"

"Geez, Louise," Bobby moaned.

Alex concentrated as she absently watched the Asian family file out disconsolately into the night. "There has to be a reason behind this. Someone we haven't discovered yet. Dang, I wish tomorrow wasn't Sunday! All the libraries will be closed."

"What're you thinking of doing?" The lieutenant's voice was dubious. Bobby was looking at her as though she were a highly suspicious package that might explode at any moment. Charles simply let her reflect.

Picturing the ever-more-complicated genogram in her mind, she said, "There are still some question marks, lieutenant. You're looking into the Florida cousins, right?"

"Right. Should hear something Monday if there's anything to hear."

"Well, there's another possibility." Alex explained about William Williams's first marriage.

"How many kids did that old geezer have, anyway?"

"Let's sit down," Charles suggested, indicating the places left vacant by the Asian family. Scratching his head, the lieutenant made his way over to the brown Naugahyde chairs. The doors burst open, and two EMTs pushed in a gurney carrying a black-haired man who was hooked up to an IV on wheels. They pushed him straight to the elevator doors where the suave Dr. Nguyen met them.

Alex tried to bring her exhausted mind to bear on the task at hand. "Well, there was his illegitimate son, Jonathan Crowell, Joey and Frances's ancestor. He had a sister, Portia, but she doesn't come into this yet. Then there was William Williams Jr., who supposedly died of accidental drowning." She seated herself next to Charles, counting the children on her fingers. "After him came Lloyd, who was murdered by someone for some reason we don't know. His sister was Gwenyth, who was disinherited because she married a German. Now we've discovered this first child, sex unknown, who could've died at birth."

"You know," Charles said meditatively, "if that child were a girl, possibly her descendants are trying to get rid of everyone else so the money would come to them. They might have thought they had an easy job with just Gladys and her family. It makes sense that they'd be a little upset with you for continuing to discover new descendants."

"A girl?" Bobby and the policeman echoed blankly.

Alex looked at Charles. He was as bright and alert as though it were first thing in the morning, his light blue eyes speculative.

"You know, you could be right," she said. "If it was a *boy*, all his descendants would have to do would be to come forward to claim the inheritance, supposing they knew about it." She hunched forward, her elbows resting on the knees of her jeans. "Think about it. If the child lived, he or she was probably raised by the mother's family. The mine owners, remember. They might have written William off when he left town."

Bobby was shaking his head. "I don't get any of this."

"I'm sorry," Alex apologized. "It's sort of like coming in on the middle of a play." She patted his knee. "The main thing is that Frances is going to be okay. We'll see to that, I promise."

With these words, Frances walked through the swinging doors. Looking around the room, she spotted them and came over.

"He's going to be fine," she said, her green eyes still wet and red-rimmed. "The CAT scan just came back. It's a concussion, but he's conscious now, and the internal bleeding has stopped. They've got him packed in ice."

Alex drew a profound sigh of relief as her heart beat free of the fearful vise that had gripped it. Things were bad, of course, but they could have been so much worse.

Bobby had stood and now enveloped the girl in his arms, pulling her to him protectively. "Thank God," he said reverently.

"Yes," she agreed, seeming to give into her weariness as she leaned against her boyfriend.

"Will you come home with Charles and me, Frances?" Alex asked. "I feel like we owe it to you to keep you safe."

"She's coming home with me," Bobby said stubbornly.

Frances pulled back and looked up into his face. "You know I can't do that, Bobby. Uncle Joey wouldn't like it."

"These guys are involved with murderers, Frances. And kidnappers. I've been listening. They think there are at least three. What do you want to mix yourself up with them for? No amount of money's worth your life."

Lifting her chin at his preemptory tone, she said, "I want to find whoever it was who did this to Uncle Joey. I can't stay with you, and I don't think it's a good idea to stay by myself."

"My mother would love to have you, Frances," Alex said.

Bobby looked Charles up and down, seeming to weigh whether or not he could be trusted. "I suppose you live somewhere on the North Shore," he said scornfully.

Alex heard another ambulance scream into the drive in front of the emergency room. The African-American doctor came running through the double doors and out into the cold in his scrubs and white coat.

"I'm a fellow rugger player, though you wouldn't think it to look at me," Charles replied. "And I row. You can trust me to take care of Frances."

"Oh, I'll just bet I can!" Bobby sneered.

"Bobby!" Frances said sharply. "Charles isn't interested in a girl like me."

"Not now, maybe," the young man said. "But when you have money . . ."

"I have plenty of money, thank you very much," Charles replied, his voice level and reasonable. "And I don't prey on young girls."

Frances stood apart from Bobby, scowling at him. "Honestly, Bobby . . ."

"Wait a minute," Alex said, trying to think how Briggie would handle the situation. "We're all tired, and Frances has had a very trying day. She's still in danger . . ."

Lieutenant Laurie unexpectedly entered the fray. "Look, kid, Mr. Lamb doesn't have a thing for your girlfriend. Get a grip. Let her go with them and get some sleep."

After another look at the discouraging countenance Frances showed him, Bobby gave in with bad grace. "At least give me the phone number. I want to be able to get in touch with you. I don't suppose you'll be at my match tomorrow?"

"Grow up, Bobby," Frances said with disgust. "News flash! My uncle almost died today. No, I am not going to be at your match tomorrow."

With those words, she left him behind, marching out of the hospital. Alex threw Bobby an apologetic look and followed her.

Chapter Twenty-Four

At 4 A.M. Alex had Frances tucked up in her bed. Wearily, she donned her own nightgown again and crawled into bed beside her mother.

"What?" Amelia inquired sleepily.

"Go back to sleep, Mother," Alex told her. "I'll tell you about it in the morning."

At 8:30 A.M. she was awakened without ceremony by Briggie. "Why are you sleeping in here?" she demanded. "Aren't you going to church?"

"Oh, Briggie . . ." Alex rolled over, away from her friend, and buried her head in the goose down pillow. Instantly she was fast asleep. She didn't even hear Briggie walk out of the room.

When she next woke, it was noon by her mother's bedside clock, and she was still tremendously weary. Gradually, a feeling of urgency penetrated her grogginess. *Frances. Joey. The man without the tortoiseshell glasses.*

She sat up, her head heavy. Was Charles awake? Did anyone even

226

know about poor Frances? Good grief! There were certainly draw-backs to having a man in the house. She was going to have to pull herself together before she went downstairs.

However, when she did get downstairs half an hour later, dressed in black slacks and sapphire turtleneck, it was to find only Frances and her mother having a comfortable chat by the sitting room fire. Professor Moriarty was perched on the redheaded girl's shoulder, and to Alex's surprise, the grieving Tuppence was in her lap. "Feather your corners!" the parrot advised.

"I'm so glad you brought Frances to us, Alex," her mother said. "She's just been telling me about school. Did you know the music conservatory at Roosevelt has one of the most prestigious percussion departments in the country?"

Amelia looked sunny in her lavender wool slacks and ivory twin-set. She was clearly delighted with her guest. Frances, wearing jeans and a maroon sweatshirt with the Roosevelt University logo, glanced up at her. "Hey," she said, "the hospital says Uncle Joey's still stable."

"That's great news. Is Charles still asleep?"

"He went to church with Briggie," her mother told her.

Alex was mildly stunned. "Really? That's interesting." But she couldn't deal with the ramifications of Charles going to church right now. "I suppose someone told you about last night?"

Amelia nodded. "We've got to find out who's behind this, Alex. Now more than ever."

"I know." Alex sank onto the couch. "We've got to find out about that child in Pittsburgh. I don't even know where to begin." Lord Peter came in and nosed her palm. She patted his head absently.

When Briggie and Charles walked in a few moments later, she found they had the matter well in hand.

"The bishop found the phone number of one of the bishops in Pittsburgh for me," Briggie told her, pulling off her red wool stocking cap. Her white hair stood on end with static electricity. Alex wondered what in the world she had told the bishop of the North Shore Ward. She had a way of making things larger than life. That was one of the reasons why she loved her. "Charles told me about his suspicions, and I think they make sense. I'm going to call this bishop and get the name of a little old lady who does genealogical research."

"A little old lady like you?" Alex asked, smiling. With Briggie's arrival, she felt her exhaustion lift. They were on the chase again. They would succeed. They always had before.

"You know I'm not old," Briggie objected. "Just getting ripe. Why don't you ask Charles how he liked church?"

Charles was grinning. He looked absolutely stunning in a charcoal gray suit, pale blue shirt, and silver pinpoint tie. Alex lifted her eyebrows in a silent query.

"I found it very interesting. About as different from an Anglican service as it could possibly be," he told her. "The principal speaker was a nineteen-year-old boy."

"A missionary farewell?" Alex asked Briggie.

"Yep. A fine one, too. Kid's going to Ukraine. Real fired up."

"I'll say," Charles said. "Either he's barmy or he actually believes in what he's doing. Ukraine's a dangerous place these days. And not terribly hospitable to religion."

"I have a ham in the oven," Amelia interjected, patting her coiffure with new serenity. "And I've made your father's favorite cornbread, Alex. Do you remember? It's like cake."

"You're turning into quite a chef," Alex said, surprised. "Do you think maybe once upon a time you actually liked to cook?"

"I'm beginning to wonder," her mother said.

After a surprisingly good dinner of ham, three-bean vinaigrette salad, baked potatoes, cornbread, and German chocolate ice cream, Charles offered to take Frances to visit her uncle.

"Oh, that would be great," the girl said, turning toward Charles. Frances reminded Alex vividly of a sunflower. She suspected that no matter what she had told her boyfriend, Frances had developed a crush on Charles. "I've got to see when they're going to let him come home. He doesn't have any insurance."

"Don't worry about that now," Briggie said, patting her hand. "You're probably going to have yourself a nice little inheritance."

Alex frowned at her. Why was Briggie raising what could be false hopes?

"I just have a feeling," Briggie said stoutly.

Alex knew Briggie's feelings. "Frances, don't worry about it in any case. It's my fault your uncle was hurt. I *am* coming into an inheritance. I'll see that his bill is paid. Let him stay in there as long as he needs to. There might be complications because of his liver and everything."

Frances began to protest, but Charles ushered her firmly out of the room. "Come, come, child. Don't be tiresome."

After he was gone, Alex helped Briggie with the dishes, and then they sat down in Amelia's sitting room with the genogram to figure out when William Williams's first child would have been born. Amelia sat by the fire, ready to take part.

"Let's see," Briggie said, taking her notes out of her denim briefcase. "William was born in 1850, according to the history Robert Harrison wrote." She adjusted the half-glasses on her short nose. "That means he would have been about twenty in 1870. Should we start there?"

"It's a rum go," the Professor opined.

"I don't know," Amelia said, toying with the silver bracelet at her wrist. "I think some of those coal miners married young. I wouldn't be surprised if he married at eighteen."

"Okay. We'll start with 1868. Right." Picking up the phone, she punched in the number of the Pittsburgh bishop. He referred them to Mary Tomblin, who turned out to be the vivacious head of the Pittsburgh Stake Family History Library.

"Of course, I'd *love* to help you with your research!" Alex could hear her clearly from across the room. "My husband and I just love doing genealogy! It's so much fun to be retired and have nothing else we *have* to do."

Briggie grinned at Alex and Amelia. "Well, Sister Tomblin . . ."

"Oh, call me Mary!"

"Well, Mary, do you think you could do a search for us at the Allegheny County Courthouse? We need some birth and marriage information, but we're not sure of the year."

"Of course! The family history library is only open Tuesday through Thursday, so I have the whole day tomorrow."

"That's kind of you," Briggie said. "Of course we'll pay you . . ."

"No need. I do it because it's fun, I tell you. Now who are we searching for?"

"Well, the name's kind of common. William Williams. He married someone somewhere around 1868 to 1873 or so. And they had a child. Or anyway she died in childbirth. We're not exactly sure if her child lived or not. We're checking to see if this William Williams had any descendants in Pittsburgh."

"Okay. So you want a marriage certificate for this man and a possible birth certificate for his child, born when?"

"Well, we don't know exactly. Sorry. It was probably a year or so after they married."

"Oh, I love a puzzle. This is going to be fun!"

"You'll be doing us a real favor," Briggie assured her.

Before Charles and Frances returned, Alex received a call from Daniel. When her mother told her who was on the line, Alex came down to earth with the proverbial thud. Her single-minded pursuit of the case had succeeded in dulling the poignancy of Daniel's defection. Reluctant to plunge herself back into this thorny patch of her life, she took the call upstairs in her mother's room, lying down on the bed. The dachshund followed her, exploring the smells in her mother's closet. Surely Daniel wouldn't phone just to resume their quarrel?

"Have you shaved off that ridiculous beard?" she asked by way of greeting. She intended to keep this light.

"No. Alex, can you ever forgive me?" His voice sounded weary.

"You gave me a bad night, Daniel," she told him, at once sobered by his tone. Her sleepless night seemed an eon ago, but it had left a deep wound. She didn't want to reopen it or venture anywhere near that emotional place again.

"Not nearly as bad as the one I had. I had to sit up in O'Hare all night and eat vendor hot dogs. I kept thinking what an absolute idiot I'd made of myself."

"I'm sorry."

"I knew I had hang-ups, but that was really inexcusable."

She felt relieved. This was more like the Daniel she had always known. The fragile stitches holding her laceration together were secure. "You must have been frozen by the time the taxi arrived."

"I was. And one of your neighbors kept looking out the window at me. I'm sure she thought I was casing the place."

"Especially with that beard."

"Okay, okay. The beard goes tomorrow morning. Friends?"

"Friends," she agreed carefully.

"So. How's the case coming?"

Glad to leave behind more personal topics, Alex brought him up to date.

"My gosh, woman! Murder and calumny follow wherever thou goest!"

"You don't need to tell me that. Frances is now a guest, and heaven only knows what we're going to do with her uncle when he's released. Not to mention all of Gladys's pets. I never thought I'd say it, but thank goodness for Briggie's deer rifle."

"Maybe I need to send my father up," Daniel said with a chuckle. The weariness had gone from his voice.

"The havoc he would create with Briggie is not something I think I can deal with right now." Alex closed her eyes against the memory of past scrapes Briggie and Daniel's father had passed through together.

"How is what's her name? Holly, is it?"

"I've actually been taken off the case by her mother, so I can't go visit her anymore. I'm working ad hoc for the hospital now. But I'm really coming to believe that her parents were right to put her somewhere safe."

"It sounds like it." He paused. "You know, I don't have any patients in crisis. I could take a couple of days off . . ."

"No," she said quickly, heading him off at the pass. "Your instincts were right, and mine were wrong. I admit it. I think you and Charles would be like oil and water. I can't deal with any added drama at the moment."

"So there *is* something going on . . ."

"Are you kidding? With people dropping like flies all around us? You're as bad as Bobby."

"And who, pray tell, is Bobby?"

"An overgrown adolescent with an inferiority complex."

"Ouch."

Alex felt better than she had since Friday afternoon. "How's Maxie?"

They spoke in a light vein about Briggie's cat, and Alex managed to regain her equilibrium. But she would never again make the mistake of taking Daniel for granted. She realized that even though they hadn't resolved anything, she had narrowly averted disaster.

But what, after all, was she to do with Charles?

This question kept her lying on the bed, alone in her mother's room, except for Lord Peter, who had gone to sleep in the closet on top of Amelia's fur slippers. She didn't want to face the man who was so clearly, in every way, the answer to any maiden's prayer. His magnetism was undeniable. It frightened her. The more she learned about him, the more heroic he became. Did *he* have any weaknesses?

Why must she always probe for weaknesses? Talk about an inferiority complex. She felt desperately in need of a shield. Having Charles at this close proximity over an extended time was wearing her resistance thin. He had a way of regarding her as though she were someone unique, someone he had been looking for all his life. So she simply couldn't be like every other woman in the world and give in to his overpowering physical attraction.

Exhausted by the very idea of battling Charles, Alex fell asleep.

* * *

Briggie had Scotch taped several pieces of notebook paper together and drawn an enormous genogram with all the names, places, dates, and question marks on it. It was spread out on the kitchen floor, and she and Frances were on their knees examining it when Alex came downstairs. Tentatively helping them with their inquiry was Tuppence, who kept close to Frances. Charles was seated at the butcher block, doing the Sunday crossword puzzle. He looked up when she came in, his blue eyes searching hers.

"Have a nice nap?" he inquired.

"Lovely," she murmured. "Where's Mother?"

"I think she's stretched out on the divan in her sitting room. That dinner rather took it out of her, I think."

"Yes," Alex said, conscience stricken. It had become hard to remember that her mother was actually ill. She hadn't complained once, but it must be awfully taxing to have all these people and pets in her house. Not to mention having been knocked out and kidnapped. Tiptoeing to the door of the sitting room, she saw Amelia asleep on her couch. Her mother looked years younger when she was asleep. Alex had never seen her so seemingly carefree. Shutting the door softly, she went back to join the others.

"How's your uncle, Frances?"

"His liver's all messed up," she replied with a sigh. "They've got him on some IV fluids. He probably should have gone into the hospital a long time ago. They're running all kinds of tests."

"I'm sorry."

"They're just going to tell us what they told us before. He needs a transplant." The girl's shoulders drooped, and she wiped a tear out of the corner of her eye. "I should have studied accounting, for Pete's sake. Then I would have had a prayer of making a living. What did I want to go and be a jazz drummer for?"

"Because you love it," Briggie said reasonably. "There are people who love accounting, but you're not one of them. My husband was, bless his practical soul. Look here," she said, pointing to the genogram. "Tell me about your folks. I want to fill in all my spaces. By the way, it seems to me that that cat's got some family sense. Must know you're related to Gladys."

"What's a five letter word for an 'attendant spirit'?" Charles asked.

The telephone rang. It was Dr. Goodwin, her voice more agitated than Alex had ever heard it.

"I thought you ought to know. Holly was out on a group pass this afternoon, bowling. She managed to give the tech the slip, and she's disappeared."

Chapter Twenty-Five

In shock Alex took the telephone to the butcher block and sat down next to Charles. "But how could she have gotten away? Is there any chance someone kidnapped her?"

"Good gracious!" Dr. Goodwin exclaimed. "I never even thought of that. Is it a possibility?"

Resting her forehead on her palm, Alex said, "Unfortunately, it is. The Westons were right to be afraid for Holly." She related to the doctor the events of the past few days, including her mother's kidnapping and the attack on Joey.

"And you have no idea who's behind this?"

Alex was growing extremely tired of this question. Charles regarded her in anxious concern, his pencil tucked absurdly behind his ear. "We're working on it, Dr. Goodwin. What did the tech say about Holly's disappearance?"

"One of the girls said she went to the rest room. They didn't realize she was gone until they were ready to leave."

"Was there a window in the rest room?"

"Yes. It would have been easy to get out that way. They found it pried open."

"And where exactly is this bowling alley?"

"In Mt. Prospect."

Sighing, Alex thought of the magenta-haired girl, alone on the cold winter streets of suburbia.

"Did she have a coat?"

"She evidently left it in the coat room."

The world suddenly seemed a frozen, hostile place, far removed from the friendly, warm kitchen where the smell of honey-baked ham lingered and Briggie and Frances examined the complicated genogram on the floor.

"What is being done to find her?"

"The police are patrolling the streets. Her description has been circulated. She didn't have any money. We don't think she could have gotten far, but there's no trace of her."

"This doesn't sound good, Dr. Goodwin. It's twenty degrees out there."

"I'm fully aware of that fact," the doctor snapped. Then she said, "Sorry. I've just had the Westons on my case all evening, and I don't have anything to tell them. The treatment center has failed Holly. That's all there is to it."

"Have you tried the homeless shelters?" Alex asked, feeling increasingly anxious.

Her mother entered the kitchen. Amelia was white and tired and looked at Alex inquiringly.

"That's the first place the police went when they couldn't find her on the streets," Dr. Goodwin said. "I've wondered if she really *was* on drugs, Alex, and that she knows someplace to go to get them."

"I don't think that's likely," Alex said. "Holly really did feel imprisoned. I only hope no one's taken her."

"Please continue with your research, Alex. I can't help but feel it's more important than ever, now."

After Alex had explained Holly's situation, the five of them adjourned to Amelia's sitting room, built up the fire, and outlined the plan of attack for the next day.

"No one can go off alone or be left alone," Charles said firmly.

"But I have school," Frances objected. "And work in the afternoon."

"She's a sweet goer," the macaw said.

"I'm sorry," Alex told the girl. "We'll try to work this out as soon as possible, but in the meantime, you need protection. There's a policeman on watch outside your uncle's room, isn't there?"

"Yes, he was there when Charles and I went to visit."

Alex suggested that Frances spend the following day with her uncle where she would be safe. Reluctantly, the girl agreed, after casting a languishing look at Charles, who was sitting next to her on the couch.

"You know, maybe we need to look at Gladys's death from our original point of view," Briggie said suddenly. "She might have been killed because she was an heir. But I don't think it's coincidental that she was killed right when we started investigating. She must have known something."

"I feel sure you're right, Briggie," Amelia agreed. "Those men who kidnapped me definitely wanted you to stop your digging."

"Well, I don't think she knew anything about the Crowells," Alex observed. "She had a flare for the dramatic, and a story about an illegitimate son would have been right up her alley if she knew it."

"What were you going to talk to her about the day she was killed?" Charles asked.

All at once Alex sat upright in her mother's desk chair. "The

Williams family Bible. She was going to show us the Williams family Bible!"

"Alex!" Briggie struck the heel of her hand against her forehead.

"Touched in her upper works," Moriarty contributed.

"I'd forgotten," Alex told her. "Her disappearance put it out of my mind." She pondered a moment. "She would have had it by her in the living room, don't you think?"

Frowning, her little brown eyes vague as she cast her mind back, Briggie said, "All that was in that living room was the afghan she was crocheting. A cream-colored thing with maroon roses. She was scalloping the edges. There was no Bible there that I could see."

"No," Alex agreed. "I wonder if the family Bible belonged to her grandfather. It might have had the details about this first marriage."

"You know," Charles observed, his face complacent, "I begin to be very hopeful about that idea of mine."

"Yes," Briggie agreed. "But that means there's nothing for us to do but sit on our hands until we hear from Mary tomorrow."

Amelia stirred in her leather armchair by the fire. "We could always go up to Lake Forest library and have another look at those articles on Lloyd and William Jr. I know there's something there that's important, if I could just remember what it was."

Alex looked at her mother. Her skin was so translucently pale that she could see the blue veins at her temple. "Maybe we should just take the day off tomorrow and rest," she suggested.

Briggie glanced at her in surprise. "In the middle of a case? No, I say we go for it. Lieutenant Laurie's checking on the Florida cousins, though they seem less and less important to me. Mary's up to good works in Pittsburgh. I say we go to Lake Forest. We can clear up that little mystery at least."

* * *

The next morning, after Charles returned from taking Frances into Chicago to sit with her uncle, Amelia, Briggie, and Alex joined him in the Range Rover for the trip to Lake Forest. The day was heavily overcast and cold in the way only a winter day on the lake could be. The snow had reached the gray and dirty stage, exactly matching the sky. Unable to help thinking about the missing Holly, Alex devoutly hoped that the girl was somewhere warm, at least. Of course, if she were dead, it hardly mattered what the weather was. She shuddered.

Across from her in the driver's seat, Charles said, "Goose walking over your grave?"

"Don't mention graves, for heaven's sake. I was just thinking of Holly."

He was very natty this morning in a camel's hair coat with a red wool scarf. "All we can do about Holly right now is to try to get on with the job," he observed.

"That's right," echoed Briggie. "We're close. I feel it."

Alex just stared out the window at the depressing landscape. Sometimes Briggie was so single-minded it annoyed her. But, after all, what *could* she do for Holly?

Her mother, who to Alex's relief seemed much more rested today, said, "Don't worry, dear. You'll only make yourself ill. You're doing everything you possibly can."

The Lake Forest Library actually had a wood-burning fireplace with leather armchairs on either side. Alex wouldn't have been surprised to find that they served coffee and hot chocolate. Its homey atmosphere—a combination of Turkish carpet, shelves of books, and a bowl of weathered pomegranates at the checkout desk—was a welcome respite from the winter day. Alex felt cheered at some level and was suddenly anxious to go to work.

"Mrs. Borden!" The librarian clearly recognized her mother. Alex remembered her improbable red hair and carmine red lips from their previous visit to search out the Williams Foundry history.

"Yes," her mother said, smiling warmly. "How nice that you remember me, Mrs. Simmons. This is my daughter, Alex, and our cousin Charles Lamb from England." She turned to Briggie, whose costume of cherry red sweats contrasted sharply with her own mink coat and knee-high Italian leather boots. "This is Brighamina Poulson, my daughter's business partner. We've come to have another look at those newspaper articles I was researching last week."

"Ah, yes. I remember. All about the Williams family. That was ghastly about poor Gladys's death. She was a member of our guild, you know." The librarian addressed Alex. "And of course, a tremendous reader, living alone as she did. Now what were the dates we were looking at?"

"The fifth of July, 1929, and the first week in September, 1936," Amelia answered promptly.

"If you just want to wait over there in the corner by the microfilm machine, I'll get the films," the matron said.

Amelia proudly led the way over to the machine that was ensconced awkwardly in its more traditional surroundings. Charles threw Alex an amused glance. "She's having the time of her life," he whispered in her ear. She could smell his Polo cologne, and her ear felt warm from his breath. Moving away from him, she stood on the opposite side of the machine.

The first article was short and straightforward:

VICTIM OF TRAGIC MISHAP

On the Fourth of July, William Williams, Jr., eldest son of steel foundry owner William Williams, died
by accidental drowning. Entertaining on board his

yacht moored behind his house in Lake Forest, the younger Williams was washed overboard when stormy weather caught him unaware. His brother, Lloyd, and friends Ann Perkins and Cynthia Downing were witnesses to what authorities are calling an accidental death.

Unmarried, Williams is survived by his father, William Williams, Sr., his mother, the former Angela Duncan, as well as his younger brother, Lloyd, his sister, Gwenyth, two nieces and two nephews. The funeral will be private.

"That's it!" exclaimed Alex's mother, pointing at a name. "Cynthia Downing."

"Downing Street," Charles said. "Prime minister. Clever of you, Amelia."

"But what about Cynthia Downing?" Alex asked, puzzled.

"Wait until you see the other article," her mother told her, hastily removing the microfilm and placing it in its box. Removing a second spool, she threaded the machine, her hands shaking a little. In a moment, she had scrolled to the second article, the headlines of which almost screamed:

BRUTAL MURDER TAKES LIFE OF LOCAL CITIZEN

Late Monday night, Lloyd Williams, Sr., of this town was discovered in his bed, dead of a gunshot wound, by his daughter, Gladys. Police, unable to find any weapon, are referring to the crime as murder.

Mrs. Williams, away in Canada visiting friends at the time, came home today to comfort a shocked and grieving son and daughter.

Authorities say that little is known about the night
of the murder, aside from the fact that a bridge party
was given earlier that evening. Present were guests Mr.
and Mrs. George Jensen and Miss Cynthia Downing.

Police are said to be following up all clues in their
possession. As yet, no arrests have been made.

"Hmm," Alex reflected. "I see what you mean, Mother. Cynthia
Downing was present at both occasions."

"And Lloyd's wife wasn't," Amelia added cheerfully.

"Clear as can be," Briggie announced. "Blackmail."

"What in the world are you talking about?" Alex asked. They had
obviously reached the point in the case where Briggie was jumping
to conclusions only her Miss Marple-like mind could follow. That
they generally proved to be wrong never stopped her.

"Lloyd Williams killed his brother," Briggie stated. "Should never
have inherited from his father because you can't benefit from a crime.
This Cynthia Downing was there. Saw him push his brother over. She
was blackmailing him."

"And she murdered Lloyd because . . . ?" Alex asked.

Briggie looked at her sternly. "Haven't quite worked that part out
yet. But his descendants shouldn't have that money."

At that moment, Alex's cell phone rang. She looked at her watch.
One o'clock. Could it be Mary already?

It was. "May I speak to Briggie Poulson, please? She gave me this
number. This is Mary Tomblin." Alex handed the telephone to
Briggie.

The cell phone didn't amplify the cheerful voice in the same way
the home telephone had. But whatever it was saying, it caused Briggie
to signal for a pencil and paper. Pulling her steno pad out of her

Coach leather handbag, Amelia gave it and her gold Cross pen to Alex's colleague.

Scrawling down names and dates, Briggie said, "Excellent, Mary. Really fine work. That's just what we need. Now. Can you find a marriage for Naomi? And trace her descendants?" She listened. "Yes. I agree. The census would be better for the descendants, but if she was born in 1871, the first census she would probably show up on as a married woman would be the 1890, and we all know what happened to the 1890 census."

Amelia and Charles looked at Alex questioningly. Alex mouthed, "Burned," and turned her attention back to Briggie's interesting call.

"Yes. Well, try for a marriage certificate, and then, if you find it, we'll look up the 1900 census on this end. Thanks, Mary. You're our good angel. This is really important."

"A daughter?" Alex asked as she took the phone from Briggie.

"Yes." Briggie looked triumphant, her eyes sparkling like polished agates. "Charles, you were right. Naomi. Born August 1, 1871. Mother: Chloe Beverly. Father: William Williams. They were married March 10, 1870."

Alex wandered over to the fireplace and sat down on the blue leather armchair. "Well," she said finally. "Since the child was a girl, at least Frances and Joey are still in the running for their money."

"Yes," Charles said, looking smug. "And we've got another possibility for murdering cousins."

Amelia was handing the microfilms to the bemused librarian. "Thank you so much," she said. "I don't suppose you've ever heard of a Cynthia Downing? She was present at both deaths, you see."

The woman laughed. "I'm not *that* old. If she was a contemporary of Lloyd and William, she'd be almost a hundred."

Amelia frowned. "And married, too, I expect. Well, never mind."

Alex could only be thankful that Briggie, in light of this new discovery, seemed to have completely dropped her blackmail idea. She had insisted that they head south immediately to be in place at the Newberry to look at the 1900 Soundex if Mary called with Naomi's marriage information.

They stopped for a late lunch at the house. Lord Peter wagged his entire hind end in greeting. Tuppence was back on top of the refrigerator. "Are you tired, Mother?" Alex asked, as she made the one thing she knew how to make really well.

Her mother's eyes were glittering with nervous excitement, and she looked almost feverish. "No. This is the most fun I've ever had since your father and I bicycled through France."

"You bicycled through France?" Alex held up the lid of a tomato soup can.

"What can I do to help?" Charles asked. She passed him cans of split pea and mushroom soup along with the can opener.

"When did you do that?" she asked, unable to imagine her mother on a bicycle.

"When your father was training for the Tour," Amelia said, smiling mistily.

"The Tour de France? He cycled in the Tour de France?" Alex was incredulous. Her father had been a great swimmer and tennis player, but she had never known he cycled.

"No. As a matter of fact, he fell during practice and injured his knee. He was never able to attain that particular dream. But that was after our lovely summer. We cycled all through the Rhone River Valley." Her voice had taken on an odd, pleading tone. She looked pointedly at Alex. "That was the trip when your father fell in love with Paris. We both did. It was the happiest time of our lives. *La vie en rose.*"

So, thought Alex, standing with her can of crab, staring at her radiant mother, *that* was why when they sent her away they had sent her to Paris. They had been happy there.

"I wish I had known that," she said, handing the can to Charles. The mystery and all its attendant characters dropped away for a moment, and she remembered her pie-shaped apartment on the Left Bank, reeking of garlic, and her skinny, sinuous roommate, Mika, with her penchant for Modigliani.

"Alex?" Charles asked. "What do I do with all these cans?"

This wasn't then. This was here and now, and she had a mother again and a mystery to solve. And Charles.

"We mix them all together," she told him. "Add milk to taste. It'll turn out to be crab bisque, I promise."

Raising an eyebrow, he dumped all the soups together in the saucepan and began stirring.

It was 3:30 by the time they were in place at the Newberry and Mary called them back.

Chapter Twenty-Six

Briggie took the call as they sat around a heavy oak table in the rear of the library. This place, too, was a refuge from the gray weather. One of the reasons Alex loved genealogy was the feel and scent of libraries. They were such a cache of miracles. Hidden in books and microfilm were scattered families waiting to be linked, stories waiting to be told. The Spirit of Elijah hovered over and around anything to do with genealogical research, kindling a unique thrill of discovery. Now there was an urgency behind their search, which involved the lives of people—Holly, Frances, Joey—who had become important to her. She was anxious that they all be safe from their enemies. Someone had perverted what should have been the loving task of finding one's roots.

"Yes, Mary!" Briggie caroled into the little cell phone. "What do you have for us? Uh-huh. Yes. Great. Thank you so much. You've really helped us. People's lives may depend on this." Punching the End button, she handed the phone back to Alex and turned her writing pad around so everyone could see it.

Naomi Williams m. Elijah Frueh, 3 November 1888. An almost audible ping went off in Alex's head. "Briggie, did you bring that big genogram you did last night?"

Her business partner nodded and pulled from her denim briefcase the big chart that was folded into quarters. Spreading it out on the table, she watched Alex scan it eagerly.

"There," Alex said, pointing to Robert Harrison's name. "Look at his parents. We got them from the marriage certificate."

"Eliza Frueh and Walter Harrison!" Amelia crowed, causing patrons around her to look up and grin knowingly. "My heavens, Alex, do you think Gladys's husband was descended from William Williams, too?"

"We'll soon find out," she said. "Let's hit the Soundex."

Charles was shaking his head. "What a shatter! How on earth would he have met Gladys?"

"By design, I expect," Alex told him, remembering the pride in Gladys Harrison's eyes as she displayed Robert's picture. The memory became suddenly painful. "I hate to think of her being deceived. It's absolutely sickening. She was only nineteen. He told her that the minute he set eyes on her, he knew he was going to marry her." She looked at Charles, anger making her defiant.

"Well, don't look at me," he said. "I didn't have anything to do with it, my dear girl."

His affronted face made her smile. "Sorry. But I really liked Gladys."

The 1900 Soundex for Allegheny County, Pennsylvania, confirmed Alex's guess. In the household of Elijah and Naomi Frueh was a child of eleven years old: Eliza. There were no other children.

"Well," said Briggie. "That's all very interesting, but it doesn't get us any further forward."

"Not unless Robert had siblings," Charles observed. "How can we find that out? The 1910 census?"

Alex checked her watch. It was 4:30. "I think we might just have time, if we hurry."

Amelia was quietly recording William Williams's descendants on the genogram that was spread on the table behind the microfilm reader. Briggie hustled off to request the correct 1910 Soundex roll. Alex felt as though her head had left her shoulders in search of a saner perch.

And then she saw him. Nike Man, lately from Ernie's Grill in Waukegan, was gazing at her malevolently from across the library. His wide mouth was set in a determined line and his little eyes, set close together under thunderous heavy brows, were beady and intense. As soon as he registered her notice of him, he turned abruptly and disappeared in the direction of the stacks. She put her hand on Charles's arm. "We've been followed," she said in a low voice. "We've gotten so caught up in this chase, we forgot to watch our tail!"

Her cousin stiffened like a bird dog on point. "You saw someone?"

"The man that was so interested in William Williams's will the day Briggie and I were in Waukegan. He was standing right over there in a black raincoat." She indicated the spot. "He just disappeared into the stacks."

Charles was off in a moment, moving like a sleek panther in search of prey. He had just gone out of sight when Briggie returned.

"Where's Charles?" she asked.

"Gone after our watcher from Waukegan." Alex glanced at her watch. "We have to hurry. They'll be shutting down soon. Let's look at that Soundex." She felt the rush of adrenaline that often kept genealogists researching into the night. Unfortunately, the Newberry kept business hours.

But the Soundex revealed only one child in Eliza and Walter Harrison's family: Robert, age ½.

"They could have had other children later, but we don't have time to check the 1920 Soundex today," Alex said, frustrated. Then she realized Charles had not returned. Out of the corner of her eye she saw a bald man with a prominent nose approaching them. Quickly, she assembled her papers and stuffed them into her carryall.

"Grab the genogram, Briggie," she said. "Come on, Mother. We're out of here."

Alex shepherded her mother and Briggie down to the street. The air was bitter with cold and the gasoline fumes of rush hour.

"But where's Charles?" her mother asked fretfully.

"We can't wait for him," Alex said shortly. Luckily, a yellow cab cruised close to the curb and she hailed it. Someone was watching out for them.

"Dang!" she said, as she climbed inside. "I left the microfilm on the reader! He could see just what we had found!"

"Who, Alex?" Amelia wanted to know. Her movements were halting as she climbed into the cab. With three of them, the backseat was crowded, but Alex instructed the driver to take them to the train station. He was a tiny Hispanic man who could scarcely see over the steering wheel.

As the cab inched along, threading its way through cars, she said, "We had two watchers at the library. Charles went after one of them. The other was closing in." Looking out the back window, she said, "I think we lost him."

Briggie, shrouded in her L. L. Bean parka, was clutching her briefcase to her ample middle. "This is getting serious."

"I hope Charles is okay," Amelia said, grasping Alex's hand and squeezing tight.

"He's going to be fine," Alex told her, trying to sound confident. After all, what could a middle-aged man do in a library to a man in Charles's peak physical condition? *Shoot him and run,* she thought. Did these guys have guns? So far all they'd done was hit people over the head.

A vision of Charles lying unconscious and freezing to death in a Chicago back alley suddenly petrified her. She almost commanded the man whose taxi license declared him to be Alejandro Fernandez to drive them back to the Newberry. But she had her mother's safety to consider. Amelia was shrinking beside her, obviously terrified. She had already been victimized once.

"You are afraid, no?" the little man said. "Someone follows you?"

"Si, Señor Fernandez," Briggie told him. "Drive fast."

Their driver turned his head around, his wide grin displaying a gold front tooth. "Like the movies! I dream of this!" Facing his task with new enthusiasm, he began to maneuver skillfully between cars, whose drivers objected strongly with their horns, until he found an alley between buildings. Turning into it, he laid rubber on the pavement as he accelerated to fifty miles an hour for the space of one block. Then he turned sharply to the right, and once again horns blared as he cut between cars and then ran a yellow light that was just turning red.

Alex's mother clutched at her. "Was it the man with the bald head?" she asked feebly.

"It might have been. There are lots of bald men in the world. I could have just freaked out," Alex admitted. "But the man Charles was following was definitely the man Briggie and I saw in Waukegan. When I saw a bald man coming towards us . . ."

"You did the right thing," Briggie said, clutching her briefcase tighter. "They're moving in."

"Oh, my gosh!" Alex exclaimed suddenly. "Frances! She must wonder where in the heck we are!" Pulling out her cell phone, she punched in 411 for information. "Northwestern University Hospital," she requested.

When she was connected to the hospital, she asked for Joseph Jacks's room and was told that he had been released. Though she had been keeping it at bay, panic now assailed her with full force, and she began rooting through her carryall for the Chicago policeman's card.

Señor Fernandez continued his erratic progress to the train

station. It was dark, and sleet was beginning to fall. Alex felt as though the buildings of the Chicago Loop were closing in, imprisoning her downtown. Would they never reach the station?

At last she found Officer Hambleton's card. Dialing the number on it, she heard, "Officer Hambleton."

"Officer, this is Alex Campbell. You questioned me at the Northwestern Hospital about the Joseph Jacks's assault?"

"Oh, yes, Mrs. Campbell. What can I do for you?"

"It's about Mr. Jacks. He's been released from the hospital, and his niece is with him." Alex swallowed and forced herself to go slowly. She unfortunately had no faith in this policeman's ability to grapple with too many facts at once. "I'm worried about them. We're in a taxi on the way to the train station. We saw two of the men who've been following us . . ."

"Whoa there, Mrs. Campbell. Two of the men, you say? How many are there?"

"Well, we know of three, for sure. We still don't know who they are. The point is, the third man could be after Joe and Frances Jacks . . ."

"I see. I'll send a squad car over to Mr. Jacks's apartment."

"Or they might have gone to Frances's place. Do you have her address?"

"No."

"She lives in Roger's Park. She's listed in the phone book under F. Jacks."

"Right. I'll send another squad car over there."

"Thanks. Can you call me back at this number when you find something out? It's a cell."

"Okay. Shoot." She gave him her number.

They had reached the train station at last. Alex wished more than anything she could name that Charles had a cell phone.

The rush hour journey seemed endless. They had just caught the train as it was closing its doors and were therefore unable to get seats. As her mother swayed next to her, holding on to the back of the seat beside her, Alex wondered how her legs were holding up. Amelia seemed to have shrunken in her fear, and her eyes darted nervously from passenger to passenger. All of them were sitting in coats, hats, gloves, and mufflers, wearing their train faces and staring at their evening papers or reading thrillers. A gallant gentleman in a black wool topcoat rose and offered Amelia his seat. Breathing a sigh of relief, Alex thanked him. Her mother closed her eyes and sank further into her mink. Her face was dead white.

The train rushed into the night through the seedy outer reaches of the city. Just as they were pulling out of Evanston, their first stop, her cell phone rang.

"Where the devil are you?" Charles demanded.

"There was another man," Alex said. "We caught a taxi, and now we're in the train. What happened?"

"I've had quite a chase. The fellow gave me the slip at the Hancock Building. He got into a lift full of people just as it was closing."

Picturing the hundred-story black glass building on the north end of Michigan Avenue, she said, "I'm sorry, Charles. Bad luck. But listen." Instinctively she lowered her voice. "Joey was released from the hospital. I've sent the police to his apartment and Frances's. They could be in danger. I haven't heard back from Officer Hambleton."

Alex realized at this point that several passengers had lowered their papers and were regarding her curiously.

"I'll stop by Frances's," Charles said. "But I have no idea where Joey lives. I'm at the pay phone down the street from the Newberry, so it'll take me a while to get there. The traffic looks bad."

"It is bad. But thank heavens you're okay." The obvious interest of her onlookers prevented her from telling him that she had been picturing him dead in an alley. "If you find Frances and Joey, bring them to the house."

"Aye, aye, Captain Campbell."

His jocularity caused her to relax slightly. She hadn't realized just how worried about him she'd been. "You're proving to be a very able accomplice, Charles."

"Yes, well, I must say it's been a humbling experience. Cheerio."

When their taxi finally pulled up to the house in Winnetka, Alex looked carefully up and down the street but couldn't distinguish any lurking figures in the darkness. She helped her mother out, feeling the fragility of her slight frame beneath her mink coat. Amelia began to limp toward the house.

"Briggie . . ." Alex flashed a message at her, nodding in Amelia's direction as she fished in her carryall for her wallet. Her friend caught up with her mother and put a supporting arm around her.

"Easy does it, Amelia," she said. "We're almost there. It's been a long day."

The house welcomed them with the familiar pampas grass and Picasso in the entryway. In her whole life Alex had never been so relieved to be home. What used to seem empty and impersonal was now vital and inviting because it housed a woman whom she loved. Not to mention Lord Peter, who was running around her in circles. Carefully helping her mother off with her coat, Alex led her back to her sitting room.

"Briggie, if you light the fire, I'll call Officer Hambleton and then see if I can find anything for dinner."

Someone knocked at the front door. The little dachshund ran off at top speed, barking.

Chapter Twenty-Seven

Alex froze in the act of tucking an afghan around her mother's legs. Who could possibly be at the door? Probably the best thing to do was to ignore it, she decided. It was bolted.

But would a killer knock? She didn't think so.

"Briggie, someone's at the front door. Where's your deer rifle?"

"In the kitchen," Briggie said. "I'll get it, and we'll go together."

With her colleague behind her, rifle loaded, Alex called through the door, "Who's there?"

"Oh, please, Alex. We're freezing! It's Frances and Joey."

Relief released the constriction in her chest, and she unbolted the door and flung it wide. "For goodness sake, come in! How did you get here?"

"Bobby brought us," she explained, coming inside, her hands clenched inside the cuffs of her sweatshirt. Her uncle followed her, still dressed in the black, rhinestone-spangled performance costume he must have worn to the hospital. Deep black circles showed beneath his tired eyes. "He's out at the curb," Frances continued.

"Angrier than I've ever seen him. He wanted us to go to his place. But he's got school tomorrow. And anyway, I feel safer here."

"Well, he can at least come in for something hot to drink," Briggie said.

"He won't." Frances pulled a face. "He's mad at me."

Alex waved her forearm towards where Bobby's old Pontiac sat waiting at the curb. Recognizing Frances, Lord Peter had run outdoors to bark at the car. The young man drove off with a squeal of his tires.

"Never mind," Alex said. "I'm so glad to see you. When we called the hospital and found out your uncle had been released, we had no idea where you'd gone." She ushered the two into the hall, an arm around each of them.

"What's that?" exclaimed Joey, staring at Briggie.

"Deer rifle," her friend answered. "We've had some trouble today."

"Trouble?" Frances's brow contracted. Briggie bolted the door after the little dachshund reentered. He was sniffing Joey with interest.

"People following us. No one was hurt," Briggie reassured her.

"Where's Charles?" Frances asked, peering into the hallway.

"He'll be right along," Briggie said. "Don't fret. Now, Joey, I understand you've had a knock on the head. How're you feeling?"

"Seedy," the man said sadly. It was clear he was not his normal convivial self.

"I think we'd better get you to bed," Alex told him. Where was she going to put him? It would have to be her father's bed. Charles would have to go back to the Lawsons' or sleep on the couch. "Briggie, make them some hot bouillon. I'll go change the sheets." Opening the hall closet, she took out her father's heavy black wool overcoat. "Here, Joey, put this on to keep you warm. You look like you're freezing to death."

He accepted it gratefully, looking around, his black eyes lighting on the Picasso. "Nice place you've got here."

. After Joey had drunk his bouillon and been put to bed, Charles finally arrived. Frances's face lit with the smile of a damsel welcoming her hero home from the wars. "Charles! You're back!" She was cradling Tuppence in her arms.

Alex, surprisingly overwhelmed by the air of masculine vitality that radiated from him, turned away, hiding her own relief. The picture of him dead in the alley hadn't quite left her until now.

"Dinner is going to be frozen pizza, I'm afraid," she said, opening the freezer door. To her surprise, Charles came up behind her, put his hands on her shoulders, and kissed the back of her neck. "Hello to you, too, Alex," he breathed into her ear.

Staring hard at the pizza box, she fought the urge to turn in his arms. She was *not* a character in a romance novel!

Reality returned. Who did he think he was? Kissing her like it was his natural right?

"Joey's upstairs in your bed," she said prosaically. "He's not in very good shape. Bobby brought them."

Charles let his hands drop and turned to face Frances. "Hello, drummer girl. You showed good sense to come here. We've been worried about you."

"But if Uncle Joey's in your bed, where will you sleep?" Frances asked, sounding stricken.

"There's a perfectly lovely sofa in the living room," he told her. "Now, did anyone think to inform the police that you are safe?"

Briggie came striding into the room, deer rifle under her arm. "Charles. Good to see you. Amelia's had a rough day. She's back in her sitting room. I think she'd like a word."

"I'll call the police," Alex said. "Thanks for reminding me."

Dinner was rising-crust pepperoni pizza. Fortunately, Alex had found three in the freezer. Everyone was ravenous. Frances, Charles, and Alex ate at the butcher block. Amelia had a tray in her sitting room and watched the news. Briggie ate upstairs with Joey to keep him company.

Charles filled in an interested Frances on what they had found out that day.

"So you're telling me that this Robert Harrison was another cousin of mine and that he actually followed Gladys to Hollywood and married her?"

"That's it."

"Hmm. That was pretty cold-blooded," the girl observed.

"What makes it interesting is that he may have had brothers and sisters. They may be the ones who are raising havoc," Charles told her.

"How do you find out?"

Charles turned to Alex. "Here's the expert."

"We've got to look at the 1920 census." Her cousin's nearness was pulling at her, coaxing her to cling to him. Moving slightly away from where his arm rested next to hers on the butcher block, she forced herself to think about the case.

They needed to solve this. Now. Holly was missing. They were all in danger. "I have an idea," she said suddenly, pushing away from her dinner. "I need to talk to Briggie."

Running upstairs, she found her colleague chatting to Joey. "Yeah, Ray Charles was good, but I'm more into Sinatra."

Joey was sitting up in bed, her father's rosewood writing desk supporting his paper plate with a half-finished slice of pizza on it. *His pompadour must be glued in place,* Alex thought irrelevantly. It was as smooth as ever.

"Briggie, do you think there's any chance Mary might have a copy of the 1920 Allegheny County Soundex on permanent loan to her family history library?"

Her colleague turned, her seamed face lighting up. "We could call her and ask. She's so gung ho, she might just check it for us tonight."

"That's what I was thinking."

"Well, I'm finished eating. I'll give her a call. And you'd better call Lieutenant Laurie about those Florida Crowell cousins, just to make sure."

"I forgot to tell you. Lieutenant Laurie left a message on the answering machine." Alex smacked her forehead. Charles's kiss had turned her mind to mush. She was surprised she could think at all. "Zach Crowell has a police record, but he's in prison right now for robbing a convenience store, so he can't be behind this. The police down there are going to question him about his sister and father, but that's a pretty unlikely angle. His father would be elderly. We're after middle-aged men, I think."

"Right. I'll go call Mary. Need to check on Amelia, too."

"Yes," Alex said. "She's a little shut down. What did she want to talk to Charles about?"

"She made him promise to look after you. She's worried, Alex. She doesn't care about herself or what might happen to her, but she cares about you."

Mary Tomblin told Briggie, in tones of ecstasy that sounded throughout Amelia's sitting room, that they did indeed have the 1920 Soundex for Allegheny County at her library.

"Look," Briggie explained, "you've done a lot of work today already, but there are some pretty desperate characters after us. We need to know who they are, pronto. Would you be willing to go down tonight and open up the library and do a search for us? Every minute counts."

Mary apparently was willing.

"We need the family of Walter and Eliza Harrison," Briggie told her. "Pittsburgh. They'll have a ten-year-old son Robert. What we need to know is if they have other children."

Sister Tomblin said she'd get on to it immediately and would call them as soon as she found anything.

Amelia sighed from her couch. "What a good soul she is. Now we won't have to go back to the Newberry tomorrow."

"You're tired, aren't you, Mother?" Alex said, sitting on the side of her couch.

"Sweet goer," the Professor said. Alex could swear his tone was tender. Amelia's eyes filled with tears. "I'm sorry. It's just that all of a sudden I can't keep up."

"It's not surprising," Alex told her. "Briggie has the constitution of an ox. I can scarcely keep up with her, and I'm thirty years younger than she is. I think it's her Mormon pioneer blood. Her ancestors crossed the plains by handcart, you know."

Briggie laughed. "I think Mary Tomblin's must have, too. That woman is a real trooper."

"Are you ever going to tell me about the Mormon church, Alex?" her mother inquired tentatively.

"I didn't know you wanted to know about it." Alex was surprised. When she first came back to Winnetka, her mother had had scathing things to say about her new religion. What had changed her mind?

"You and Briggie have something special. I guess I want to be part of it."

Alex held back a sigh of disappointment. Put that way, it sounded suspiciously as if her mother's interest arose from her feeling that she was outside the bond that held Alex and Briggie together. She patted her mother's arm. "You and I have something special, too, you know."

"Yes, yes," her mother said impatiently, "but there's something about the two of you . . . you're so sure of yourselves or something. Oh, I can't put it into words."

"We'll get the missionaries to come in as soon as this is wrapped up," promised Briggie.

Charles strode into the room, Frances and Tuppence at his heels. "I've been neglecting my duty shamefully, Alex. Come with me to the Lawsons' to check on the house."

"We're waiting to hear from Mary," she told him. "She's got the 1920 Soundex down at her library."

"Well, it'll only take a few minutes if we go right now. Come along."

"But, Mother . . ."

"Go with him, Alex," her mother told her.

Realizing she could do nothing except refuse him outright in front of everyone, she rose reluctantly and went to get her pea coat.

They made the drive to the Lawsons' in silence. Since Charles's return tonight, the atmosphere had simmered between them. The night outside showed brilliant contrasts of light and dark, now that the afternoon's storm had passed. A full moon reflected on the snow, and stars punched through the blackness like winking silver through velvet.

"All right, Alex," Charles said, as he pulled into the driveway, leaving the comfortably warm car running. "Ever since Friday night, you've scarcely spoken to me. What happened? What did I do?"

Bowing her head beneath this reproach, she couldn't think of what to say. She couldn't possibly tell him about Daniel.

"It was after you came back from the airport," he reminded her. "You wouldn't even look at me, and you went straight up to bed." She felt his eyes, no longer cool but warm and caressing, trying to see inside her. The car suddenly seemed an intimate place. They were closeted together against the night.

Then, seeing herself succumbing to an attraction she couldn't help but feel, she told herself to buck up. Raising her chin, she said, "You assume too much, Charles."

"And what do you mean by that?" His voice was not indignant but gentle, teasing.

"You can have any woman in the world by snapping your fingers," she told him, reminding herself at the same time. "And you seem to think that should work with me, too."

"Have I snapped my fingers?" he inquired softly. "I'm sorry if you think so. I thought there was rather more than just the normal physical attraction between us."

He reached across and put a finger under her chin, turning her to face him. One look at those eyes, tenderly gazing at her, stirred feelings inside her she didn't know she had, and she was lost. She felt her resistance vanish as if it were being burned out of her.

Her gaze must have told him, for he took her hand and, raising it to his lips, kissed the inside of her wrist. She just stared at him. "I love you, Alex," he said. "You and your Jeanne Moreau eyes."

His words jolted her, and the reference was obscure. Confused and amazed, she said, "*Mata Hari?*"

"Yes," he replied, holding her hand. "The French film. One couldn't help championing her. You have her look—tragic and frightfully vulnerable. But brave with it."

"But I'm not," she protested, disturbed by this vision of herself.

"Eyes don't lie," he said simply.

As he got out of the car and went to check the house, she sat, bemused. Charles in love with her? Attracted to her, certainly. But in love? And what about her? This head-over-heels feeling wasn't what she'd felt for Stewart or Daniel. Even as her mind urged caution, her heart winged away from it.

When they got back to the house, Charles removed her pea jacket as though it were a costly fur and followed at her elbow back to her mother's sitting room. The gentle sound of blues piano music wafted through the air from the Bordens' Steinway grand in the living room. Running around the two of them, Lord Peter seemed to realize they were a couple. Amelia looked from Charles to Alex and back again. Then she smiled a self-satisfied smile and sat up on the couch, throwing back the afghan from over her knees. Briggie, seeming to catch something of the atmosphere, looked up from Stewart's book, which she had apparently taken from the coffee table. Her little brown eyes clouded.

"Where's Frances?" Alex asked, feeling all at once like a schoolgirl who had stayed out too late.

"She's with Joey," Briggie said. "Can't you hear the piano? Couldn't keep him in bed for love or money. The two of them were like to go crazy without their instruments."

"Has Mary called?"

"Not yet. You were only gone twenty minutes, for Pete's sake." Her colleague's voice was irritated.

A lot could happen in twenty minutes. The gentle, melancholy strumming of the piano invited Alex to the living room. "Why don't we all go listen to Joey?" she asked.

Mary called while Joey was singing his soulful rendition of "Cry Me a River."

Chapter Twenty-Eight

Everyone gathered around the butcher block as Briggie took the call, pencil in hand.

"Yes. Got that. Okay. Hmm. Just as we figured. Mary, you're a brick. I don't know what we would have done without you today. Thanks." Briggie hung up the phone, and Alex could hear the grandfather clock in the hall strike nine o'clock.

"Well?" she said. Her colleague was looking puckish.

"I think we're onto them," Briggie said. "Walter Harrison had two more children. A son, Jacob, who was nine in 1920, and a daughter, Theresa, who was five. Those bozos who've been chasing us must be their kids."

"So what does this mean?" asked Joey, seating himself on a stool. "Are we still heirs or not?"

"Yes," said Alex. "The Williams money was willed to the oldest son. That's your grandfather. These people are descendants of his first marriage, but they came through a daughter, not a son."

"So what would happen to the money if all of Great-grandfather's heirs were wiped out?" Frances asked, moving closer to Charles as if for protection.

"That's a question for Richard," Briggie decided, "the estate lawyer we work with. We'll call him right now."

Picking up the phone, she punched in a number from memory.

"Put him on the speaker phone, Briggie," Amelia said. "I want to hear this straight from the horse's mouth."

"How do I do that?"

Amelia showed her, and soon the whole room could hear the phone ringing.

"Hello."

"Richard? Brighamina."

"Hey, watching the game?"

"What is it, basketball?"

"Of course. Bulls vs. Pacers. Bulls are getting beaten pretty badly, I'm sorry to tell you. Is my son up there with you still?"

"Daniel? No. He never came."

"What? I took him to the airport myself."

Alex bit her lip. Charles was looking at her. How could she have forgotten Daniel? The hurt he would surely feel if she were to marry Charles lanced through her. Marry Charles? What was she thinking?

"He had a last-minute emergency," Briggie told him. "Client or something."

"That's odd." There was a pause. "Well, are you behaving?"

Briggie chuckled. "As well as can be expected. Haven't had to use my deer rifle yet, but it's been a close thing, I can tell you. We're in a spot, Richard."

"And you need my help? Do you want me to come up there?" Alex didn't miss the hopeful note in his voice.

"No, thanks. We just need some advice."

Briggie explained about the will. Then she asked, "If there were no children of the oldest son left, would the trust be broken?"

"The will specifically mentions children, not heirs?"

"Yes. And it says something about if the property reverts to his other children, under no circumstance is it to be allowed to go to his youngest daughter, Gwenyth, or to her children."

"So he had other children?"

"A daughter by his first marriage, another son, and an illegitimate daughter besides the daughter he specifically disinherited."

"Well, that's a nice little problem. Not too complicated. The estate would probably be divided between the heirs of the two daughters and the other son."

Briggie and Alex exchanged a look. It was to everyone's advantage that the Crowell line be wiped out.

"So," Richard said in a jovial tone. "Has anyone been murdered yet?"

"Afraid so," said Briggie. "And a couple of attempts, too."

"And Daniel's not there? What's the boy thinking? I can be there in the morning. First thing. There's a flight at seven." He hung up before Briggie could say another word.

"For Pete's sake," said Briggie, looking blankly at the speaker. "What have I done?"

"Where are we going to put him?" Amelia moaned.

Alex was stricken. She *couldn't* let Richard know the status of things between herself and Charles. She couldn't bear to have Daniel hear about them secondhand. Or over the phone. She was going to have to watch herself.

Charles sensed her discomfort. "He can stay at the Lawsons'," he said. "I'm sure they wouldn't mind."

"What did all that mean?" Joey asked querulously. His face was yellow and strained.

Briggie put a hand on his shoulder. "It means we've got to take mighty good care of you. If anything happens to you and Frances and your Florida cousins, the money's up for grabs."

"The Westons are in danger, too," Alex observed. "I think I'd better go see them in the morning and explain things to them. These people might have taken Holly."

"Who's Holly?" Frances wanted to know. She had linked her arm closely through Charles's.

Alex sighed. "She's the one who started the whole thing. It's her genealogy we were doing. She's the granddaughter of the woman who was murdered. She's been missing since last night."

Amelia said, "I'm going to make up a descendancy chart of William Williams before I lose my mind trying to keep it all straight."

"I think we'd better call Lieutenant Laurie, now that we have a pretty good idea who's behind this," Charles said. "He needs to know about what happened today and who's in danger. Do you have a fax machine?"

Amelia nodded. "In my husband's office."

"We'll fax him a copy of your descendancy chart."

"You take care of that, Charles. I'm a girl who needs a hot fudge sundae in the worst way," Briggie told him.

Alex lay in bed next to her mother, tossing from one side to the other. The complicated case and all of its ramifications seemed to have retreated into the background. One moment she was reliving the life-altering minutes in the car with Charles, the next she was envisioning Daniel in her car Friday night, his normally gentle eyes hard and implacable. He had known. She could almost not bear it that she was going to hurt him. And she couldn't picture life without Daniel.

"For heaven's sake, Alex," her mother murmured finally. "What is it?"

Williams Descendancy Chart

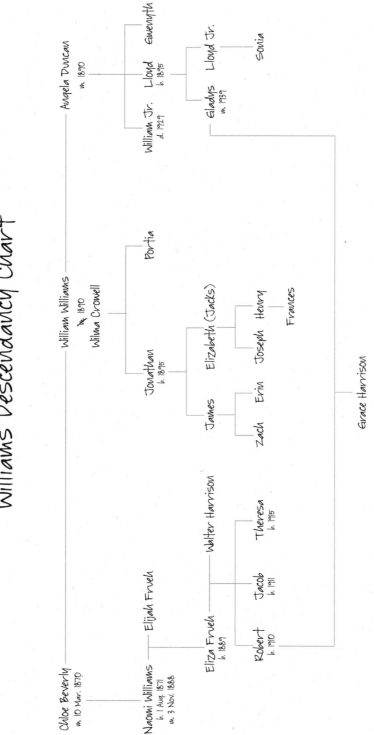

Chloe Beverly
m. 10 Mar. 1870

William Williams
m. 1890
Wilma Crowell

Angela Duncan
m. 1890

Naomi Williams
b. 1 Aug. 1871
m. 3 Nov. 1888

Elijah Frueh

Jonathan
b. 1895

Portia

William Jr.
d. 1929

Lloyd
b. 1895

Gwenyth

Eliza Frueh
b. 1889

Walter Harrison

James

Elizabeth (Jacks)

Gladys
m. 1939

Lloyd Jr.

Robert
b. 1910

Jacob
b. 1911

Theresa
b. 1915

Zach

Ervin

Joseph

Henry

Frances

Sonia

Grace Harrison

"I'm sorry, Mother. Go back to sleep." Slipping out of bed, she put on her robe. "I'm just going downstairs."

She went to the linen closet in the hall and removed sheets, a down comforter, and a pillow. Padding down the stairs to her mother's sitting room, she made up a bed on the couch.

"A bit top lofty," was Moriarty's quip. Wondering if the parrot was right, she fell asleep some time after the hall clock struck 2 A.M.

Alex was awakened by sounds in the kitchen. Struggling to sit up, she noticed that it was scarcely light outside and tried to put her day in context.

Charles. Richard. Daniel. *Oh, I can't deal with that now!* Throwing a forearm across her eyes, she tried in vain to go to back to sleep, but whoever it was in the kitchen had started to whistle. That let out her mother and Briggie. She finally recognized the "Promenade" from *Pictures at an Exhibition.* That let out Frances and Joey. It could only be Charles.

Scrunching into a ball, she told herself she must think about the case. Holly was missing. Frances and Joey were in acute danger. The Westons. She was going to warn the Westons about the renegade heirs of Naomi Williams. Checking her watch, she saw that it was seven o'clock. She would have to hurry if she were going to catch George Weston before he left for work.

She sneaked to the stairway and then ran up to her bedroom. Frances stirred as Alex opened her closet.

"What time is it?"

"About 7:00. I've got to go out. I think Charles is in the kitchen making breakfast, if you want to go down and join him."

"Where are you going so early?" the girl inquired.

"Remember when I told you about Holly?"

"The girl who started all of this?" Frances asked, swinging her legs over the side of the bed. For pajamas she wore sweatpants and a New Orleans Hard Rock Café T-shirt. "The one who's missing?"

"Yeah. I think I know who took her. I'm going to tell the Westons, her parents."

Frances shivered. "I sure hope she's not dead. They almost killed Uncle Joey."

"I hope not, too. I think the Westons know something about all of this. Something they haven't told anyone yet. There's some reason they put Holly in the treatment center. I'm going to see if I can find out."

"I hope you find out something. As much as I love staying here and doing nothing, I've got to get back to my life or I'm going to flunk out of school and lose my job."

Alex had been swiftly dressing in gray wool slacks and a matching turtleneck. Jeans wouldn't do for Mrs. Weston. Carefully combing her riot of ringlets, she noticed Frances watching her in the mirror.

"Charles is in love with you, isn't he?" Frances inquired, moving back into the bed and tucking her knees under her chin, enclosing her bent legs with her arms.

Alex felt herself blushing. "What makes you say that?" she asked.

Frances sighed heavily. "It's pretty obvious by the way he looks at you. I wish someone would look at me like that. Like I was a rare piece of silver or something." She stared down at her work-roughened hands with displeasure. "But I'm just plain, freckled Frances Jacks."

Overcoming her discomfiture, Alex went to the girl and tousled her red hair. "You're anything but plain, sweetie. You've got more personality in your little finger than most girls have in their whole body. Go ahead and flirt with Charles. He eats it up."

Frances grinned ruefully.

Alex managed to get out of the house without Charles being any the wiser. Presumably bewitched by Charles's whistling, Lord Peter had not stirred from the kitchen. The man had now progressed to "Für Elise."

Richard would be on his way to Chicago right now. She still didn't know how she was going to face him.

A front had moved in over the lake, and dark clouds hovered over the shore, warning of malevolence. But there was no wind, and the temperature wasn't as bitterly cold as it had been for the past week. Alex realized that this probably presaged snow and most probably, knowing January in Chicago, lots of it.

It was just 7:30. Hopefully, George Weston hadn't yet left for work.

As she hammered the brass ring that was the knocker of the gray stucco modernistic mansion in Wilmette, she wondered if anyone would answer. At length, a small Hispanic woman in a white uniform, her hair dressed in a tight bun at the nape of her neck, opened the door. Her large brown eyes were narrowed in disapproval.

"*Nada. No queremos nada,*" she said with finality.

Alex translated this as meaning she didn't want to buy anything or have anything to do with her. Before the maid could slam the door, however, Alex stepped over the threshold. "Señor Weston," she said boldly. Rustling through her carryall, she came up with a business card and handed it to the woman, who took it dubiously and, leaving Alex standing in the doorway, went off to deliver it.

A few moments later, Grace Weston, shockingly bedraggled in a pink velour housecoat, her blonde hair unrestrained and falling about her face in wisps, came into the front hall. To Alex, she looked like a blurred watercolor of her former self. There was no makeup to define her features, and her watery dark eyes seemed sunken in her head.

"You," she said without heat. Every bit of her starch had wilted.

"I think I know who has Holly," Alex told her gently. "And I think you do, too. Have they been threatening you?"

The woman's eyes filled with tears. "George promised me this wouldn't happen. He said he'd take care of it." The tears rolled down her face, and she hastily dabbed at them with a used tissue from her pocket.

"They're Jacob Harrison's children, aren't they? And they want part of the fortune, don't they?"

Grace nodded, her misery clear. "George said he'd work out a deal with them. But then Holly . . ." She couldn't go on.

"You were afraid of them, weren't you? That's why you put Holly in the treatment center."

This time Holly's mother put her hands up to her face and commenced sobbing uncontrollably.

"Look, Mrs. Weston," Alex said as her unwilling hostess started to turn away. "I'm sorry to bother you right now, but the fact is, there are other people who are in danger, too. We've got to catch these guys. Could I talk to your husband?"

Grace blew her nose. "He's just finishing his coffee. He has to go to work. I wouldn't advise you to see him. He's in a very black mood."

"But he just might know something. If he's talked to these people . . ."

"Don't you think he'd do anything he can to get Holly back?" she demanded. "Don't you think I've asked him and asked him?"

"Maybe I have some information he doesn't have," Alex persisted. "Maybe if we put our heads together . . ."

"Oh, all right. Emma?" She turned to find the little maid hovering in the background, counting the beads of her rosary, her lips soundlessly moving. "Show this woman into Mr. Weston's library."

The woman bowed her head to her mistress and, pocketing the rosary unobtrusively, led Alex down the hall into a darkened room off the main hall. As the maid threw back the drapes to let in the overcast morning light, the first thing that caught Alex's attention was a black book with gold-tooled lettering sitting squarely in the middle of the desk. It was a Bible.

Chapter Twenty-Nine

lex's brain went into instant overdrive. Looking over her
shoulder, she crept swiftly to the desk and whisked open the
first few pages of the book until she came to an elegantly
illuminated family tree.

The Family Tree of William Williams

Born February 7, 1850

Llanegryn, Wales

Footsteps sounded on the black marble tile of the hall. Hastily
shutting the book, mind whirling, Alex sat down on a black leather
chair in a corner by a thriving cactus whose three branches reached
skyward.

How did George Weston get Gladys Harrison's family Bible
between the time she disappeared and the time the police broke into
the locked house? In an instant the man was before her, his brows
drawn into a frown, his eyes fierce. This expression was so different
from the bland one she remembered that she was momentarily taken
aback. He reminded her forcefully of someone.

"You wanted to see me, Mrs. Campbell? About my unfortunate daughter?"

"Uh, yes," she stammered. "Your wife says you know all about Jacob Harrison's heirs. They've been threatening you."

Strolling around the modern rosewood desk, he appeared to notice the Bible for the first time. With seeming casualness, he picked it up and inserted it into the bookcase behind him between *Rand McNally's Illustrated Atlas of the World* and *Webster's Collegiate Dictionary*.

"Yes," he said, the fierce expression in his eyes leaving suddenly, as though he were relieved that her questioning had taken this direction. He rolled his shoulders, adjusted the knot of his cranberry-colored tie, and appeared to pull himself together. "They seem to think they have some sort of right to half my wife's fortune."

"Do you think that's why they've taken Holly?" she pressed him. "As a bargaining chip? Have you heard from them?"

"No, I haven't heard from them, as a matter of fact. I've been expecting to. The whole thing's odd."

"Well." Alex was frustrated by his attitude. Didn't this man *care* about what had happened to his daughter? "How did they get in touch with you before? Do you know how to get hold of them? Where do they live?"

He looked at her blankly, as though these questions had never occurred to him. "I have no idea. Don't you think I'd have told the police if I did?"

Alex bit her lip. He hadn't answered her first question. This interview was not going at all as she had expected it would. She had the sensation of being stonewalled.

"Why did they think they were entitled to part of the Williams fortune? During my research, I found the trust. The money clearly goes to the eldest son, not his daughter."

A glint like a flame kindled in the man's eye. "Just why are you here, Ms. Campbell?"

"I'm worried about Holly. I guessed that the Harrisons were behind it. I didn't know if you knew that."

He settled back in the blood-colored leather swivel chair, apparently unmoved by her own sense of urgency. "And just why do *you* think they had a motive?"

She hesitated. Did he know anything about the Crowells? She could hardly explain without bringing them into it. She decided to risk it. "There's been a development," she said. "I think you should know that some new heirs have turned up."

He laughed heartily. "My dear young woman. Next you'll be telling me that the money doesn't belong to my wife at all." In this room with its Oriental rug, floor-to-ceiling bookcases stuffed with expensive hardbacks, and what she now recognized as Georgia O'Keefe originals on the walls, George Weston appeared unassailable. She should have given thought to how the man would react to having the source of his wealth disappear.

"That's just what I am telling you," she said quietly. "The fortune doesn't legally belong to you or the Harrisons."

The brows came down and the eyes grew hard and calculating. Not surprised. Not angry. But definitely calculating. Then he seemed to morph before her—the gray hair on his head turning white, the goatee disappearing, and a high white collar replacing his button-down blue oxford cloth shirt. The eyebrows had wiry hairs springing from them, curling and making a familiar hedge. *William Williams.* George Weston looked just like William Williams.

"You can't expect me to swallow that. Who do you think you are?" he demanded, his cool tones now abrupt and threatening.

She gulped down the fear in her throat. "The legal heir to William

Williams's fortune was his firstborn son, Jonathan Crowell. He has living descendants here and in Florida."

There was no shock on the man's face. But he leaned across the desk on his elbows, a mocking gleam in his little black eyes. "They'll never prove it," he told her. "If Williams had meant them to inherit, he would have left proof." Abruptly, he swiveled around in his chair and pulled out the family Bible. Opening it on the desk so that she could read it, he displayed the Williams family tree. "See?" he said, pointing with a nicotine-yellowed finger. "His daughter by his first marriage is there, Naomi, but the only sons are Lloyd and William. And, of course, there's Gwenyth. But she's been blotted out."

"And where do you come in, Mr. Weston?" she asked, suddenly bold. "Are you, by any chance, Theresa Harrison's son? Did she marry a Weston?"

Now there *was* shock in his face. "What gave you that idea?"

"Genetics," Alex said, glad to have scored off him at last. "When you came in here, you reminded me of someone. It took a moment, but now I see that you're exactly like your great-great-grandfather William Williams. Those Welsh genes must be powerful. I'm surprised Gladys never saw it."

He fumed but said nothing.

"Does your wife know?" she asked. "Does she know it's your own cousins who've taken Holly?"

Now he scowled and, picking up a gold-bladed letter opener, began to turn it in his hands. "They didn't take Holly. They swear it."

Now it was her turn to be surprised. Surely, if they were trying to force the Westons' hand, they would have told them they had Holly.

"Then where is she?" Alex demanded.

"I have no idea. She's simply disappeared." His mouth was grim beneath his goatee.

Was it possible? Alex wondered, once more jolted by this upset of her theories. If the Harrisons hadn't taken her, where could she be?

She returned her gaze to the Bible. "Did Gladys's husband know about you?"

He grinned his insinuating grin. "Who do you think put me onto a good thing? What was good enough for uncle was good enough for me. Perhaps I should mention that we are a very close-knit family. I told you that first day. Just like *Leave It to Beaver.*"

"Almost indecently close-knit," she rejoined before she could think. "When did you take the Bible?"

His eyes lost their humor, and he stiffened. His wariness hit her like a wave. Little prickles, like the sharp spines from the cactus next to her, started in the small of her back and spread up to her neck and shoulders. In that instant she saw the truth.

George Weston had murdered Gladys and taken the Bible with him.

"Take it from where? Grace has always had it," he challenged her.

Alex was silent, hoping that the pounding of her heart was not audible. She had no illusions about the danger she was in. The effusively friendly woman with her menagerie of pets and her pride in her family history had never known she had spent her life surrounded by snakes. What had precipitated her murder? And would Alex herself be able to get out of this alive? She had only her wits and her karate.

"Lost your tongue?" her host asked caustically. "I can see the wheels turning. What is it you think you know?"

Above all, Alex knew she must feign innocence. "Did your cousins kill Sonia Williams?" she improvised wildly.

He narrowed his eyes. "That was a hit-and-run."

"Then why did you put Holly in the treatment center? What were you afraid of?"

Leaning back in his chair, he let out a slow breath, never taking his eyes off hers. She could see that he was calculating again. He scratched his goatee idly with the letter opener, thinking. "Well, you see, Terrence is a little, well, off the wall. Sonia had just taken up genealogy, and she found out about us. Her father had had a copy of that history, you see, and she'd made contact with the boys."

"The boys?"

He shrugged and gave a short laugh. "That's how I always think of my cousins. Christopher, Stanley, and Terrence—Jacob's sons. A more bumbling bunch of nobodies you've never seen. Terrence suddenly got this bee in his bonnet that Sonia would find out about the Crowells." He leaned forward in his chair. "We always knew about Jonathan Crowell, you see, but just thought it was best to let sleeping dogs lie. His heirs knew nothing about the will, obviously, or they would have stepped forward years ago."

"But Terrence got nervous?" Alex guessed, trying to appear merely interested but clenching her fists inside the cuffs of her pea coat.

"Yeah. He drives a semi for a living and decided to take her out." He heaved another sigh. "Mind you, if you accuse him of it, I'll deny it."

"But I'm still confused," Alex said, grateful that her ploy was working. "Why did they think they had any right to the money?"

He looked down, casually running the paperknife along the seam of rosewood. "Well, I have to admit they were blackmailing me. They threatened to tell Grace who I was and that I had married her for her money." He glanced up briefly, his eyes assessing her. "I pay them. If the money dries up for me, it dries up for them. Terrence made an almighty mess out of that attack on Joey Jacks, I hear."

"Your wife said they were threatening you. What does she think they can do?"

He gave a sigh of exasperation and managed to look goaded. "Yeah, well, she doesn't understand the trust. She thinks they have a legitimate right to the money. And she knows Terrence killed Sonia. She thinks he's going to kill all of us so the money can come to him."

With this speech, it occurred to Alex that he had become far too voluble. He was telling her way too much to allow her to get away from him. Adrenaline jolted through her. She began to study her options. Her fright had disappeared, and everything stood out in crystal clarity. The sage green cactus at her shoulder with its sharp little spines. The collection of Tom Clancy first editions, still in their dust covers, to the left of George Weston's head. The delicate gray shading on the cow skull in the painting on the righthand wall. Her life depended on her keeping a cool head. Could she get hold of that letter opener?

"It didn't help when her mother died. I suspect, though I'll never be able to prove it, of course, that they're the ones who killed her."

She should have just appeared to accept these words, but the vision of Gladys calmly stroking Tuppence wouldn't let her stay silent. "Why?" she asked.

This question appeared to stymie him. Pulling himself together, he said at last, "I think she must have found out about the Crowells."

"How would she do that?" Alex leaned forward in her chair. He had put the letter opener down. It lay between them on the desk. Could she spring for it?

He put a hand to his goatee and stroked it, regarding her. Eyes didn't lie. She remembered Charles's words. The snow had started to fall outside the window, and the room seemed suddenly cut off from the world. There was cold-blooded murder in George Weston's eyes. He was trying to figure out how to kill her.

At the same moment, they both reached for the letter opener. He grabbed it first, but she gave his wrist a sharp karate chop, causing him to drop it. Snatching it up, she held it like a dagger, backing towards the door.

George Weston had taken a bunch of keys out of his pocket and was unlocking a drawer of his desk as she gripped the doorknob. She opened the door, turned, and sprinted down the black marble hall. Her boots echoed loudly on the floor, and Alex looked back to see if the murderer of Gladys Harrison was really going to let her get away. She barreled straight into the man with the tortoiseshell glasses.

"Hold on to her, Terrence," George Weston instructed from behind her. "She knows you killed Sonia."

The man's grip on her arms tightened. He smelled like stale sweat and cigarettes. Alex trod sharply on his instep with her boot, and he momentarily relaxed his hold. Wrenching free, she brought up her hand and chopped his neck sharply. As he staggered, she hit him in the solar plexus with a roundhouse kick, plunging him to the marble floor where she heard his head crack soundly. His glasses went flying, and he lay immobile. Whirling, she faced George Weston. He now had a revolver in his hand. Grace was standing behind him, her mouth gaping as she looked from Alex to the gun in her husband's hand to Terrence sprawled on the floor.

"But he kidnapped Holly, George," she said. "Why are you pointing that gun at her? I certainly hope you have a license for it."

"Grace, leave this to me. You were right. This woman is a pest. It's because of her that Holly's in danger."

George's wife turned burning eyes on Alex. "You! What have you done?"

Alex decided to gamble. He surely wouldn't shoot her in front of his wife. "George Weston is your cousin. He's Terrence's cousin, too. He killed your mother."

A succession of expressions passed across the woman's face, the rigidity of shock, followed by the horror of disbelief, and finally the implacability of anger. "Shoot her, George. She shouldn't be allowed to say such things! The idea!"

Ducking, Alex rushed for the man's legs. She was quick. Before he realized what she was doing, he was sprawled on the floor. But Grace Weston was quick, too. She grabbed for the gun and fired.

Her bullet went wide. She fired again, this time winging Alex in the shoulder.

She felt the burn of the wound but had no time to pay attention to it. Rapping Grace Weston's fragile wrist before she could fire again, she watched as the gun clattered to the ground. Alex grabbed it. The murderer was staggering to his feet.

Suddenly, behind her she heard a commotion. Everyone looked up.

"*No, no! No es posible que* . . ." The little maid was screeching as Charles and Briggie rounded the corner into the corridor. Briggie took one look at the scene before her and raised her deer rifle, squinting into its sight. "Hands up!" she commanded. "Unless you want your ugly head stuffed and mounted on my living room wall."

Chapter Thirty

Alex, her shoulder expertly bandaged by EMTs, Charles, Briggie, Amelia, Frances, and Joey entertained the lawyer with the leonine mane of white hair in the living room. Chasing his tail and barking in the middle of the gathering, Lord Peter was showing off.

"I can't believe I missed the action," Richard Grinnell was saying indignantly, eyeing Briggie with disfavor.

The snow was still falling outside, and Amelia had a turkey in the oven. Weather reports predicted record-breaking snowfall. Alex, securely gripping her mother's hand while sitting in the circle of Charles's arm, looked at Richard wearily. She knew vaguely that she should spare a thought for Daniel, but it felt so good to have Charles's cherishing arm around her just now.

"Why would he kill his mother-in-law?" the lawyer wanted to know. "Briggie has shown me that impossible family tree, but that doesn't explain it."

Joey, unable to remain sitting long anywhere but at the piano,

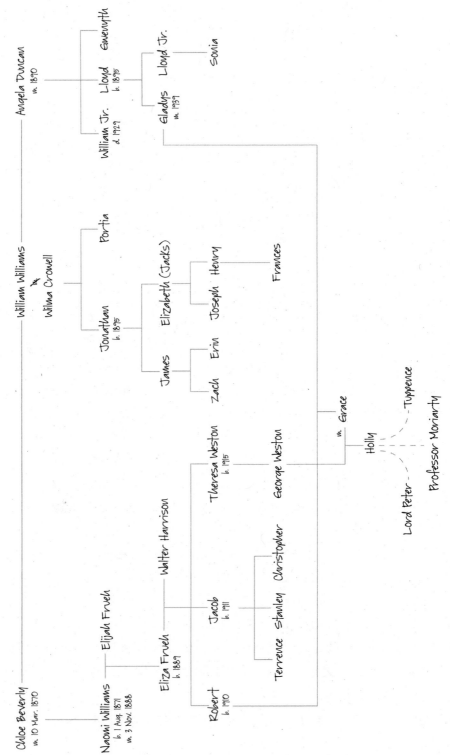

walked over to the Steinway and began playing softly. Alex recognized "Georgia on My Mind." Frances, looking very small in a pair of Briggie's royal blue sweats, sat with Tuppence on her lap, gazing at the genogram, which was now spread on the floor. "I don't think I understand, either," she said.

"Well," Alex primed herself once more to explain. Lieutenant Laurie had taken some convincing. "I don't know if we'll ever really know unless he confesses, but my guess is that he didn't intend to kill her. He just wanted to get that family Bible away from her before she could show it to anyone. You see, she phoned Grace that morning for a ride to the airport, and she happened to mention that we were coming by to look at the Bible. He knew we would figure out who he was once we started working on Naomi Williams's descendants."

"And he couldn't afford for his wife to find out that he had married her for her money," Briggie explained patiently, as though to a small child. "Very proud, Grace Weston. She would have cut him off without a penny."

"I should have figured out that George Weston had to be behind the men tailing us," Alex said, absently stroking her mother's hand. "Nike Man, Briggie. The very day after I spoke to George Weston the first time."

"Nike Man?" Charles said.

"AKA Stanley Harrison, I guess. Earlene, the waitress up in Waukegan, warned us about him. And the bald man. Charles, remember when we met for dinner? The bald man at the next table was Christopher Harrison. Didn't you recognize him?"

Lieutenant Laurie had rounded up all the Harrison cousins, once he had Terrence in custody. Christopher Harrison was being charged with kidnapping Amelia. Terrence was being charged with murder. As yet there were no charges against Stanley Harrison.

"I wasn't looking at anyone else that night, Alex," Charles said fondly.

Richard harrumphed and turned to Briggie. "Brighamina, you still haven't explained how you figured out Alex was in danger."

"It was Charles, actually," Briggie admitted. "I was a little slow."

"You should have seen George Weston's face when Briggie turned that deer rifle on him," Charles laughed. "Priceless. Absolutely priceless. She threatened to send him to the taxidermist."

Richard beamed at Briggie, showing an almost proprietary pride. One would never guess he was opposed to hunting.

"But how did you know, Charles?" Alex said. "I walked into that situation completely blind. All I could think of was Holly . . ." She stopped, holding up a hand to forestall conversation. "Holly! We still don't know where she is. No one kidnapped her, Briggie. She must have escaped on her own."

"Where would she go?" her colleague asked.

Alex put her fingertips to her temples, thinking. "She didn't have any money . . . she would have had to have some kind of transportation. She could have phoned someone to pick her up outside the bowling alley before they left the hospital." She massaged her temples in slow circles. "Yes. That must have been it. Now, who?"

"If it had been me," Frances said unexpectedly, "I would have called Bobby. Did Holly have a boyfriend?"

Alex looked at her sharply. "An old boyfriend. But I don't remember . . ." She stood up and looked at the snow out the window, still falling. It didn't seem so cozy now. It could be life-threatening to Holly. "I've got to get in touch with Grace. She may hate me, but she still loves Holly."

Walking into the kitchen, she called information for the number of the Lake County Jail where George Weston was being held. In the background, she recognized that Joey had moved on to "Sittin' on the

Dock of the Bay." Charles wandered into the kitchen and kissed her tenderly on the cheek as she listened to the telephone ring at the jail.

Grace Weston wasn't there. The attendant told Alex that she had never been there.

"She must have come out of denial," Alex said, punching in 411 one more time. She requested the number of the George Weston residence in Wilmette.

The little maid, Emma, answered. "'ello?"

"Emma, this is very important. I am trying to find Holly. Is her mother there?"

"Señora Weston 'ospital."

Hospital? What about Holly? What was she going to do? "Maybe you can help," Alex said, her mind racing. "Do you know the name of Holly's boyfriend?" She searched in her mind for the word in Spanish. She remembered it from her favorite mystery novel. "Holly's *querido.*"

"*Pedro,*" Emma said without hesitation.

Yes. That was it. Peter. "What's his family name? *Familia?*"

"*Familia* Connor. Next door," Emma told her.

"Papa Connor?" Alex asked, holding up crossed fingers for Charles to see. "Name?"

"*Roberto.*"

"*Muchas gracias,* Emma," Alex said, hanging up quickly.

Peter Connor was at home and seemed relieved that someone cared about Holly. "That's such bad news about her old man," the boy said. "I've been wondering, like, if I should go tell her or something."

"Where is she, Peter?" Alex asked. "You can trust me. Holly won't have to go back to the treatment center. The guys her mother was afraid of are in jail."

"That's awesome. Now she can come home. She's at her grandma's house."

Alex was stunned. "Her Lake Forest grandmother?"

"Yeah. She said she knew her grandma liked her."

"Thanks, Peter. You've been a great help."

Turning to Charles, she thought desperately. Holly must be sheltering in the playhouse! "We've got to go to Lake Forest. It's a good thing you've got four-wheel drive."

The drive up Sheridan Road to Lake Forest was agonizingly slow. The snow was a foot deep, and the plows hadn't been able to keep up with it. Charles drove through near white-out conditions, his headlights picking up the ruts in the snow just ahead.

"She'll be frozen after two days in that little house," Alex said, her agitation making her grip the seat convulsively. "It only has a little gas fireplace."

"We should have just called the police," Charles repeated somewhat wearily as he peered through his windshield.

"I don't want her to find out about her father from the police," Alex said again. "I started this whole mess by poking around . . ."

"You didn't put Holly in the treatment center," Charles said, exasperation sounding in his voice. Alex couldn't tell if it was with her or with the weather. "You didn't kill her grandmother."

"No, but . . ."

"George Weston is a rotter," her cousin said roundly. "He was undoubtedly a terrible father."

Alex thought this over. Then she asked, "How *did* you know about George Weston, Charles?"

"It wasn't anything on the genogram," he said. "I don't think along those lines. At least, not yet." He gave her a brief grin that made her think that perhaps his exasperation was with the weather. "I just put it together, falsely as it turns out, that if this guy was being threatened and knew who was doing it, he wouldn't stand for them taking his daughter. It didn't make any sense. He could have had the police on to them in a flash. Either he wasn't being threatened or he knew his daughter was safe. No matter how I looked at it, it seemed ominous."

He glanced at her again and grinned his megawatt grin. Reality shifted like the turn of a kaleidoscope. Alex wasn't driving through a terrible snowstorm in the middle of a Chicago winter. She was sitting in a boat, being punted down the Cherwell in high summer at Oxford. The sun was shining hot on her back, and her heart was melting in the light of that smile.

"I wasn't taking any chances with the woman I love," he added. "And, of course, Briggie was game."

Alex laughed, temporarily forgetting all the Westons and their terrible family plight. A little bubble of warmth inside her made her forget even the throbbing of her arm. She was loved and, because all her walls had finally come down, she could feel it. In a burst of euphoria, she realized how much she owed to the Shepherd who had carried her on His shoulders when she couldn't walk on her own. She had forgiven her mother, reclaimed her past, and was being healed.

And then she knew that, in the long run, Holly was going to be all right. The rotten piece had been cut out of her life. She was young, and love was powerful. Now that Alex knew that herself, she could be the Savior's hands and help the young girl with the magenta hair pick up the pieces of her life.

Epilogue

A lex," her mother said, as she watched her daughter folding laundry preparatory to packing. "There's something we've left undone."

She turned at the determined note in her mother's voice. Holly, sitting on the end of the bed, her spiky hair looking a bit odd with clean jeans and the gift of Frances's favorite T-shirt ("White girls get the Blues"), glanced up. Tuppence, finally in the arms of someone she knew, purred like a small motor.

"That old murder. We never solved it."

Sighing, she said, "You've been around Briggie too long. We're really not a detective agency, you know." She looked meaningfully in Holly's direction.

"What old murder?" the girl inquired.

Amelia went on remorselessly. "But I have a feeling that if we could trace Cynthia Downing, we might find something important."

Briggie strode in at this point. Alex had taken over her own room again with the departure of Frances. She was sharing it with the fractured Holly and her three pets, whom she wouldn't let out of her sight. Richard had arranged a temporary guardianship for Holly with Frances and Joey as her closest relatives because Grace Weston had collapsed and entered the psych hospital. The girls had taken an immediate liking to each other and so, when Alex left for Kansas City, she was going to drop Holly and her pets off in Roger's Park. It would be a very different existence for the teenager, but Alex was confident that Holly would learn from a practical teacher how to stand on her own two feet.

"Earlene got me the goods at the courthouse," Briggie told Amelia. "Cynthia Downing married Earl Winchell in 1939. The marriage certificate says she was twenty-nine when she married. So she'd be in her mid-eighties now. Chances are fair she's still alive."

"Then it looks like a call to my friend Mrs. Simmons at the Lake Forest Library is in order," Amelia decided, moving towards the door, her steps lagging only a little. "She is definitely plugged in to Lake Forest society. I bet she'll know all about Cynthia Winchell."

"Fine little filly," the Professor informed them.

"Who is Cynthia Winchell?" Holly demanded. "Like haven't you finished with all that genogram stuff?"

Alex realized she had no choice but to try to explain the vagaries of genealogists to the shell-shocked Holly. "My mother's looking for the last piece to your family puzzle. Who murdered your great-grandfather."

Holly rolled her eyes. "This is really weird, you know." She stuck her hand out and snapped her fingers. Lord Peter jumped up on his short hind legs and licked her hand with enthusiasm.

"I know. Like I told you, I've been through it myself," Alex said. "But you've got to get all the junk out where you can look at it before you know what you're dealing with."

She also realized that she didn't mind delaying her return to

Kansas City. She was dreading the inevitable confrontation with Daniel. It could certainly wait. Though she couldn't deny what existed between her and Charles, her relationship with Daniel was deeply rooted in her. She had no idea how she was going to feel when she saw him.

The red-haired librarian informed Amelia over the phone that Cynthia Winchell had indeed been a bright light in Lake Forest society, heading the Episcopalian Altar Society, the Hospital Guild's Tumor Clinic fundraising arm, as well as being a talented hostess and bridge player. Mrs. Simmons believed she had retired to the elite assisted living facility, Deerfield Crossing.

"We have time to go up there, don't we?" Amelia inquired. "The missionaries aren't coming until dinnertime, and I've got the chicken marinating. Charles is coming at six."

Alex sighed, looking at her mother fondly as she set aside the last of her laundry. "I think I've created a monster," she said.

"Just think of me as the northern branch of RootSearch, Inc.," she said, laughing. The sparkle in her eyes was new and gave another dimension to her face. It no longer appeared fragile but had the undergirding firmness of one who had passed through trials and refused to be defeated by them.

Deerfield Crossing looked like someone's idea of a hunting lodge. Large, with Tudor-esque half-timbering and stucco, it had extensive grounds and was set in a little wooded park. Alex imagined it would cost the earth to retire here.

Mrs. Winchell was allowed visitors only with her doctor's approval. Amelia approached the matronly woman at the front desk confidently.

"This is a very serious matter, my dear. It has to do with a murder that was committed when Mrs. Winchell was a young woman. She's the only one who can help us."

The matron looked alarmed. "Does that mean *her* life is in danger?"

"Oh, I don't think so," Amelia said. "But we're working for the family involved, and I think you'll agree that they need some sort of closure after all these years."

"Well, I'll call the doctor. I'm sure I don't know what he'll say. Perhaps you could just wait in the lounge."

They adjourned to a large sitting room that was in keeping with the hunting lodge decor. Leather chairs, heavy beams overhead, a cheerful fire burning in the grate, and thick, chocolate brown carpeting created an atmosphere that almost made Alex forget she was visiting a place where frail old people were dying by degrees.

The matron returned shortly with the information that Mrs. Winchell could be visited if there were a nurse present in the room but that she could only receive two visitors at the most.

After a brief consultation, Briggie decided that Amelia and Alex should go. Holly had declined to accompany them, preferring instead to talk to Peter on the telephone, her cat in her lap. When she had learned of her next-door neighbor's role in her rescue, that romance had definitely begun to blossom again.

Following the matron down the carpeted hallway behind a set of closed walnut doors, they were met by a woman they presumed to be a nurse, though she wasn't dressed in the traditional white starch. Instead, she wore a navy blue suit with a red vest and white blouse.

"I understand you have a few questions for Mrs. Winchell?"

"Yes," Amelia answered. "I hope we won't tire her, but it is rather important."

"So I understand, but I do hope you won't agitate her. She has a weak heart."

"Oh, I don't think it will agitate her," Amelia assured the nurse. "It's not about anyone close to her."

Cynthia Winchell was the tiniest of ladies, resembling a small flower in her bed of fragrant pink satin sheets. Her face lit up at the sign of visitors.

"Do I know you?" she asked frankly.

"No," Amelia said. "We are genealogy detectives and have come to ask you some questions. We are hoping you can help us."

Alex watched her mother in some amusement. Even after all they had been through, Amelia still viewed this as a kind of game. In her heart of hearts, Alex expected this encounter would come to nothing, but she knew her mother had high hopes.

"We've come to ask you some questions about a family you knew a long time ago," Amelia proceeded, seating herself in a velveteen-covered chair the color of old roses. "Do you remember a man by the name of Lloyd Williams?"

The little woman's look of serenity was instantly replaced by something else. Looking away from Amelia, she began to pull at her blankets and twist ineffectually in her bed. She did not answer at once. Finally she said, in a voice so low it was almost a whisper, "What's this all about?"

"It's about his murder," Alex's mother told her. "You see, over the years the family has suffered a great deal because of the consequences of that murder. You were friendly with the family. Can you tell us anything that might help?"

Cynthia Downing Winchell sighed, as though preparing to lift a great burden. "I don't suppose it matters now. My husband's dead, and my children wouldn't care." She looked away again, but when she looked back at Amelia, there were tears in her eyes. "I was Lloyd Williams's lover. It was wrong, terribly wrong, and I've regretted it all these sixty years. But I was young and so very foolish." Folding her hands on the bedspread, she appeared to compose herself. "The night of the murder, we had arranged that I should come back after the bridge party. I had my own key."

Alex held her breath. *There was something. Mother had been right.*

"As soon as I got down the hall, I heard voices raised in his study. It didn't take long to figure out that he was having an argument with someone. This man was calling Lloyd a disgusting, penny-pinching tyrant. I didn't listen long, because I didn't want to be caught there." The woman seemed to writhe at the memory. "He was a cousin of Lloyd's, apparently, and thought Lloyd owed it to him to help him start his law practice or at least give him a job in the company." She sighed. "But Lloyd could be very arbitrary and dismissive, I'm afraid. He was giving the man pretty short shrift. When the man lost his temper and threatened Lloyd, I ran."

A cousin. A law practice. Robert Harrison. It must have been Robert Harrison. The snake who had gone after Gladys and married her once she'd become an heiress.

Amelia placed her hand over the trembling hands of Cynthia Winchell. "It must have been very frightening for you when you found out he was murdered that night."

"Yes. I couldn't tell anyone I'd been there, because it would have ruined my reputation completely. Besides, I hadn't a clue who the man was. Do you?"

"Yes." Alex's mother looked at her across the patient's bed. "I think we do. But you must rest now. You've helped us very much. Thank you for deciding to tell us."

"If I had told it before, would it have made a difference?"

Amelia looked at Alex, her eyebrows raised. "I don't think so," Alex said. "They didn't have the information we do."

"My dear," said Amelia on the way back to Winnetka, "I do believe that family was even more messed up than ours."

Briggie was driving, and Alex sat behind her mother in the

backseat of the Bronco. She put her hand on her mother's shoulder. "We've learned that families can be healed, Mother. Holly and Frances are a new generation. They can break the pattern."

"It's love that breaks the pattern," Briggie said. "The Savior's love. We're not finished with those two girls."

Alex smiled to herself, remembering the bleak winter day four years ago when Briggie had first swooped down upon her, a new widow, hailing her with a delighted smile and a surprising light in her agate-bright eyes. "We're family," she'd said. "My third great-grandfather was a Campbell. Do you want to help me find him?"

The rest, as they say, is history.

About the Author

The adventure of writing this book could well be called *The Case of the Forgotten Manuscript.* G. G.'s last book in this series, *Of Deadly Descent,* was published in 1996. Soon afterward, she became very ill, was hospitalized, and underwent a procedure that caused her to lose her memory and her ability to write. In 2006, she was miraculously healed, but her memory was not restored. One day she received the impression that she should search the computer for an idea she had once had about a third mystery in her Alex and Briggie series. To her surprise, she found an entire novel she didn't remember writing, buried deep in the computer. With a stronger testimony of the Lord's healing powers, she rewrote the manuscript that has become *Tangled Roots.*

G. G. and her husband, David, have three children and one grandchild. A dedicated genealogist, G. G. serves as an ordinance worker in the Provo Utah Temple of The Church of Jesus Christ of Latter-day Saints. Her previous works include *Voices in Your Blood, Cankered Roots,* and *Of Deadly Descent.* She is also a regular columnist for *Meridian Magazine.*

Visit G. G. at ggvandagriff.com.